STS

山田社

STS

山田社

完全攻略 英檢
初級 中級
必考文法

320

English

Good
gram game

General English Proficiency TEST

里昂 著

英語考試權威助陣，權威文法，就是這麼威！ **MP3**

超強漫畫式學習，有趣就能有效記住！

說明完全掌握必考重點，贏得高分！

打破時間之牆，【文法＋單字＋句型：3效學習】省時省力，
讀完一遍就記住！

用耳朵的記憶力背文法，只用零碎時間，照樣取得高分！

英檢、托福、多益100%必考文法

山田社
Shan Tian She

超強漫畫式學習，有趣就能有效記住！

說明完全掌握必考重點，贏得高分！

打破時間之牆，【文法+單字+句型：3效學習】省時省力，讀完一遍就記住！

用耳朵的記憶力背文法，只用零碎時間，照樣取得高分！

英檢、托福、多益100％必考文法！

《完全攻略英檢初級、中級必考文法320》秉持著「有趣就能有效記住」的原則，把枯燥的初、中級英檢文法，融入趣味橫生的插圖故事中，讓讀者輕鬆理解，記憶深刻，想忘都難。

完全攻略英檢初級、中級必考文法320》為了把iBT，SAT，GRE，TOEIC，GEPT國內五大考試，所有可能出現在考題中的初、中級文法一網打盡。參考財團法人語言測驗訓練中心的英檢文法範圍，以及包括台灣、美國、日本、韓國，甚至非洲各國等國小至高中常考英語文法，為您精心分析、用心整理出必考文法，成為一本小辭典！更讓您考試如虎添翼，百發百中。

看了這本書讀者會有：

1. 超強漫畫式學習，有趣記得就快

   每項文法下面各帶出一個例句，再輔以活潑的插圖。把枯燥的文法融入插圖的故事中，讀者絕對會有「原來如此」文法真有趣，真簡單的感覺！

2. 說明完全掌握必考重點，贏得高分

   為了紮實對文法的記憶，對每一文法項目意義明確、清晰掌握。說明中不僅對每一文法項目的意義、用法、語感、近義文法項目的差異，及關連的近義詞、反義詞、慣用語等方面進行記述以外，還分析不同的文法項目間的微妙差異。也就是讓您完全掌握必考重點，贏得高分！

3. 打破時間之牆，【文法+單字+句型：3效學習】省時省力，讀完一遍就記住！

   網羅英檢初級到中級的文法・句型・單字，每個文法項目，都帶出4個例句，每個例句都是生活、工作、財經、甚至是報章雜誌常出現的，不論是情境或是自然度，都經過精心編寫，都能突顯出文法的意思，讓讀者對文法架構有正確的認知。不僅如此，例句中更包括初級到中級的單字，這樣就可以3效學習文法、單字和例句，可說是最實用的英語文法書。並能快速讓您強化實力、高分通關。

4. 用耳朵的記憶力來背文法，只用零碎時間，照樣取得高分！

   本書附贈由專業美籍老師錄製的朗讀MP3，文法例句全都錄！不僅幫助讀者在英檢聽力項目取得高分，更讓讀者善用「耳朵」的記憶力來學習文法！手上

沒有書，照樣記文法！開車聽、洗澡聽、刷牙聽、走路聽，睡覺也可聽！就是只用零碎時間，英檢證照一樣輕鬆到手！

　　本書廣泛地適用於一般的初學者、大學生、碩·博士生、參加國內五大考試的考生，以及出國旅遊、生活、研究、進修人員，也可以作為英語翻譯、英語教師的參考書。可說是人手一本，必備的文法書。

目錄

壹、初級

一、be動詞·一般動詞

四、冠詞、形容詞跟副詞

五、句型·各種句子

11

十、分詞

十一、主詞的各種型態

十二、介係詞

一、be動詞・一般動詞：1.動詞種類─be動詞（現在1）

➜ 想說「A（主詞）是B」的時候，也就是表示「A=B」的關係時，A跟B要用特別的動詞來連接起來，這個動詞叫「be動詞」，而「be動詞」以外的動詞叫「一般動詞」。後面可以接名詞，用來介紹自己的姓名、職業及國籍等。

I am Mary.
我是瑪莉。

➜ 例句

1 I am a driver. | 我是個司機。

2 I am a businessman. | 我是個商人。

3 We are students. | 我們是學生。

4 He is a fan of chocolate. | 他是個巧克力迷。

2.動詞種類─be動詞（現在2）

➜ 在 be動詞的後面，跟主詞可以劃上等號（＝），有對等關係的詞叫「補語」。補語除了名詞（表示人或物的詞），也可以接形容詞（表示狀態或性質的詞）。

I am tall.
我個子高大。

➡ 例句

1	I am poor.	我貧窮。
2	I am glad.	我很高興。
3	I am handsome.	我很英俊。
4	I am angry.	我很生氣。

● 3.動詞種類─be動詞（現在3）

➡ 前面說過了，am這個 be動詞要接在 I的後面，至於 are是接在 You的後面，is是接在he（他）、 she（她）、 it（它）和所有單數名詞的後面。

初級
Level

I am a boy.
我是個男生。

➡ 例句

1	You are short.	你個子矮小。
2	He is my friend.	他是我的朋友。
3	Tom is my son.	湯姆是我的兒子。
4	That is my notebook.	那是我的筆記本。

● 4.動詞種類─be動詞（現在4）   CD1- 2

➡ 主詞是複數（2人以上、2個以上），代表性的如： you（你們）、 they（他們）、 we（我們）和所有複數名詞時， be動詞要用 are。這時候 be 動詞後面的名詞就要變成複數形了。

We are brothers.
我們是兄弟。

⟹ **例句**

1 You are teachers.

你們是老師。

2 They are my brothers.

他們是我的兄弟。

3 These are goats, not cows .

這些是山羊，不是牛。

4 You and I are good baseball players.

你跟我是優秀的棒球選手。

5.動詞種類—一般動詞（現在1）

⟹ 表示人或物「做了什麼，在什麼狀態」的詞叫「動詞」。be動詞（am, are, is）以外的動詞叫「一般動詞」。英語中主詞後面接動詞。一般動詞也就是動詞的原形，用來表示現在式這個時態。

I swim.
我游泳。

⟹ **例句**

1 I walk.

我走路。

2 You run.

你跑步。

3 We draw.

我們畫畫。

4 Birds fly.

鳥會飛。

● 6.動詞種類──一般動詞（現在2）

➡ 動詞分及物和不及物兩種，它們的分別是在「後面能不能接受詞」。什麼叫及物呢？及物是指動作會影響到他物，所以後面要接承受這個動作的目的物（也就是受詞）。及物動詞後面要接受詞，不及物動詞後面不接受詞。我們先看及物動詞。

I ordered a steak.
我點了一客牛排。

➡ 例句

1 He rides horses. | 他騎馬。

2 Mike touches the cat. | 麥克觸碰那隻貓。

3 George has an office. | 喬治有一間辦公室。

4 His dog catches the ball. | 他的狗接住球。

● 7.動詞種類──一般動詞（現在3） CD1- 3

➡ 動作不會影響到他物，而不用接受詞的動詞叫不及物動詞。不及物動詞最大重點就是，後面不能直接加上受詞。

I wait.
我等待。

➡ 例句

1 I win. | 我勝利。

2 I sing. | 我唱歌。

3 I jump. | 我跳躍。

4 I see. | 我明白了。

● 8.動詞種類─第三人稱 ・ 單數s（1）

➜ 我、你以外的人或東西叫「第三人稱」，也就是說話者與聽話者以外的所有的人或物。主詞是第三人稱，而且是單數（一個人、一個）的時候，一般動詞後面要接s，這叫「第三人稱・單數的s」。

He runs fast.
他跑得很快。

➜ 例句

1 She likes flowers.　　　　　　　她喜歡花。

2 My uncle plays golf.　　　　　　我叔叔打高爾夫球。

3 Ann washes her hair everyday.　　安每天洗頭。

4 Jim always cooks his dinner.　　　吉姆總是自己做晚餐。

● 9.動詞種類─第三人稱 ・ 單數s（2）

➜ 主詞雖然是第三人稱，但為複數（兩人以上、兩個以上）時，動詞不加s。

They like Christmas.
他們喜歡聖誕節。

➜ 例句

1 We have a new computer.　　　　我們有部新電腦。

2 Her parents know Ann.　　　　　她的父母認識安。

3 They drink coffee in the morning.　他們早上喝咖啡。

4 Tom and Judy like popcorn.　　　湯姆和茱蒂喜歡爆米花。

● 10.動詞種類─第三人稱 · 單數s（3） CD1- 4

➡ 主詞是「第三人稱單數」時，一般動詞規則上要接s，但是也有不在這個規則範圍內的情況。一般動詞要接 -s, -es的情況是：1.主詞是第三人稱；2.主詞是單數；3.時態是在現在。

She goes to bed early.
她睡得很早。

➡ 例句

1	He teaches English.	他教英文。
2	Mr. Lee studies hard.	李先生努力學習。
3	Tom has to stay at home.	湯姆得留在家。
4	My father has a new car.	我父親有台新車。

初級
Level

● 11.名詞─主詞 · 目的語 · 補語（1）

➡ 表示人或物的詞叫「名詞」，名詞可以成為句子的主詞。通常主詞後面接動詞，所以《主詞＋動詞》就形成了句子的骨幹啦！

Tom exercises.
湯姆運動。

➡ 例句

1	She cried.	她哭了。
2	He writes.	他寫東西。
3	They laugh.	他們笑。
4	We dance.	我們跳舞。

● 12.名詞─主詞・目的語・補語（2）

➡ 名詞會有各種修飾詞，其中比較具代表性的有，修飾名詞的 a, the, my, your, that。

There is a new house.
那裡有一間新房子。

➡ 例句

1 Mary is my aunt. ┃ 瑪莉是我的阿姨。

2 He is your cousin. ┃ 他是你的表弟。

3 My brother plays the piano. ┃ 我弟弟彈鋼琴。

4 She kept her promise. ┃ 她遵守了她的承諾。

● 13.名詞─主詞・目的語・補語（3）　CD1- 5

➡ 名詞也可以做動詞的受詞。受詞就是接在動詞後面，成為主詞動作對象的詞。要記得喔！及物動詞一定要接受詞。

I love you.
我愛你。

➡ 例句

1 I like pets. ┃ 我喜歡寵物。

2 I bought a pair of shoes. ┃ 我買了一雙鞋子。

3 My brother changed his plan. ┃ 我弟弟改變了他的計畫。

4 They built that tower. ┃ 他們建造了那座塔。

● 14.名詞—主詞　目的語　補語（4）

➡ 名詞也可以是動詞的補語。什麼是補語呢？補語就是出現在be動詞，或一般動詞的後面，用來補充說明主詞，跟主詞有對等（＝）關係的詞。

Mary is a singer and she sings well.
瑪莉是一個歌手，而且她唱得很好。

➡ 例句

1 Jack is a wise lawyer.｜傑克是個有智慧的律師。

2 They are very hard-working students.｜他們是很努力的學生。

3 My major is modern art.｜我的主修是現代藝術。

4 My boyfriend becomes a doctor.｜我男朋友成為一名醫生。

初級
Level

● 15.代名詞—人稱代名詞（1）

➡ 代替名詞的叫「代名詞」，而用來代替人的代名詞叫「人稱代名詞」。當你不想再重複前面提過的名字時，可以用人稱代名詞來代替。

Nick is my brother. He likes music.
尼克是我的弟弟。他喜歡音樂。

➡ 例句

1 Mary is an American. However, she can't speak English.｜瑪莉是美國人。然而，她並不會說英文。

2 I have a dog. It has gray fur.｜我有一隻狗。牠的毛是灰色的。

3 Jack and I work in a senior high school. We are teachers.

傑克和我在一所高中工作。我們是老師。

4 Patty and Iris are my friends. They feed my fish.

派蒂和愛瑞斯是我的朋友。他們餵我的魚。

16. 代名詞—人稱代名詞（2） CD1-6

➡ 人稱代名詞也可以單獨當作主詞使用。人稱代名詞分： 第一人稱：自己是說話者之一，例如：I（我），we（我們）。第二人稱：說話的對象，例如：you（你）。第三人稱：he（他），she（她），It（它），they（他們）。

We hate vegetables.
我們討厭蔬菜。

➡ **例句**

1 You are a speaker.

你是一位演說家。

2 He comes from the USA.

他從美國來的。

3 She is very careful with the patients.

她對待病人很小心。

4 They are just teenagers.

他們只是青少年。

17. 代名詞—人稱代名詞（3）

➡ 人稱代名詞也可以是動詞的受詞，這時候叫「受格」，也可以稱做受詞。人稱代名詞當受詞時，大都會有變化。

My dog likes me.
我的狗喜歡我。

➡ 例句

1 These are fresh strawberries. I love them. | 這些是新鮮的草莓。我很喜歡它們。

2 Lily likes the song. I like it, too. | 莉莉喜歡這首歌，我也喜歡它。

3 The baby is cute. We love her. | 這個小嬰兒很可愛。我們很喜歡她。

4 These cakes are so delicious. I can eat them all. | 這些蛋糕太好吃了。我可以吃光它們。

● 18.代名詞—人稱代名詞（4）

初級 Level

➡ 記一下受格人稱代名詞的人稱及其單複數。例如，單數：I→me；you→you；he→him；she→her；it→it；複數：we→us；you→you；they→them。

Mary pleases us.
瑪莉讓我們開心。

➡ 例句

1 We know her. | 我們認識她。

2 Target it. | 瞄準它。

3 Lucy hates him. | 露西恨他。

4 Don't tell them. | 別告訴他們。

19.形容詞—兩種用法（1） CD1- 7

➡ 表示人或物的性質、形狀及數量的詞叫形容詞。形容詞接在名詞的前面，可以修飾後面的名詞，讓後面的名詞有更清楚的表現。

She is a good singer.
她是一個很好的歌手。

➡ 例句

1 This city has a long river.

這城市有一條很長的河川。

2 I have four brothers.

我有四個兄弟。

3 That is a big car.

那是一輛大車子。

4 This is an interesting book.

這是一本有趣的書。

20.形容詞—兩種用法（2）

➡ 一個名詞前面可以有多個形容詞來修飾。

I have a beautiful blue ring.
我有一個美麗的藍色戒指。

➡ 例句

1 She is a big, tall girl.

她是個又高又大的女孩。

2 The two young boys are my brothers.

這兩個年輕男孩是我的弟弟。

3 Jack is a kind and cute boy.

傑克是一個善良又可愛的男孩。

4 Ruby is a beautiful young lady.

露比是一個漂亮的年輕少女。

● 21.形容詞—兩種用法（3）

➡ 形容詞也可以當作 be動詞的補語。這時候，只要把形容詞接在be動詞的後面就行了，後面不用接名詞。就像這樣：《主詞＋be動詞＋形容詞》，這裡的形容詞是用來修飾前面的主詞。

Jane is fantastic.
珍很棒。

● 例句

1 The doll is lovely.

這玩偶很可愛。

2 My sister looks happy.

我妹妹看起來很快樂。

3 That building is old.

那棟建築物很老舊。

4 He is very famous.

他非常有名。

● 22.副詞—讓表現更豐富（1）　　CD1- 8

➡ 用來修飾動詞，表示動作「在哪裡」、「怎麼樣」、「什麼程度」、「在什麼時候」等各種意思的詞叫「副詞」。

I throw hard.
我丟得很用力。

● 例句

1 He speaks English slowly.

他慢慢地說英文。

2 She works hard.

她工作努力。

3 I got up early.　　　　　　　我起得早。

4 Kate eats a lot!　　　　　　　凱特吃很多！

● 23.副詞—讓表現更豐富（2）

➡ 副詞不僅修飾動詞，也可以放在形容詞前面修飾形容詞。

That is a very long bridge.
那是一座很長的橋。

➡ 例句

1 The test was very easy.　　　　這考試很簡單。

2 This beer is cool enough.　　　這啤酒已經夠涼了。

3 You are too lazy.　　　　　　你太懶散了。

4 Mary is much taller than my sister.　瑪莉比我妹妹高多了。

● 24.否定文—be動詞（1）

➡ be動詞（am, are, is）的否定句，就是在be動詞的後面放not，表示「不…」的否定意義。

I am not George the engineer.
我不是工程師喬治。

➡ 例句

1 He is not an Englishman.　　　他不是個英國人。

2 You are not his niece.　　　　妳不是他的姪女。

3 This is not my shirt.　　　　這不是我的襯衫。

4 It is not a pig.　　　　　　牠不是一隻豬。

25.否定文──be動詞（2）　　　CD1-9

➡ be動詞的否定文常用縮寫的形式，要記住喔！isn't是is not的縮寫；aren't是are not的縮寫。

I'm not stupid.
我不笨。

➡ **例句**

1 He's not heavy.　　　　　　他不重。

2 Louis isn't smart.　　　　　路易斯不聰明。

3 You are not fat.　　　　　　你不胖。

4 We aren't baseball players.　　我們不是棒球選手。

26.否定文──一般動詞（3）

➡ 表示「不…」的否定說法叫「否定句」。一般動詞的否定句的作法，是要在動詞前面加do not（=don't）。do not是現在否定式。

I don't read books.
我不看書。

➡ **例句**

1 You don't like this city.　　　你不喜歡這個城市。

2 They don't study English.　　　他們不念英語。

3 We don't eat breakfast.

我們不吃早餐。

4 You don't have a pen.

你沒有筆。

● 27.否定文—一般動詞（4）

➡ 主詞是「第三人稱・單數」時，do要改成does，而does not（=doesn't）後面接的動詞一定要是原形動詞。does not是現在否定式。

She doesn't play tennis.
她不打網球。

➡ 例句

1 He doesn't like music.

他不喜歡音樂。

2 She doesn't have any brothers.

她沒有任何兄弟。

3 She doesn't read novels.

她不看小說。

4 Kitty doesn't have a book.

凱蒂沒有書。

● 28.疑問句—be動詞（1）　CD1- 10

➡ be動詞的疑問句，只把主詞跟動詞前後對調就好啦！也就是《be動詞＋主詞…》，然後句尾標上「？」。配合主詞，要正確加上be動詞喔！回答的方式是：「Yes, 代名詞+ am/are/is.」、「No, 代名詞+am not/aren't/isn't」。

Are you a nurse?—Yes, I am.
你是護士嗎？—是，我是。

➡ 例句

1 Are you American?—No, I'm not.

你是美國人嗎？—不，我不是。

2 Is this your uniform?—Yes, it is.

這是你的制服嗎？─是，它是。

3 Is the Earth round?—Yes, it is.

地球是圓的嗎？─是，它是。

4 Is that a park?—Yes, it is.

那是座公園嗎？─是，它是。

● 29.疑問句──be動詞（2）

➡ 會問問題也要會回答喔！回答疑問句，要把主詞改成人稱代名詞。

Does Ann celebrate Christmas?—No, she doesn't.
安慶祝聖誕節嗎？─不，她不慶祝。

➡ 例句

1 Is Mary unhappy?—No, she isn't.

瑪莉不開心嗎？─不，她沒有。

2 Is your sister healthy?—Yes, she is.

你姊姊健康嗎？─是，她健康。

3 Are those children yours?—No, they aren't.

那些都是你的小孩嗎？─不，他們不是。

4 Are those boys smoking?—Yes, they are.

那些男孩正在抽煙嗎？─是，他們在抽煙。

● 30.疑問句──一般動詞（3）

➡ 表示「…嗎？」問對方事物的句子叫「疑問句」。一般動詞的疑問句是在句首接Do，句尾標上「？」。回答的方式是：「Yes, 代名詞+ do.」、「No, 代名詞+ don't」。

Do you like comic books?—Yes, I do.
你喜歡漫畫書嗎？—是，我喜歡。

➡ 例句

1 Do you live in New York? —No, I don't.

你住在紐約嗎？—不，我不住那裡。

2 Do you use a computer? —Yes, I do.

你用電腦嗎？—是，我用。

3 Do they save money? —Yes, they do.

他們存錢嗎？—是，他們存錢。

4 Do they drink water? —No, they don't.

他們喝水嗎？—不，他們不喝。

31.疑問句—一般動詞（4）

➡ 主詞是「第三人稱單數」時，不用do而是用does，而且後面的動詞不加-s、-es，一定要用原形喔！回答的方式是：「Yes, 代名詞+ does.」、「No, 代名詞+ doesn' t」。

Does Mary like steak?—Yes, she does.
瑪莉喜歡牛排嗎？—是的，她喜歡。

➡ 例句

1 Does he have brown eyes?—No, he doesn't.

他有褐色的眼睛嗎？—不，他沒有。

2 Does your brother understand English?—Yes, he does.

你弟弟懂英語嗎？—是，他懂。

3 Does Ann live in Taiwan?—No, she doesn't.

安住在台灣嗎？—不，她不在。

4 Does it taste good?—Yes, it does. | 那吃起來好吃嗎？—是，好吃。

● 二、動詞跟助動詞：1.過去式—be動詞（1）　CD1-11

➔ 要表達動作或情況是發生在過去的時候，英語的動詞是要改成「過去式」的！be動詞的過去式有兩個，am, is的過去形是was，are的過去形是were。

I was busy yesterday.
昨天我很忙。

➔ 例句

1 She was tired last night. | 她昨天晚上很累。

2 You were absent yesterday. | 你昨天沒來。

3 There were some girls there. | 當時那裡有幾個女孩。

4 We were in Seoul last week. | 上星期我們在首爾。

初級
Level

● 2.過去式—be動詞（2）

➔ 表示過去並沒有發生某動作或某狀況時，就要用「過去否定式」。be動詞的「過去」否定式，就是在was或were的後面加上not，成為was not（=wasn't）, were not（=weren't）。

The reporter was not tired.
那記者當時不累。

➔ 例句

1 He wasn't married. | 他當時未婚。

2 She wasn't at the bookstore. | 她當時不在書店。

3 They weren't afraid.

他們當時不害怕。

4 We weren't in town last week.

上星期我們不在鎮上。

● 3.過去式—be動詞（3）

➡ be動詞的疑問句，是把be動詞放在主詞的前面，變成《be動詞＋主語…？》，過去式也是一樣喔！回答是用 "yes"、"no" 開頭。

Was the road flat?—No, it wasn't.
馬路平坦嗎？—不，不平。

➡ 例句

1 Were you hungry?—No, I wasn't.

你那時餓嗎？—不，我不餓。

2 Were you at home last night—Yes, I was.

你昨晚在家嗎？—是，我在。

3 Was it rainy in Taipei yesterday?—Yes, It was.

昨天台北一直下雨嗎？—是，一直下雨。

4 Were the roses pretty?—Yes, they were.

那些玫瑰花漂亮嗎？—是，它們漂亮。

● 4.過去式—一般動詞（1）　　CD1- 12

➡ 英語中說過去的事時，要把動詞改為過去式。一般動詞的過去形，是在原形動詞的詞尾加上-ed。

She helped me.
她幫了我。

➡ 例句

1 I checked his homework. | 我檢查了他的作業。

2 We danced last night. | 我們昨晚跳舞。

3 They watched TV last Sunday. | 他們上星期天看了電視。

4 My mother used my bag last Monday. | 我母親上個星期一用了我的包包。

● 5.過去式──一般動詞（2）

➡ 原則上一般動詞是在詞尾加-ed的，但也有在這原則之外的。如字尾是e直接加d；字尾是子音＋y則去y加 "-ied"；字尾是短母音＋子音的單音節動詞：重複字尾再加 "-ed"，

I lived in the center of the city.
我住在市中心。

➡ 例句

1 They decided to clean the road. | 他們決定了要清理馬路。

2 He grabbed a pen and then corrected the tests. | 他抓了一枝筆然後改了考卷。

3 They copied my homework! | 他們抄我的作業！

4 John married her a month ago. | 約翰一個月前娶了她。

● 6.過去式──一般動詞（3）

➡ 一般動詞的過去式中，詞尾不是規則性地接-ed，而是有不規則變化的動詞。這樣的動詞不僅多，而且大都很重要，要一個個確實記住喔！

初級
Level

I bought a couch yesterday.
我昨天買了個躺椅。

➡ 例句

1 I wrote a sad story. | 我寫了一個悲傷的故事。

2 My daughter drew a picture. | 我女兒畫了一張畫。

3 Mary gave George a present. | 瑪莉送了一份禮物給喬治。

4 Kay sat on the table. | 凱坐在桌子上。

● 7.過去式─一般動詞（4）　　　　CD1- 13

➡ 上述的動詞叫「不規則動詞」，與其相對的，詞尾可直接接-ed變成過去式的就叫做「規則動詞」。

She cooked dinner.
她做了晚餐。

➡ 例句

1 I washed the dishes. | 我洗了盤子。

2 My children wanted a bigger house. | 我的孩子們想要大一點的房子。

3 I used some eggs. | 我用了一些蛋。

4 We joined a new club yesterday. | 我們昨天新加入了一個社團。

● 8.過去式──一般動詞（5）

➡ 要說「我過去沒有做什麼、沒有怎麼樣」，就要用過去否定的說法。一般動詞的「過去」否定，是要在動詞的前面接did not（=didn't）。訣竅是無論主語是什麼，都只要接did就可以啦！

I didn't watch TV last night.
我昨晚沒有看電視。

➡ 例句

1 I didn't read the book.

我沒看這本書。

2 She didn't come.

她沒有來。

3 He didn't catch the last bus.

他沒有趕上末班公車。

4 We didn't stay at the hotel.

我們並沒有待在飯店裡。

● 9.過去式──一般動詞（6）

➡ 一般動詞的「過去」疑問句，要把Did放在句首，變成《Did＋主詞＋原形動詞…？》。

Did you receive the gift yesterday?—No, I didn't.
你昨天收到禮物了嗎？一不，我沒有。

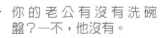

➡ 例句

1 Did your husband wash the dishes?—No, he didn't.

你的老公有沒有洗碗盤？一不，他沒有。

2 Did he kiss her last night?—Yes, he did.

他昨晚有沒有親吻她？一是的，他有。

3 Did you finish your homework?—No, I didn't.

你已經寫完你的作業了嗎？－不，我沒有。

4 Did she pick the purple one?—Yes, she did.

安是否選了紫色的那個？－是，她選了。

● 10.進行式—正在…（1）   CD1- 14

→ 《be動詞＋…ing》表示動作正在進行中。…ing是動詞詞尾加ing的形式。現在進行式，用be動詞的現在式，表示「（現在）正在…」的意思；過去進行式，用be動詞的過去式，表示「（那時候）在做…」的意思。

I am walking to the library.
我正在走路到圖書館。

→ 例句

1 Helen is making a name list.

海倫正在列名單。

2 We are cooking beef now.

我們現在正在煮牛肉。

3 We were just starting the game.

我們當時才正要開始比賽。

4 She was talking to her boss.

她當時正在和老闆說話。

● 小專欄

→ 動詞後面接ing時叫「ing形」，ing形的接法跟規則動詞「ed」的接法很相似。ing形的接法如下：
1.詞尾直接接ing
2.詞尾是e的動詞，去e加ing
3.詞尾是「短母音＋子音」的動詞，子音要重複一次，再加ing。

1.詞尾直接接ing

1 He is playing soccer now. | 他現在正在踢足球。

2.詞尾是e的動詞，去e加ing

2 I am making a cake. | 我正在做蛋糕。

3.詞尾是「短母音＋子音」的動詞，子音要重複一次，再加ing。

3 We were running with his dog. | 我們那時正跟著他的狗跑。

● 11.進行式─正在…（2）

➔ 要說現在並沒有正在做什麼動作，就用進行式的否定形。進行式的否定句是在be動詞的後面接not。這跟be動詞否定句是一樣的。順序是《be動詞＋not＋…ing》，這跟be動詞的否定句是一樣的。

初級
Level

I'm not lying!
我並沒有在說謊！

➔ 例句

1 She isn't cooking lunch. | 她沒有在做午餐。

2 They aren't buying a new house. | 他們沒有要買新房子。

3 We weren't talking with Ann. | 我們那時沒有在跟安說話。

4 He wasn't taking a bath. | 他那時沒有在洗澡。

● 12.進行式─正在…（3）

➔ 進行式的疑問句，是把be動詞放在主詞的前面，順序是《be動詞＋主詞＋…ing？》，這跟be動詞的疑問句也是一樣的。

Are you listening?—Yes, I am.
你在聽嗎?—是的,我在聽。

➡ 例句

1 Is she moving the table?—No, she isn't. | 她在移動桌子嗎?—不,她沒有。

2 Is it raining now?—Yes, it is. | 現在正在下雨嗎?—是的,正在下。

3 Were they coming with Tom?—Yes, they were. | 他們那時跟湯姆一起來嗎?—是的,他們有。

4 Were you cooking at that time?—No, I wasn't. | 你那時候在做飯嗎?—沒有,我沒有。

13.未來式(1)　　　CD1- 15

➡ 在英語中要提到「未來」的事,例如未來的夢想、預定或計畫…等,動詞不用變化,而是用《will＋動詞原形》,表示「會…」、「將要…」。這叫「單純未來」。

He will come tomorrow.
他明天會到。

➡ 例句

1 He will be busy tomorrow. | 他明天會很忙。

2 We will have exams next month. | 下個月我們有考試。

3 They will be right back. | 他們馬上就回來。

4 It will rain tomorrow. | 明天會下雨。

● 14.未來式（2）

➡ 這個will是表示將來的助動詞，它還有表示未來將發生的動作或狀態，相當於「（未來）將做…」的意思。這叫「意志未來」。

I will go to the soccer game tonight.
我準備去看今晚的足球賽。

➡ 例句

1 I will attend the meeting. | 我會參加會議。

2 I will end this conversation. | 我準備結束這個對話。

3 She will get the mail. | 她會收到郵件。

4 We will call on him after school. | 我們下課後準備去他家。

初級
Level

● 15.未來式（3）

➡ 未來式的否定句是把not放在助動詞will的後面，變成《will not +動詞原形》的形式。助動詞跟原形動詞之間插入not成為否定句，可以應用在所有的助動詞上喔！對了，will not的縮寫是won't。

I won't go to the party.
我不準備去參加宴會。

➡ 例句

1 You will not find a pack of cigarettes here. | 你在這裡不會找到一包煙。

2 She won't clean the windows. | 她不願打掃窗戶。

3 My children won't bathe. | 我家小孩不洗澡。

4 They won't work on Sunday. | 他們星期天不工作。

16.未來式（4）

CD1- 16

→ be動詞的未來形，跟一般動詞的作法是一樣的。be動詞的（am, are, is）的原形是「be」，所以一般句子是《will be…》，否定句是《will not be…》。

I'll be twenty next month.
我下星期就二十歲了。

→ 例句

1 I hope you will be happy here. | 希望你在此一切滿意。

2 You will be late. | 你會遲到。

3 He will not be here on time. | 他不會準時到這裡。

4 I won't be here tomorrow. | 我明天不會在這裡。

17.未來式（5）

→ 每個人都喜歡詢問未來。英語中的未來式的疑問句，是將will放在主詞的前面，變成《will+主詞+動詞原形…？》的形式，相當於「會…嗎？」的意思。回答的方式是《Yes, 代名詞+will.》、《No, 代名詞+won't.》

Will he go abroad?—Yes, he will.
他會出國嗎？—是的，他會。

→ 例句

1 Will Jim have time to send the letter? —Yes, he will. | 吉姆有時間寄那封信嗎？—有，他有。

2 Will we arrive in Tokyo on time? —No, we won't. | 我們會準時到東京嗎？—不，我們不會。

3 Will you call me? —Yes, I will.

你會打給我嗎？ 一會的，我會。

4 Will you buy a microwave? —Yes, I will.

你會買個微波爐嗎？ 一會的，我會。

● 18.未來式（6）

➡ be動詞的疑問句也跟一般動詞一樣。由於be動詞的原形是「be」，所以是形式是《will+主詞+be…？》。

Will you be free tomorrow?—Yes, I will.
你明天有空嗎？—有，我有空。

➡ **例句**

1 Will he be on time this afternoon?—No, he won't.

他這個下午會準時到嗎？ 一不，他不會。

2 Will you be here in time?—Yes, I will.

你會及時到這裡來嗎？—會的，我會。

3 Will Mary be able to see him off on Sunday?—Yes, she will.

瑪莉星期天可以去送機嗎？—是的，她可以的。

4 Will you be nice to your sister?—Yes, I will.

你會好好對待妹妹嗎？—是，我會的。

● 19.未來式（7）　　CD1- 17

➡ 句型《will you…》在此並不是「你會…嗎？」的意思，而是「可以幫我…嗎？」的意思，是一種委婉的請求。回答的方式也很多。

Will you shut the door? —Sure.
可以麻煩你關門嗎？—沒問題。

初級
Level

例句

1 Will you please be quiet?—Sorry.

可否請你安靜一點？—對不起。

2 Will you carry my groceries?—Yes, I will.

可否請你幫我拿我買的雜貨？—好的，我幫你。

3 Will you mow the yard?—I'm sorry, I can't.

可否請你把院子的草割一割？—對不起我沒辦法。

4 Will you take out the garbage?—All right.

可否請你把垃圾拿出去倒掉？—可以啊！

20.未來式（8）

句型《will you…》也有勸誘對方，「要不要做…」的意思。回答的時候，要看當時的情況喔！

Will you watch the video with us? —Yes, I will.
要不要和我們一起看錄影帶？—好啊！我要。

例句

1 Will you talk about your hobbies? —Yes, I will.

要不要聊聊你的興趣？—好啊！我要。

2 Will you sing the song for me? —No, I won't.

要不要為我唱這首歌？—不，我不要。

3 Will you have some coffee?—Yes, please.

來杯咖啡如何？—好的，麻煩了。

4 Will we go to the market, Tom?—Yes, let's go.

湯姆，我們去市場吧！—好，我們走吧。

21.助動詞─can, may等（1）

放在動詞的前面，來幫助動詞表達更廣泛意義的詞叫「助動詞」。助動詞的後面，一定要接原形動詞。助動詞can有：（1）表示「可能」、「有能力」的意思，相當於「會…」；（2）表示「許可」的意思，相當於「可以…」。

I can live without you.
我沒有你也能活。

➡ 例句

1 She can use the knife well. | 她很會使用刀子。

2 You can call me Mary. | 您叫我瑪莉就行了。

3 You can use the car, really. | 你可以用這車子，真的。

4 Mary can drive a car. | 瑪莉會開車。

22.助動詞─can, may等（2）　　CD1- 18

助動詞may有：（1）表示「許可」的意思，相當於「可以…」；（2）表示「推測」的意思，相當於「可能…」。

You may look around.
你可以四處看看。

➡ 例句

1 You may come next Thursday. | 你可以下禮拜四過來。

2 You may watch TV on weekends. | 週末的時候，你可以看電視。

3 It may rain today. Take an umbrella with you.

今天可能會下雨。你帶把傘吧。

4 The towel may be wet.

那毛巾可能是溼的。

23.助動詞—can, may等（3）

➡ 助動詞must有：（1）表示「義務」、「命令」、「必須」的意思，相當於「得…」；（2）表示「推測」的意思，相當於「一定…」。

I must help my mother.
我得幫助我母親。

➡ 例句

1 You must follow the rules.

你必須遵守規則。

2 They must not make noise.

他們不應該製造噪音。

3 I must be crazy!

我一定是瘋了！

4 She must be very lonely.

她一定很寂寞。

24.助動詞—can, may等（4）

➡ 助動詞should有表示「義務」的意思，語含勸對方最好做某事的口氣。相當於「應該…」、「最好…」。

We should keep our promises.
我們應該信守諾言。

➡ 例句

1 You should be honest.

你應該要誠實。

2 You should hurry up. | 你應該加緊速度。

3 You should share your toys with others. | 你應該跟別人分享你的玩具。

4 You should do the right thing. | 你應該做對的事情。

● 25.助動詞─否定句（1）　　　　CD1- 19

➡ 助動詞的後面接not就變成否定式，can的後面接not表示「不會…」、「不可能…」、「不可以…」的意思，可縮寫成 can't或是cannot。

I cannot play basketball.
我不會打籃球。

➡ 例句

1 I can't paint. | 我不會畫畫。

2 He can't be only eighteen years old. | 他不可能才十八歲。

3 You can't be hungry already. | 你不可能已經餓了。

4 You can't do that again. | 你絕不可以再那麼做了。

● 26.助動詞─否定句（2）

➡ may not是「可能不…」、「不可以…」，must not是「不可以…」的意思。must not比may not有更強的「禁止」的語意。

He may not notice.
他可能不會注意到。

➡ 例句

1 It may not be true.

這可能不是真的。

2 You may not go camping tomorrow.

你明天不可以去露營。

3 You must not touch that bee.

你不可以碰那隻蜜蜂。

4 They must not enter my room.

他們不可以進我的房間。

● 27.助動詞─疑問句（1）

➡ can的疑問句，是把can放在主詞的前面，變成《Can+主詞+動詞原形…？》的形式。意思相當於「會…嗎？」。回答「是」用《Yes, +代名詞+can》；回答「不是」用《No, +代名詞+can't》。

Can you ride a horse? —No, I can't.
你會騎馬嗎？─不，我不會騎。

➡ 例句

1 Can you use chopsticks?—Yes, I can.

你會使用筷子嗎？─是，我會用。

2 Can you fix the lamp?—No, I can't.

你會修檯燈嗎？─不，我不會。

3 Can you remember anything?—No, I can't.

你能記得任何事嗎？─不，我不記得了。

4 Can you see that tree?—Yes, I can.

你看得到那棵樹嗎？─是，我看得到。

● 28.助動詞─疑問句（2）

➡ may（可以）或must（必須）的疑問句，跟can一樣是《助動詞+主語+動詞原形…？》。

May I sit down?—Sure.
我可以坐下嗎？─當然可以。

➡ 例句

1 May I send an e-mail?—Yes, of course. | 我可以寄封電子郵件嗎？
─沒問題。

2 May I open the window?—No, you may not. | 我可以打開窗戶嗎？─不，你不可以。

3 Must I carry the bag?—Yes, you must. | 我一定要帶這個包包嗎？─是的，你要。

4 Must Dolly have an operation?—No, she doesn't need to. | 桃莉一定要開刀嗎？─不，她不需要。

● 29.be動詞的另一個意思─「存在」（1） CD1- 20

➡ be動詞還有表示「存在」的意思，相當於「在」、「有」等意思。

The book is on the table.
書在桌上。

➡ 例句

1 John is at home. | 約翰在家。

2 We are in the car. | 我們都在車裡。

3 The children are on the playground | 孩子們都在運動場。

4 I was there last night. | 我昨晚在那裡。

英語文法・句型詳解

● 30.be動詞的另一個意思──「存在」（2）

➡ 表示「在」、「有」的意思時，否定句跟疑問句的形式，跟be動詞是一樣的。

The card is not on the table.
卡片不在桌上。

➡ 例句

1 John is not in the bathroom. | 約翰不在浴室。

2 They were not at the airport. | 他們當時不在機場。

3 Is he at the beach?—Yes, he is. | 他在海邊嗎？─是呀，他在。

4 Am I in America?—Yes, you are. | 我在美國嗎？─對呀，你在。

● 31.be動詞的另一個意思──「有」（1）

➡ there原本是「那裡」的意思，但是「there+be動詞」還有表示存在之意，相當於中文的「有（在）…」。單數時用《There is…》；複數時用《There are…》。

There is an orange in the basket.
籃子裡有顆橘子。

➡ 例句

1 There is a little milk in the glass. | 玻璃杯裡有些牛奶。

2 There are twenty girls in my class. | 我們班有二十個女生。

3 There are too many hills here. | 這兒有太多山坡。

4 There were many shops in Michigan. | 密西根州有很多商店。

● 32.be動詞的另一個意思—「有」（2）

➡ 否定句是在be動詞的後面接not，疑問句要把be動詞放在句首，變成《Is there…？》的形式。

There isn't a clock in my room.
我房裡沒有時鐘。

➡ 例句

1 There isn't a black car by the gate.　　門旁邊沒有黑色的車子。

2 There isn't a piano in the classroom.　　教室裡沒有鋼琴。

3 Is there chalk on the table?　　桌上有粉筆嗎？

4 Are there any cookies in the box?　　盒子裡有餅乾嗎？

初級
Level

● 三、名詞與代名詞：1.名詞的複數形（1）　CD1- 21

➡ 我們常說二個以上要加s，這是英語的特色。英語中人或物是很清楚地分為一個（單數）跟二個以上（複數）的。人或物是複數時，名詞要用「複數形」。一般複數形要在詞尾加上-s。

Many plants come alive in spring.
很多植物在春天都會活起來。

➡ 例句

1 I got eighty points.　　我得了八十分。

2 I have four baseball caps.　　我有四頂棒球帽。

3 I have two notebooks.　　我有兩本筆記本。

4 Mr. Brown has three children.　　布朗先生有三個小孩。

● 2.名詞的複數形（2）

把單複數弄清楚，說起英語會更道地喔！名詞的詞尾是ch, sh, s, x, o時，複數形要加-es。

He ate three sandwiches.
他吃了三個三明治。

➡ 例句

1 Dad broke five dishes.　　　　　爸爸打破了五個盤子。

2 Sam collects pictures of foxes.　　山姆收集狐狸的照片。

3 There are three big boxes.　　　　那裡有三個大盒子。

4 I have six potatoes.　　　　　　　我有六個馬鈴薯。

● 3.名詞的複數形（3）

詞尾是「子音+y」時，y要變成i，然後加-es。這裡的-es發音是[z]。

The babies are sleeping.
寶寶們正熟睡著。

➡ 例句

1 Maybe I know those ladies.　　　　我可能認識那些女士。

2 We saw five flies.　　　　　　　　我們看到五隻蒼蠅。

3 The toy needs batteries.　　　　　這件玩具需要電池。

4 America and Canada are big countries.　美國跟加拿大是大國家。

50

● 4.名詞的複數形（4）　　　　　CD1- 22

➡ 名詞的複數形也有不規則的變化，如man跟men（男人）、foot跟feet（腳）、mouse跟mice（老鼠）。也有單數跟複數是一樣的如sheep（羊）、deer（鹿）跟fish（魚）。

He has five bad teeth.
他有五顆不好的牙。

➡ 例句

1 There are three mice. | 有三隻老鼠。

2 Do you know the women? | 你認識那些女人嗎？

3 I want to buy two fish. | 我想買兩條魚。

4 Are there many sheep in the field? | 草原上有很多羊嗎？

初級
Level

● 5.可數名詞跟不可數名詞（1）

➡ 名詞大分為「可數名詞」跟「不可數名詞」兩類。可數名詞複數（2人或2個以上）時，要用複數形。另外，單數（1人、1個）時，前面常接a或an。

I have a camera.
我有一台相機。

➡ 例句

1 She gave me an apple. | 她給了我一顆蘋果。

2 I have a banana and an apple. | 我有一根香蕉跟一顆蘋果。

3 Swimming is a good sport. | 游泳是個好運動。

4 They are my good friends. | 他們是我的好朋友。

● 小專欄

➡ 不可數名詞一般不接表示「單數的」a或an，也沒有複數形。不可數名詞基本上有下列三種。

　　1.固有名詞（唯一的，大寫開頭的人名、地名等）
　　2.物質名詞（沒有一定形狀的空氣、水、麵包等）
　　3.抽象名詞（性質、狀態籠統，無形的愛、美、和平、音樂等）

　　4.固有名詞（人名、地名等）

1 I live in Paris. ｜ 我住在巴黎。

　　2.物質名詞（空氣、水、麵包等）

2 I want a glass of water. ｜ 我想一杯水。

　　3.抽象名詞（愛、美、和平、音樂等）

3 We love peace. ｜ 我喜歡和平。

● 6.可數名詞跟不可數名詞（2）

➡ 不能用1個、2個來計算的名詞，也可以用表示「量」的形容詞，來表示「多或少」。如：some（一些）, much（很多）, little（很少）, a little（一點點）, no（沒有）, a great deal of（很多）, a lot of（很多）…。

I want some apple juice.
我想要一點蘋果汁。

➡ 例句

1 I need a lot of food. ｜ 我需要很多食物。

2 I would like some salad. ｜ 我想要一些沙拉。

3 She has no money. ｜ 她沒有錢。

4 He has a great deal of clothes. | 他有很多衣服。

● 7.可數名詞跟不可數名詞（3）　　CD1- 23

➜ 不可數名詞在當作單位名詞時，有時變成可數的。

I want two glasses of milk.
我要兩杯牛奶。

➜ 例句

1 Give me a cup of coffee. | 給我一杯咖啡。

2 She has a slice of bread. | 她吃一片麵包。

3 There is a sheet of paper. | 那裡有一張紙。

4 Would you like a glass of fresh juice? | 你要不要來一杯新鮮的果汁？

● 8.指示代名詞（1）

➜ 指示眼睛可以看到的東西或人叫「指示代名詞」。指近處的東西或人，
　單數用this（這個），複數形用 these（這些）。

This is my eraser.
這是我的橡皮擦。

➜ 例句

1 This is a great plan. | 這計畫很棒。

2 These seats are taken . | 這些位子有人坐了。

3 This is a big surprise! | 這是個大大的驚喜！

4 Are these your magazines? | 這些是你的雜誌嗎？

初級 **Level** 英語文法 · 句型詳解

● 9.指示代名詞（2）

➡ 指示較為遠處的人或物，單數用that（那個），複數用those（那些）。

That is my father.
那位是我的父親。

➡ 例句

1 That is your coat.　　　　　　　　　那是你的外套。

2 That's a large sweater!　　　　　　　那真是件大毛衣!

3 That was the best movie of the year!　那是年度的最佳電影!

4 Those books are the same.　　　　　　那些書都是一樣的。

● 10.指示代名詞（3）　　　　　　CD1- 24

➡ this從「這個」的意思，發展成「（介紹人說的）這位是…」、「這裡是
…」、「今天是…」及「（打電話指自己）我是…」的意思。

This is George, my second cousin.
這是我第二個表兄弟，喬治。

➡ 例句

1 This is the national theater.　　　這是國家劇院。

2 This is my nephew.　　　　　　　這位是我外甥。

3 This is the kitchen.　　　　　　　這裡是廚房。

4 Hello, this is Ann.　　　　　　　你好!我是安。〈打電話時〉

● 11.指示代名詞（4）

➡ 指示眼前較為遠處的事物的 that，也表示「那、那件事」的意思。

That's a special gift.
這是個特別的禮物。

➡ 例句

1 That's her third book.		那是她的第三本書。
2 That is a huge department store.		這家百貨公司真大。
3 That's a good idea.		那真是個好主意。
4 That's an interesting question.		這是個有趣的問題。

初級
Level

● 12.名詞及代名詞的所有格—表示「的」的詞（1）

➡ 表示「…的」的形式的叫「所有格」。表示人或動物的名詞，以接
《…'s》表示所有格。

My father's car is red.
我父親的車子是紅色的。

➡ 例句

1 The dog's name is Kant.		這隻狗的名字叫康德。
2 That is my brother's dictionary.		那是我哥哥的字典。
3 My uncle's house is near the station.		我叔叔的家離車站很近。
4 Have you seen Anna's brother before?		你以前看過安娜的弟弟嗎？

初級 **Level**

英語文法・句型詳解

13.名詞及代名詞的所有格—表示「的」的詞（2）

➤ 表示人或動動以外，無生命物的名詞，一般用《of…》的形式來表示所有格。of…修飾前面的名詞。

We broke the legs of the desk.
我們弄壞了桌腳。

➤ 例句

1 It is raining hard in the south of Taiwan. | 台灣南部正下著大雨。

2 Autumn is the best season of the year. | 秋天是一年中最棒的季節。

3 He was the leader of his class. | 他是班上的領導者。

4 January is the first month of the year. | 一月是一年當中的第一個月。

14.名詞及代名詞的所有格—表示「的」的詞（3）

➤ 人稱代名詞的所有格，各有固定的形式。《I→my〔our〕》、《you→your〔your〕》、《he→his〔their〕》、《she→her〔their〕》、《it→its〔their〕》。〔 〕裡是複數。

John is my classmate.
約翰是我的同學。

➤ 例句

1 He is my grandfather. | 他是我的祖父。

2 She goes out with her friends. | 她和她的朋友出去。

3 They speak English in their country. | 他們在他們的國家裡說英語。

4 The dog is shaking its head. | 那隻狗搖著牠的頭。

● 15.名詞及代名詞的所有格—表示「的」的詞（4）

➡ 指示代名詞的 this, that等，也可以當作指示形容詞，來表示「…的」的意思。但可不是「所有格」喔！

That question was simple.
那個題目很簡單。

➡ 例句

1 Who drives that truck? | 是誰開那輛卡車的？

2 You are not the king of this country. | 你不是這個國家的國王。

3 Did you buy all of those pens? | 那些筆全是你買的嗎？

4 What have you been doing during these days? | 這些日子你都在做些什麼？

● 16.所有代名詞跟反身代名詞（1）　CD1- 26

➡ 表示「…的東西」的代名詞叫「所有代名詞」，這個用法是為了不重複同一名詞。所指的「物」不管是單數或複數，所有代名詞都是一樣。所有代名詞1個字等同於〈所有格＋名詞〉。

That picture is hers.
那張照片是她的。

➡ 例句

1 These bags are yours, sir. | 這些包包是你的，先生。

2 The television is ours. | 這電視是我們的。

3 The boat is his. | 這艘船是他的。

4 The farm is not yours. It's theirs. | 這農場不是你的，是他們的。

● 小專欄

下面的相同意思，不同的說法，是考試常出現的，要多注意喔！

That is our car.
那是我們的車。
↓
That car is ours.
那車是我們的。

These are my pens.
這些是我的筆。
↓
These pens are mine.
這些筆是我的。

That is Smith's ball.
那是史密斯的球。
↓
That ball is Smith's.
那個球是史密斯的。

● 17.所有代名詞跟反身代名詞（2）

➡ 動詞的受詞等，跟句子的主詞是一樣的時候，要用表示「自己…」的特別的代名詞，叫「反身代名詞」。也就是人稱代名詞加上 -self（單數形），-selves（複數形）。

I asked myself.
我問我自己。

➡ 例句

1 You should believe in yourself.

你應該相信自己。

2 The man hurt himself.

這個人傷了他自己。

3 My friends prepared for the party by themselves.

我的朋友們自己準備了派對。

4 My sister and I often cook dinner for ourselves.

我姊姊和我通常都自己作晚餐。

● 18.所有代名詞跟反身代名詞（3）

➡ 反身代名詞也有強調主詞的作用。

58

I made the cake myself.
我親手做了一個蛋糕。

➡ 例句

1 I washed all the dishes myself. | 我自己洗了所有的碗盤。

2 He paid the bill himself. | 他自己付了帳單。

3 She picked the new house herself. | 她自己一個人挑選了新家。

4 They prepared for the party themselves. | 他們自己準備了派對。

● 19.不定代名詞—some, any等（1）　CD1- 27

初級
Level

➡ 沒有特定的指某人或某物的代名詞叫「不定代名詞」。不定代名詞的 some含糊的指示人或物的數量，表示「一些、幾個」的意思。

There are some apples in the basket.
籃子裡有一些蘋果。

➡ 例句

1 Give me some lemons, please. | 請給我一些檸檬。

2 I want some tea. | 我要一些茶。

3 I buy some books every month. | 我每個月都買幾本書。

4 Some of the test questions were too hard. | 這個考試中的部份題目真的太難了。

● 20.不定代名詞—some, any等（2）

➡ something表示「某事物」，somebody, someone表示「某人」、「誰」的意思。這些都是單數。

I smell something.
我聞到某種味道。

例句

1 I have something to tell you. | 有話要跟你說。

2 There's something I want you to look at. | 這裡有些東西我想給你看。

3 Somebody has to wake me up. | 要有個人叫我起床。

4 There is someone at the door. | 門旁有個人。

21.不定代名詞—some, any等（3）

➡ 疑問句中表示「多少個」、「多少」、「多少人」時，用 any。否定句用 not…any，意思是「一個也（一人也）…沒有」。

Do you have any wishes?
你有任何願望嗎？

例句

1 Do you want any hot dogs? | 你要不要熱狗？

2 Is there any big news today? | 今天有什麼大新聞嗎？

3 I don't have any kids. | 我沒有小孩。

4 Ms. Jolie doesn't have any friends. | 裘莉小姐沒有任何朋友。

22.不定代名詞—some, any等（4） CD1- 28

➡ 同樣地，在疑問句跟否定句中 anything是「什麼」、「什麼也」的意思；anybody, anyone是「有誰」、「誰也」的意思。

I don't know anything about the pollution.
污染的事我什麼也不知道。

➡ 例句

1 They are busy, but I don't have anything to do. | 他們在忙，但我沒什麼事可以做。
2 Well, I don't see anyone here! | 嗯，我在這裡連個人影都沒看見！
3 Anybody can make a hamburger. | 不管誰都會做漢堡。
4 Does anybody grow flowers at home? | 這裡有誰在家裡有種花嗎？

● 23.不定代名詞—all, each等（1）

➡ all是「全部」，each是「各個」的意思。其中《all of+複數名詞》被當作複數，《all of+不可數名詞》被當作單數，而 each則都是當作單數。

I know all of them.
我認識他們所有人。

➡ 例句

1 All of us agreed to do that. | 我們全都同意這麼做。
2 All of us can play cards. | 我們全都會玩牌。
3 Each of us has a car. | 我們每人都有車。
4 Each of the girls has a cell phone. | （他們之中）每一位女生都有手機。

● 24.不定代名詞—all, each等（2）

➡ both跟 either都是用在形容二個事物的時候，但是 both表示「兩者都」，被當作複數，either則表示「兩者中任一」，被當作單數。

Both of you may go.
你們兩個都得離開。

➡ 例句

1 Both my parents are fine. | 我父母兩人都很好。

2 Both of them appeared at the party. | 他們都在派對上出現了。

3 Either of the teams will win. | 那兩隊其中之一會贏。

4 Write either with a pen or with a pencil. | 用原子筆或鉛筆寫都可以。

● 25.不定代名詞—all, each等（3）　CD1- 29

➡ one除了「一個、一個的」意思以外，還可以用來避免重複，代替前面出現過的名詞。不定代名詞 one跟前面的名詞相對應，表示跟前面的名詞是「同類的東西」，常用於《a+形容詞+ one》的句型。

This cup is dirty, I need a clean one.
這片杯子很髒，我需要一個乾淨的。

➡ 例句

1 Do you have a sweater?—Yes, I have one. | 你有毛衣嗎？一有，我有一件。

2 He has a motorcycle. I want one, too. | 他有一台摩托車，我也想要有一台。

| 3 | Do you want a big apple or a small one? | 你要大的蘋果還是要小的？ |
| 4 | We could give her this old TV and buy a new one. | 我們可以把這台舊電視給她，然後買一台新的。 |

● 26.不定代名詞─all, each等（4）

→ another表示不定的「又一個東西（人）」、「另一個東西（人）」。another其實是由〈an+ other〉來的，至於the other則表示特定的「（兩個當中的）另一個東西（人）」。

I don't like this one. Show me another.
我不喜歡這個。給我看看別的。

● 例句

1	Do you want another cup of coffee?	你要不要再來一杯咖啡？
2	Will you have another piece of cake?	再來一片蛋糕如何？
3	This egg is bigger than the other.	這顆蛋比另一顆大。
4	He lives on the other side of the river.	他住在河的另一邊。

● 27.名詞其它該注意的用法─it, they等（1）

→ it除了指前接的「特定的東西」以外，也含糊地指「天氣」、「時間」、「距離」跟「明暗」等。

It's fine today.
今天天氣好。

● 例句

| 1 | It's cold outside. | 外面很冷。 |

2 It's seven-thirty.

現在七點三十分。

3 It's about twelve kilometers away.

大概有十二公里遠。

4 It's getting dark outside.

外面漸漸變暗了。

● 28.名詞其它該注意的用法─it, they等（2） CD1- 30

➔ it也可以放在句首，對應後面的不定詞（to＋原形動詞）。

It is easy to answer this question.
回答這個問題很簡單。

➔ 例句

1 It is difficult to spell the word.

要拼出這個單字很困難。

2 It is boring to stay at home all day.

待在家裡一整天是件很無聊的事。

3 It is exciting to travel to a foreign country.

到異國旅遊是件興奮的事。

4 It is interesting to chat on the Internet.

在網路上聊天是件有趣的事。

● 29.名詞其它該注意的用法─it, they等（3）

➔ we, you, they也有含糊的指「一般的人，人們，相關的人」的用法。翻譯的時候可以配合前後文。

We shouldn't take anything that is not ours.
我們不該拿不屬於自己的東西。

➡ 例句

1 Love makes you blind. | 愛情使你盲目。

2 Take your pain as a challenge. | 把你的痛苦當作挑戰。

3 You can see Jade Mountain from here. | 從這裡可以看到玉山。

4 They say he is very rich. | 據說他很有錢。

● 30.名詞其它該注意的用法─it, they等（4）

➡ 含有代名詞的片語，也要多注意喔！像是each other（互相）,one another（互相）,one after another（一個接著一個）等，都相當實用。

We call each other monthly.
我們每個月彼此互通電話。

➡ 例句

1 They hug each other for a couple of minutes. | 他們抱著對方持續幾分鐘。

2 They looked at one another and finally laughed. | 她們看著彼此，然後終於笑了出來。

3 The soldiers died one after another. | 士兵們一個接著一個死了。

4 We will never forget one another. | 我們絕不會忘記彼此的。

● 四、冠詞、形容詞跟副詞：1.a跟the（1） CD1- 31

➡ 冠詞是一種形容詞，特定指單數的「一個東西」、「一個人」時，名詞前面要接冠詞 a（an）。但是 a只用在不限定的人或物上，「限定的」人或物就要用「Point2」的冠詞 the。所以 a叫「不定冠詞」，the叫「定冠詞」

There's an elementary school near my house
我家附近有一所小學。

➡ **例句**

1 Mrs. Green is a doctor. | 格林夫人是個醫生。

2 Please stand in a line. | 請站成一直線。

3 This is a wonderful evening. | 這真是個美好的黃昏。

4 There is a huge elephant! | 那裡有一隻好大的大象!

2.a跟the（2）

➡ 在彼此都知道的情況下，指示同類事物中的某一個，也就是指示「特定的」人或物時，名詞前面要接 the，表示「那個…」的意思。

The movies starts at nine.
那齣電影九點開演。

➡ **例句**

1 Write the answer on the blackboard. | 把答案寫在黑板上。

2 Please turn to page twenty of the book. | 請翻到這本書的第二十頁。

3 They're waiting for us at the restaurant now. | 他們正在那間餐廳等我們。

4 Please close the door. | 請關門。

3.a跟the（3）

➡ 不定冠詞 a是用在不限定的單數名詞前面，所以複數名詞或不可數名詞不用加 a。

I don't like cats.
我不喜歡貓。

⊖ **例句**

1 I made some mistakes. | 我犯了些錯誤。
2 I often get headaches. | 我常有頭痛的毛病。
3 She enjoys life. | 她享受生活。
4 They drink coffee in the morning. | 他們早上喝咖啡。

4.a跟the（4）　　　　　　CD1- 32

⊖ 只要是指「特定的」人或物，不管是複數名詞或不可數名詞，都用 the。

I saw the girls at the bus station.
我在公車站看到那些女孩。

⊖ **例句**

1 I lay on the grass. | 我躺在草地上。
2 Please pass the salt. | 請把鹽遞給我。
3 I jump into the water. | 我跳進水裡。
4 Let her have the money. | 讓她拿那些錢吧。

5.a跟the該注意的用法（1）

⊖ a的後面接上「單位」，也有表示「每…」的意思。

He studies six hours a day.
他一天讀書六小時。

英語文法·句型詳解

➡ 例句

1 We go to the museum once a month.

我們每個月去博物館一次。

2 They change their menu twice a year.

他們每年會換兩次菜單。

3 I have to go to the supermarket once a month.

我每個月必須要去超市一次。

4 They go to Japan once a year.

他們每年去一趟日本。

● 6.a跟the該注意的用法（2）

➡ a也有表示「同種類的全體」的意思，也就是總稱的用法。

A rabbit has long ears.
兔子有長長的耳朵。

➡ 例句

1 A giraffe has a long neck.

長頸鹿的有長長的脖子。

2 A dream needs hard work.

夢想需要努力

3 A vacation refreshes your mind.

假期滋養人的心靈。

4 Birds of a feather flock together.

物以類聚。

● 7.a跟the該注意的用法（3）　　CD1- 33

➡ the也用在自然地被「特定」的東西之前，如「月亮」或「太陽」等獨一無二的自然物。還有only（只有一個）、 first（最初）、second（第二）等附有形容詞的名詞前。

The Sun rises in the east.
太陽從東方升起。

➡ 例句

1	The Moon goes around the Earth.	月亮繞著地球轉。
2	The Earth goes around the Sun.	地球繞著太陽轉。
3	Look! That's the best painting of DaVinci.	你看！那是達文西最好的一幅畫。
4	He won first prize.	他得了第一名。

● 8.a跟the該注意的用法（4）

➡ 同樣地，從說話者跟聽話者當時的情況，自然而然地被「特定」的事物，也用the。也就是從周圍的狀況，知道對方指的是什麼。

Pass the salt, please.
請把鹽傳過來。（指的當然是桌上的鹽）

➡ 例句

1	Look at the tiger.	看那隻老虎。（因為彼此都看到了）
2	What was that sound?	那是什麼聲音呀？（因為彼此都聽到了）
3	Explain this sentence to me, please.	請幫我解釋這個句子。
4	Give me the ticket.	給我票。

● 9.冠詞跟習慣用法（1）

➡ 在英語的成語中，冠詞也有固定的用法，下面舉出的習慣用法，一般用the。

Miss Brown can play the violin.
伯朗小姐會拉小提琴。

➡ 例句

1 He listens to the radio in the morning.　他在早上聽收音機。

2 By the way, may I have your phone number?　喔，順便一提，可以給我你的電話嗎？

3 In the end, he still didn't get the postcard.　最後，他還是沒收到明信片。

4 At that moment, she knew the truth.　在那一刻，她知道了真相。

● **10.冠詞跟習慣用法（2）**　　CD1- 34

➡ 下面的成語要用a。

Have a good time on Saturday!
星期六玩得開心點！

➡ 例句

1 Let's take a walk. −OK, let's go.　我們來散散步吧！－好啊，我們走吧。

2 Let's take a break. It will be helpful.　我們休息一下吧。那會很有幫助的。

3 Take a deep breath and you will feel better.　深呼吸會讓你舒服點。

4 He has been in Hong Kong for a long time.　他在香港好一段時間了。

● 11.冠詞跟習慣用法（3）

➡ 慣用表現中，也有省略冠詞的情況。

I go to school on foot.
我走路上學。

➡ 例句

1 He is at home because he's weak now.　　　他在家，因為他現在很虛弱。

2 Dad will come back soon.　　　爸爸馬上會回來。

3 Kate can play guitar and even write songs.　　　凱特會彈吉他，甚至會寫歌。

4 Do you go to school on Sundays?　　　你星期天要上學嗎？

初級
Level

● 12.冠詞跟習慣用法（4）

➡ 「運動」、「三餐」、「學科」等相關敘述，一般是不加冠詞的。

Let's forget about the test and play baseball!
我們忘了考試，來打棒球吧！

➡ 例句

1 We have lunch together.　　　我們一起吃午餐。

2 He majors in Chinese.　　　他主修中文。

3 Irene likes science. It's such a joy for her.　　　艾琳喜歡科學。那對她來說真是種快樂。

4 Pat doesn't like summer.　　　派特不喜歡夏天。

● 13.表示數跟量的形容詞—多・少（1） CD1- 35

➡ 「數」很多的時候用 many，「量」很多的時候用 much。many, much常用在疑問句跟否定句中。many後面要接的是可數事物，像是可以數出來的桌椅、車票…等；much是用來形容不可數的東西，像是水或果汁、很抽象的錢、時間…等。

There aren't many books in my room.
我房間裡沒有很多書。

➡ 例句

1 Are there many banks in your city? | 你的城市裡有很多銀行嗎？

2 I don't want too much butter on my toast. | 我的吐司不要太多奶油。

3 How much sugar do you need? | 你需要多少糖？

4 Is there much milk in the bottle? | 瓶子裡有很多牛奶嗎？

● 14.表示數跟量的形容詞—多・少（2）

➡ 可以同時表示「數」跟「量」很多的是 a lot of。在疑問句跟否定句以外的一般肯定句中，a lot of比 many跟 much還要常使用。

There are a lot of rules in this class.
這個班級有很多規則。

➡ 例句

1 I have a lot of problems. | 我碰到了很多問題。

2 They want a lot of water. | 他想要很多水。

3 It was a lot of work to make a map. | 做一張地圖費了好大功夫。

4 Those jeans cost a lot of money. | 那些牛仔褲花了我不少錢。

● 15.表示數跟量的形容詞—多・少（3）

➡ 表示「數」有一些時，用 a few，而且是用在複數形可數名詞上；表示「量」有一些時，用 a little，用在不可數名詞上。

I have a few friends.
我有2、3個朋友。

➡ 例句

1	It's only a few blocks away.	只不過幾條街過去而已。
2	I know only a few magic tricks.	我只會一些魔術技法。
3	I have a little money.	我有一些錢。
4	They were thirsty and drank a little coffee.	他們口渴，於是喝了一些咖啡。

初級
Level

● 16.表示數跟量的形容詞—多・少（4）

➡ 有冠詞 a的時候，含有肯定的「有一點」的語意。但是把 a拿掉只用 few, little，就含有「只有一點點」、「幾乎沒有」等否定意味。當然 few是用在「數」，而little用在「量」上。

I had few friends in the past.
過去，我沒什麼朋友。

➡ 例句

1	The kid owns few toys.	那小孩只擁有一點點玩具。
2	They took a rest and drank a little water.	他們休息了一下並喝了一點水。

3 There is little ice in the cup.

杯子裡幾乎沒什麼冰塊。

4 I have little experience.

我沒什麼經驗。

● 17.表示數跟量的形容詞—some, any等（1）CD1- 36

➡ 數詞是用來表示數目的，其中有分「計算數量」跟「表示順序」的兩種數詞。

Johnny has sixteen pens
強尼有十六支筆。

➡ 例句

1 He has two hundred kinds of stamps.

他有200種郵票。

2 He is the first son in his family.

他是家中的長男。

3 Our apartment is on the third floor.

我們的公寓在第三層樓。

4 December is the twelfth month of the year.

12月是一年中的第12個月。

● 18.表示數跟量的形容詞—some, any等（2）

➡ 表示「不特定的數或量」用 some，意思是「一些的」。中譯時有時候字面上是不翻譯的。

I want some rice.
我想要一些飯。

➡ 例句

1 There are some keys in the box.

箱子裡有幾支鑰匙。

2 Bring me some water, please.

請拿一些水給我。

3 My mother went to buy some fruit. | 我媽媽去買水果。
4 Consider it a chance to get some exercise. | 當它是個運動的好機會。

● 19.表示數跟量的形容詞—some, any等（3）

➔ 通常在疑問句和否定句中，表示「不特定的數或量」時要用 any。

Do you have any plans for the future?
你對未來有什麼計劃嗎？

➔ 例句

1 Do I have any problems with my heart? | 我的心臟有什麼問題嗎？

2 Do you have any interests? | 你有什麼嗜好嗎？

3 Do you have any ideas in mind? | 你腦子裡有什麼點子嗎？

4 Are there any serious problems? | 有什麼嚴重的問題嗎？

初級
Level

● 20.表示數跟量的形容詞—some, any等（4）

➔ any跟否定的 not一起使用時，表示「一點…也沒有」的意思。當然「數」跟「量」都可以使用。

She doesn't know any foreigners.
她一個外國人也不認識。

➔ 例句

1 I don't see any trash on the ground. | 我看不到地上任何有垃圾。

2 I didn't see any books in the package. | 我沒看見有任何書在包裹裡。

3 Sarah doesn't want any advice from a man. | 莎拉不想要從個男人那裡得到任何建議。

4 I don't have any money left this month. | 這個月我一毛錢也沒剩下。

21.副詞該注意的用法（1）　　　CD1- 37

➡ always（總是，經常）、often（常常，往往）、usually（通常）、sometimes（有時）、once（一次）等表示頻率的副詞，通常要放在一般動詞的前面，但是要放在 be動詞的後面。

He always gets up at seven.
他總是七點起床。

➡ 例句

1 I often cook noodles by myself. | 我經常自己煮麵。

2 I often go to the theater alone. | 我經常一個人去戲院。

3 I usually go to bed early. | 平常我很早睡覺。

4 He is sometimes absent from school. | 他有時會不去上學。

● 小專欄

➡ 表示「程度」的副詞，通常要放在它修飾的形容詞或副詞的前面。但是要記住喔！同樣是程度副詞的 enough（足夠），可是要放在它修飾的形容詞或副詞的後面。我們來跟另一個程度副詞 very比較看看。

He is very tall.
他很高大。

↓

He is tall enough.
他夠高大了。

This beer is very cool.
這啤酒很冰。

↓

This beer is cool enough.
這啤酒已經夠冰了。

● 22.副詞該注意的用法（2）

➡ 修飾動詞表示「很」、「非常」的時候，一般用 very much。

I enjoyed the music very much.
我非常享受音樂之美。

➡ 例句

1 Thank you very much.　　　　　　　真的很謝謝你。

2 I like the present very much.　　　　我非常喜歡這個禮物。

3 I like strawberries very much, too.　　我也很喜歡草莓。

4 He likes tennis very much.　　　　　他非常喜歡打網球。

● 23.副詞該注意的用法（3）

➡ only（僅，只）、even（甚至）也可以修飾名詞跟代名詞，放在名詞或代名詞的前面。

She came only twice.
她只來過兩次。

➡ 例句

1 It's only one o'clock.　　　　　　　現在才一點鐘。

2 It's the only way to learn.

這是學習的唯一方法。

3 Jack even wears a raincoat.

傑克甚至穿了件雨衣。

4 Laura even called the police officer.

萊拉甚至打給了警察。

五、句型・各種句子：1.有補語的句子・有受詞的句子（1）

CD1- 38

→ 一般動詞（be動詞以外的動詞）裡面，也有後面要接「補語」的動詞。
代表性的有 become（成為…）。

She became a successful model.
她成為一個成功的模特兒。

→ 例句

1 He became a teacher.

他成為老師。

2 Tom and I became the leaders of this club.

湯姆跟我變成這社團的領導人。

3 He became thin.

他變瘦了。

4 It becomes very hot in July.

七月變得很熱。

2.有補語的句子・有受詞的句子（2）

→ 後接補語的動詞，有下面幾個，要記下來喔！這些動詞的補語，常常是形容詞。

She looked great.
她看起來很棒。

➔ 例句

1	He went crazy after several months.	幾個月後他就瘋了。
2	She grew old and does not have clear thinking.	她老了並且思考不清楚。
3	She seems pretty smart.	她似乎很聰明。
4	It smells good! It must be delicious.	聞起來很香！它一定很好吃。

● 3.有補語的句子‧有受詞的句子（3）

➔ 一般動詞中，動作會影響到他物的。也就是有受詞的，叫及物動詞；動作不影響到他物，沒有受詞的叫不及物動詞。

初級
Level

I had my fourth try.
我做了第四次的嘗試。

➔ 例句

1	I write her a letter.	我寫了一封信給她。
2	I like the little monkey.	我喜歡那隻小猴子。
3	The Moon rose.	月亮升起。
4	It rains.	下雨了。

● 小專欄

➔ 到目前為止所學的句型，我們來整理一下吧！
　1.《主語＋動詞》的句子（沒有補語也沒有受詞）
　2.《主語＋動詞＋補語》的句子
　3.《主語＋動詞＋受詞》的句子

1.《主語＋動詞》的句子（沒有補語也沒有受詞）

1 He lives in Taipei. | 他住台北。

2.《主語＋動詞＋補語》的句子

2 Ann became a doctor. | 安成為了醫生。

3.《主語＋動詞＋受詞》的句子

3 I drink milk. | 我喝牛奶。

4.有2個受詞的句子（1）

CD1- 39

➡ 動詞中也有兩的受詞的。這時候的語順是《動詞+間接受詞+直接受詞》。間接受詞一般是「人」，直接受詞一般是「物」。

She gave Tom a smile.
她給湯姆一個微笑。

➡ 例句

1 Kate sent me a pink t-shirt. | 凱特寄給我一件粉紅色的T恤。

2 He paid me ninety dollars. | 他付了九十元給我。

3 I will tell you everything. | 我會告訴你所有的事情。

4 Stacy bought her mom a new refrigerator. | 史黛西買了一台新冰箱給她母親。

5.有2個受詞的句子（2）

➡ 這類的句型，常用的動詞如下。

I showed everyone my new car.
我把新車展示給大家看。

➡ 例句

1 My grandmother told me a secret. | 我的奶奶告訴我一個秘密。

2 John sent his girlfriend a tape. | 約翰寄了一捲錄音帶給他的女友。

3 He bought me a book from a garage sale. | 他在車庫特賣會買了本書給我。

4 She made me some pumpkin soup | 她為我做些了南瓜湯。

● 小專欄

➡ 《give+人+物》跟《tell +人+物》的文型，可以把表示人的受詞用 to把受詞的順序前後對調，改成《give+物+to+人》跟《tell +物+to+人》。這時候直接受詞的「物」，變成改寫句的受詞。

初級
Level

I told him the truth.
我告訴他真相了。
↓
I told the truth to him.
我告訴他真相了。

She sent me a card.
她寄給我一張卡片。
↓
She sent a card to me.
她寄給我一張卡片。

● 小專欄

➡ 《buy+人+物》跟《make+人+物》，可以把表示人的受詞用 for把受詞的順序前後對調，改成寫成《buy+物+for+人》跟《make+物+for+人》。

He made his mother a cake.
他做了一個生日蛋糕給他媽媽。
↓
He made a cake for his mother.
他做了一個生日蛋糕給他媽媽。

He sang me a song.
他唱了一首歌給我聽。
↓
He sang a song for me.
他唱了一首歌給我聽。

初級 Level

6.受詞有補語的句子（1）

➜ 一個句子如果說到受詞，還沒有辦法表達完整的意思，就要在受詞的後面，接跟受詞有對等關係的「受詞補語」。語順是《動詞+受詞+補語》。這類動詞並不多，請把它記住喔！

We made him our captain to lead us.
我們選他為隊長來領導我們。

➜ **例句**

1 We call the bear Banana.

我們叫這隻熊為香蕉。

2 The parents named their baby Pat.

那對父母替嬰兒取名為派特。

3 They named the ship Hope.

他們將那條船取名為「希望」。

4 I consider him a nice person.

我認為他是一個好人。

7.受詞有補語的句子（2）　　CD1- 40

➜ 受詞的補語，不僅只有名詞，形容詞也可以當補語。

The performance made the fans excited.
那場表演讓粉絲們很雀躍。

➜ **例句**

1 He wants me to be safe and happy.

他希望我平安而且開心。

2 I found the book quite interesting.

我發現這本書相當有趣。

3 He left the windows open except for one.

他把窗子都打開了，只剩一個（關著的）。

4 The traffic jam drove me crazy.

塞車讓我快瘋了。

● 8.受詞有補語的句子（3）

➡ 《make+受詞+動詞原形》是「讓…」的使役表現。有這種意思的動詞叫「使役動詞」。

I must make her laugh.
我一定要讓她笑。

➡ 例句

1 His mother made him stay away from us | 他母親要他離我們遠一點。

2 Perhaps a walk would make me feel better. | 也許走一走會讓我覺得舒服一些。

3 What makes you think so? | 你怎麼這麼認為呢？

4 Don't ever make your girlfriend cry. | 絕對別讓你女朋友哭。

● 9.受詞有補語的句子（4）

➡ Let 也是個使役動詞，《let+受詞+動詞原形》的句型則表示「讓…」、「允許做…」的意思。

Let me at least introduce myself.
至少讓我來自我介紹。

➡ 例句

1 Let me give you a hand. | 我來幫你。

2 Let me cut it in half. | 讓我把它切成兩半。

3 Please let me see my wife. | 請讓我見見我的妻子。

4 Why don't you let her decide? | 你為什麼不讓她決定？

英語文法・句型詳解

● 10.各種疑問句—what, who等（1） CD1- 41

➡ what表示「什麼」的意思，放在句首，以《what+be動詞+主詞…？》和《what+do+主詞+動詞原形…？》做疑問句。回答的時候不用 yes和no，而是用一般句子。另外，也可用來問事物或職業、身份等。

What does this mean?
這是什麼意思？

➡ 例句

1 What is that on your lips? | 你嘴唇上的那是什麼？

2 What are you planning to do in September? | 你九月計劃要做什麼？

3 What do you want for your sixth anniversary? | 結婚六週年慶，你想要什麼？

4 What exciting things did he say? | 那他說了什麼令人興奮的事？

● 11.各種疑問句—what, who等（2）

➡ who表示「誰」, which表示「哪些，哪一個」，是用來表示疑問的詞，叫「疑問代名詞」。who只用在問人，which表示選擇，用在人或事物都可以。

Who is that sweet girl?
那個甜美的女孩是誰？

➡ 例句

1 Who is she? | 她是誰？

2 Who cooks your meals? | 誰料理你的餐食？

3 Which do you like, black or white?

妳喜歡哪一個，黑色或是
白色？

4 Which is the right answer?

哪一個是正確的答案？

● 12.各種疑問句─what, who等（3）

➡ what和which也用在修飾後面的名詞，表示「什麼的…」、「哪個的…」
的用法。

What flowers do you like?
你喜歡什麼花？

➡ 例句

1 What time is it now?—It's 9:00p.m..

現在幾點了？－晚上九點了。

2 What size is your shirt?

你的襯衫尺寸是幾號的？

3 Which towel is mine?

哪一條毛巾是我的？

4 Which skirt suits me the best?

哪一件裙子最適合我？

● 13.各種疑問句─what, who等（4） CD1- 42

➡ 表示「誰的…」用 whose（要記住 who並沒有那個意思喔）。形式是
《whose+名詞》。

算數

Whose book is this?
這是誰的書？

➡ 例句

1 Whose belt is this?

這是誰的皮帶？

2 Whose house is on fire?

誰的房子失火了？

3 Whose jacket is gone? | 誰的夾克不見了？

4 Whose mobile is ringing? | 誰的手機在響？

● 14.各種疑問句—when, where等（1）

➡ when用在問時間，表示「什麼時候」；where用在問場所，表示「哪裡」。由於具有副詞的作用，所以又叫做「疑問副詞」。

When is your birthday?
你的生日是什麼時候？

➡ 例句

1 When does the party begin? | 舞會幾點開始？

2 When did you meet Lucy? | 你什麼時候見過露西？

3 Where can I go on Friday night? | 星期五晚上我可以去哪裡呢？

4 Where did you buy that chair? | 你在哪裡買到這張椅子的？

● 15.各種疑問句—when, where等（2）

➡ why是表示「為什麼」的疑問詞，用在詢問理由、原因。回答 why的疑問句，一般用because來回答。

Why are you so sure?
你為何如此篤定？

➡ 例句

1 Why are you still here? | 你為什麼還在這裡？

2 Why didn't I get first place? | 為什麼我沒有得到第一名？

3 Why don't we try something else?

咱們何不試試別的？

4 Why did you hang out so late?

你為什麼在外面鬼混到這麼晚？

● 16.各種疑問句—when, where等（3）　CD1- 43

➡ how是表示「如何」的疑問詞，用在詢問「方法」、「手段」時。

How do you spell the word "circle"?
「圈」這個字（英文）要如何拼呢？

➡ 例句

1 How do you know my grade?

你怎麼知道我的成績？

2 How can I get to the factory?

我要怎麼樣去工廠？

3 How did you cut your finger?

你怎麼割到手指的？

4 How will that help?

那能幫得上什麼忙？

● 17.各種疑問句—when, where等（4）

➡ how還有詢問健康、天氣「如何」的意思。

How are you and your partners?
你和你的夥伴們都好嗎？

➡ 例句

1 How is your hurt eye?

你受傷的眼睛還好嗎？

2 How is your dear mother?

你親愛的母親還好嗎？

3 How was your New Year's Eve?

你的除夕夜過的如何？

4 How was the weather?　｜當時的天氣如何？

● 18.各種疑問句—How old等（1）

➡ How的後面接 old（…歲的）或是 tall（個子高）時，可以用來詢問「幾歲」、「多高」。形式是〈how+形容詞〉。

How old is she? －She's only seventeen.
她幾歲？－她只有十七歲。

➡ 例句

1 How old is this airplane?　｜這架飛機多老了？

2 How old is the waitress?　｜那女服務生幾歲了？

3 How tall are most of the players?　｜大部分的選手有多高？

4 How tall is your brother?　｜你弟弟多高？

● 19.各種疑問句—How old等（2）　CD1- 44

➡ 同樣地，how的後面接 high（高）, long（長），可以用來詢問「高度有多高」、「長度有多長」。

How long is that railway?
這條鐵路多長？

➡ 例句

1 How long was your trip?　｜你的旅行有多久？

2 How long will you be the shopkeeper?　｜你會在這裡當多久的店長？

3 How high is the building?　｜這棟樓有多高？

4 How high is that mountain? 那座山有多高？

● 20.各種疑問句─How old等（3）

➔ How many…是「幾個的…」的意思，how much…是「多少的（量的）…」的意思，可以用來詢問人或事物的數跟量。

How many socks do you have?
你有多少雙襪子？

➔ 例句

1 How many people are dead? 死了多少人？

2 How many lessons do you have on Monday? 你星期一有幾節課？

3 How much does this computer cost? 這台電腦多少錢？

4 How much candy did you buy? 你買了多少的糖果？

● 21.各種疑問句─How old等（4）

➔ How開始的疑問句，常用的有下面的用法。

How much is this chicken?
這隻雞多少錢？

➔ 例句

1 How far is it from here to that junior high school? 從這裡到那間國中有多遠？

2 How often do you wash your face? 你多久清洗一次臉？

3 How quick his reply was!　　　　　他的答覆真快！

4 How dangerous!　　　　　　　　　多麼危險啊！

● 22.要注意的疑問句（1）　　　　　CD1- 45

➡ 疑問詞為主詞的句子，語順跟一般句子一樣是《主詞＋動詞…》。疑問詞屬第三人稱　單數，所以現在式句中的一般動詞要接-s, -es。

Who plays the piano?
誰會彈鋼琴？

➡ 例句

1 Where do your grandparents live?　　你的外祖父母住在哪裡？

2 What do you like to do when you have　妳空閒時喜歡做什麼？
free time?

3 How does he get to the train station?　他怎麼去車站的？

4 Why doesn't Mary come with us?　　為什麼瑪莉不和我們一起
來？

● 23.要注意的疑問句（2）

➡ 使用疑問詞 what 來詢問日期、星期、時間也是常用的，要記住喔！

What's the date today? ―June 6th.
今天幾號？―六月六日。

➡ 例句

1 What time is it?―It's eight.　　　　現在幾點？―八點。

2 What day is today?―It's Tuesday.　　今天星期幾？―星期二。

3 What time is it in New York? ｜ 紐約現在幾點？

4 What day of the week is today? ｜ 今天星期幾？

● 24.要注意的疑問句（3）

➔ 一般的疑問句後面加上《or…》，是表示「…嗎？還是…嗎？」的意思，用來詢問兩個之中的哪一個。回答時不用 yes, no。

Is it sunny or cloudy?
天氣是晴朗還是多雲？

➔ 例句

1 Is David 59 or 60 (sixty)years old?—He's 59 years old. ｜ 大衛59歲還是60歲？—他59歲。

2 Is this yellow or blue?—It's blue. ｜ 這是黃色還是藍色？—是藍色。

3 Is he leaving or entering?—He's leaving. ｜ 他要進來還是出去？—他要出去。

4 Do you walk or take a taxi?—I walk. ｜ 你是走路還是搭計程車？—我走路。

● 25.要注意的疑問句（4）　　CD1- 46

➔ 以 which（哪個，哪邊）為句首的疑問句，後面也有接《A or B》（A還是B）的形式。

Which do you want, beer or Coke?
你想要哪一個，啤酒還是可樂？

初級
Level

91

➡ 例句

1 Which do you like, ham or sausage? | 妳比較喜歡火腿還是香腸？

2 Which is Ann's, this or that? | 哪一個是安的，這個還是那個？

3 Which does he prefer, e-mail or telephone? | 他比較喜歡電子郵件還是電話？

4 Which season do you like, spring or summer? | 你比較喜歡哪個季節？春天還是夏天？

● 26.各種否定句（1）

➡ 不用 not也能表示否定的意思。如把副詞 never放在動詞的前面，就有「絕對沒有…」，表示強烈否定的意味。

I'll never forget that special holiday
我永遠不會忘記那次特別的假日。

➡ 例句

1 She never gets herself in trouble. | 她從沒讓自己惹過麻煩。

2 Never bite your fork like that again. | 絕對不准再像那樣咬你的叉子。

3 Never give up. | 絕對不要放棄！

4 You should never break your promise. | 你永遠都不該違背你的承諾。

● 27.各種否定句（2）

➡ not跟 very（非常）、always（總是）、all（全部的）、every（每一的）等字一起使用，就有「不是全部…」的意思，也就是部份否定。

I don't like the story very much.
我不怎麼喜歡這個故事。

➡ 例句

1 Patty didn't like the band very much. | 派蒂以前不怎麼喜歡那個樂團。

2 Iris is not always right. | 艾瑞絲並非總是對的。

3 He doesn't feel happy all the time. | 他並不是所有時候都很快樂。

4 Not every man can understand art. | 不是所有的人都能瞭解藝術。

● 28.各種否定句（3）　　CD1- 47

➡ 用形容詞的 no也可以表示否定。用《no+名詞》就有「一點…也沒有」、「一個…也沒有」的意思。No的後面，單複數都可以接。

The dog sees no color.
狗看不見顏色。

➡ 例句

1 The farmer has no children. | 那位農夫沒有小孩。

2 This doll has no nose. | 這洋娃娃沒有鼻子。

3 There are no holidays in March. | 三月沒有假日。

4 The old saying "no pain, no gain" is real. | 那句古老諺語「一分耕耘，一分收穫」是真的。

29.各種否定句（4）

➡ 用 nothing（無一物）、nobody（無一人）或 no one（無一人）也可以表示否定的意思。

I have nothing to do today.
我今天沒事做。

➡ 例句

1 She knows nothing about popular music. | 她對流行音樂一無所知。

2 Nobody took that path. | 沒人走過那條路。

3 Nobody likes losing. | 沒有人喜歡失敗。

4 No one is strong enough to move that box. | 沒有人強壯到足以移動那個箱子。

30.命令句（1）

➡ 命令對方的句子叫做命令句。命令句不用主詞，用動詞原形開始。

Take off your hat!
把你的帽子脫掉！

➡ 例句

1 Turn off the gas! | 把瓦斯關掉！

2 Move that sofa away. | 把那沙發移開。

3 Stay on the sidewalk, please. | 請待在人行道上。

4 Please protect our Earth. | 請保護我們的地球。

● 31.命令句（2）　　　CD1- 48

➡ 表示「別做…」的否定命令文，要把 don't放在句首，形式是《don't+
動詞原形…》。

Don't care too much.
別太在意。

➡ 例句

1 Don't eat the cheese. | 別吃這乳酪。

2 Don't forget our trip in May! | 別忘了我們五月的旅行！

3 Please don't pick the green one. | 拜託別選綠色的那個。

初級
Level

4 Please don't eat snacks before dinner. | 請不要在晚餐前吃零食。

● 32.命令句（3）

➡ 用《Let's+動詞原形…》（讓…吧）形式，是提議對方做某事的說法。
若回答好用「Yes, let's」，不好則用「No, let's not.」。

Let's go on a picnic!
去野餐吧！

➡ 例句

1 Let's travel north. | 我們往北方旅行吧！

2 Let's take a photo of that rainbow! | 我們來給那彩虹拍張照吧！

3 Let's go jogging in the park. | 我們到公園慢跑吧！

4 Let's go to the zoo, kids. | 孩子們，我們去動物園吧！

33.命令句（4）

➡ 命令句是用動詞原形為句首，所以 be動詞的命令句就是用 Be來開頭，表示「要…」的意思。否定的命令句，也是在 be動詞的前面接 Don't。

Be ready for the test.
準備好要考試。

➡ 例句

1 Be careful with your arm. | 小心你的手臂。

2 Be kind to animals. | 要善待動物。

3 Don't get too excited. | 別太興奮。

4 Don't trust anyone. | 別相信任何人。

34.感嘆句（1）　　　CD1- 49

➡ 用《What (+a〔an〕)+形容詞+名詞》開始的句子，然後再接《主詞＋動詞！》，就是表示強烈的情緒或感情的句子，意思是「真是…啊！」。

What a huge space!
好大的空間喔！

➡ 例句

1 What a dirty restroom! | 好髒的廁所喔！

2 What a big mouth she has! | 她的嘴巴好大喔！

3 What cheap clothes they are! | 好便宜的衣服喔！

4 What a windy day it is! | （天氣）風好大啊！

● 35.感嘆句（2）

➡ 這種表示強烈感情的句子叫「感嘆句」。感嘆文句尾要用驚嘆號「！」。感嘆句常省略主詞和動詞。

What a funny animal(it is)!
多麼有趣的動物啊！

➡ 例句

1	What a useful tool(it is)!	真好用的工具！
2	What a large garden(it is)!	好大的花園喔！
3	What a surprise(it is)!	多麼驚奇啊！
4	What a sunny day(it is)!	多晴朗的一天啊！

初級
Level

● 36.感嘆句（3）

➡ 用《How+形容詞+主詞+動詞！》表示「多麼…啊！」的意思。這時候how的後面不接a。

How lucky he is!
他真幸運啊！

➡ 例句

1	How shy you are!	你真害羞耶！
2	How polite he is!	他好有禮貌喔！
3	How difficult this task is!	這任務真困難！
4	How wonderful it is!	這真是太好了！

● 37.感嘆句（4）

➤ How的感嘆句，有時後面不是接形容詞，而是接副詞。用《How+副詞+主詞+動詞》，表示「多麼…啊！」。

How slowly that patient man does his work!
那位有耐心的男士做事還真慢啊！

➤ 例句

1 How strangely he behaves! What a strange person! | 他的行為好怪！真是個怪咖！

2 How perfectly she dresses! | 她穿得真好！

3 How late the light invented was! | 燈發明得真晚啊！

4 How quickly you found your perfect match! | 你真快就找到你的完美拍檔了！

● 六、比較的說法：1.比較級的用法（1）　CD1- 50

➤ 表示比較的形容詞叫「比較級」。用《比較級形容詞+than…》來比較兩者之間，意思是「…比…為…」。比較級一般是在形容詞的詞尾加 -er。比較的對象用 than…表示。

It is warmer inside than outside.
裡面比外面溫暖。

➤ 例句

1 Jack is a lot smarter than Pat. | 傑克比派特聰明得多。

2 The cat is almost bigger than the dog. | 這隻貓幾乎比那隻狗還大。

3 She is younger than both of you. | 她比你們兩個都年輕。

4 The English test is easier than the math test. | 英文試題比數學簡單。

● 2.比較級的用法（2）

→ 副詞也可以和形容詞一樣形成比較級。用《副詞的比較級+than…》表示「比…還…」的意思。副詞比較級的作法跟形容詞一樣。

The train runs faster than my car.
那輛火車跑得比我的車子快。

初級
Level

→ 例句

1 I can walk a little further than you. | 我可以比你走更遠一些。

2 Rob seldom studies harder than Nelson. | 羅伯很少會比尼爾森努力學習。

3 Wood can burn longer than paper. | 木頭比紙張要能燒得更久。

4 You can't drive slower than I. | 你不可能比我還開得更慢了。

● 3.比較級的用法（3）

→ 形容詞或副詞比較長的時候，前面接 more就形成比較級了。形式是《more+形容詞或副詞+than…》。

Health is more important than wealth.
健康比財富更重要。

➡ 例句

1 Laura is more beautiful than Patty. | 萊拉比派蒂更美。

2 He pulled harder than I. | 他拉得比我還要用力。

3 Bill has more confidence than any other people. | 比爾比任何人都有自信。

4 Air in the forest is fresher than that in the city. | 森林裡的空氣比城市裡的要新鮮。

● 4.比較級的用法（4）　　　　　　CD1-51

➡ 比較句中也可以省略 than…的部分。這是用在不必說出 than…，也能知道比較的對象時。

His pants are longer.
他的褲子比較長。

➡ 例句

1 I like pork better. | 我比較喜歡豬肉。

2 Her voice is louder. | 她的聲音比較大。

3 I shall run faster. | 我要跑快一點。

4 Please speak more slowly if possible. | 可能的話，請講更慢一點。

● 5.最高級的形成（1）

➡ 三者以上的比較，表示「最…的」的形容詞叫「最高級形容詞」。而在其前面加定冠詞 the，成為《the+最高級形容詞》的形式。最高級一般在形容詞詞尾加 -est。

This star is the brightest of the four.
那顆星星是四顆中最亮的。

⊕ 例句

1 She is the youngest queen ever. | 她是有史以來最年輕的皇后。

2 He is the best photographer in the competition. | 他是比賽中最好的攝影師。

3 This is the best bread in the bakery. | 這是麵包店裡最棒的麵包。

4 That is the biggest spoon I've got. | 那是我所有的最大的湯匙了。

● 6.最高級的形成（2）

⊕ 副詞也可以和形容詞一樣，形成最高級副詞。用《the+最高級副詞》表示三者以上之間的比較「最…」的意思，用法跟形容詞一樣。這時候，the常有被省略的情況。

Mike runs the fastest in group three
麥克是第三組中跑得最快的。

⊕ 例句

1 That fisherman can dive the deepest in the ocean. | 在海裡，那個漁夫能潛到最深。

2 Oliver is the best scientist in the West | 歐立弗是西方最優秀的科學家。

3 Kate sang the loudest in the chorus. | 凱特是合唱團裡唱最大聲的。

4 Mary thinks the deepest of the girls her age. | 瑪莉在同年齡的女孩中想最深入。

● 7.最高級的形成（3）　　　　CD1- 52

→ 形容詞或副詞比較長的時候，前面接 most就形成最高級了。形式是《the most+形容詞或副詞》。

This hat is the most expensive of the three.
這頂帽子是三頂中最貴的。

→ 例句

1 PE is the most interesting subject to me. | 體育課對我來說是最有趣的科目。

2 The bag is the most expensive one in the store. | 那包包是全店最貴的一個。

3 Christ is the most famous rock star in the world. | 克斯特是全世界最有名的搖滾明星。

4 Tomatoes are the most disgusting food in the world! | 蕃茄是世界上最噁心的食物！

● 8.最高級的形成（4）

→ 最高級形容詞也可以用來修飾複數名詞，用《one of the+最高級形容詞+名詞》表示「最好的…之一」。這是最高級常用的說法。

Chinese is one of the most difficult languages.
中文是最困難的語言之一。

→ 例句

1 She is one of the richest writers in the world. | 她是全世界最有錢的作家之一。

2 This is one of the most important festivals. | 這是最重要的節日之一。

3 The lion is the strongest animal in the forest. | 獅子是森林裡最強壯的動物。

4 Rita is one of the most important players in this game. | 麗塔是這場比賽中最重要的選手之一。

● 9.副詞的比較級

➡ 想要做誰「跑得比較快」、「跳得比較遠」這種動作的比較時，會用到副詞的比較級。副詞的比較級和一般的比較級差不多，同樣也是《形容詞＋er》，只是放置的位置在動詞後，用來修飾動詞。

She types faster than he.
她打字打得比他快。

➡ 例句

1 Humans think more than other animals. | 人類想得比其他動物要多。

2 Patty has hips wider than mine. | 派蒂的臀部比我的寬。

3 Sam is more powerful than you. | 山姆比你還有力量。

4 The street vendor earns more than you. | 那個小販賺的比你多。

● 10.副詞的最高級   CD1- 53

➡ 人們聚在一起常會比較個高下，要選出最好的，會用副詞的最高級。它和一般的最高級相同，同樣也是《形容詞＋est》或《the most＋形容詞》；只是位置是在動詞後，用來修飾動詞。

He does the greatest performance on stage.
他在舞台上做最棒的演出。

➡ 例句

1 Jenny has the highest income in her office. | 珍妮是全辦公室裡收入最高的。

2 I make the best spaghetti in my family. | 我是我家裡做義大利麵做得最好吃的。

3 Rita bought the most expensive violin in that shop. | 麗塔買了那家店裡最昂貴的小提琴。

4 The winner did the best of all the competitors. | 優勝者是參賽者裡最好的一位。

● 11.副詞比較級—like…better

➡ 在遇到二選一的狀況時，可以用《like…better than…》從中挑出自己比較喜愛、偏好的一項。要注意喔！like和than後面接的選項要對稱，例如：前面是名詞，後面也要是名詞。

Jill likes action movies better than comedies.
吉兒喜歡動作片勝過喜劇片。

➡ 例句

1 I like guitar better than violin. | 我喜歡吉他勝過小提琴。

2 They like natural juice better than coffee. | 她們喜歡天然果汁勝過咖啡。

3 Kim likes oranges better than guavas. | 金喜歡柳丁勝過番石榴。

4 We like this model better than the other one. | 我們喜歡這個模特兒勝過另一個（模特兒）。

12.副詞最高級─like…the best

用英文介紹自己的最愛，要這麼說：《人＋like/ love＋最喜歡的事物＋the best》，當人是《第三人稱‧單數》時，要把like或love加上s喔。

Jack likes red bean soup the best.
傑克最喜歡紅豆湯。

例句

1　We love bowling the best. | 我們最喜歡保齡球。

2　He loves cartoons the best. | 他最喜歡卡通。

3　They like Chinese culture the best. | 他們最喜歡中國文化。

4　Mandy likes crayons the best. | 曼蒂最喜歡蠟筆。

初級
Level

13.As…as

當面臨兩個選擇都不錯，又不想得罪任何一方，就說兩者都「一樣棒」、「一樣好」，是並駕齊驅的狀態，這時用《人＋be動詞＋as＋比較項目＋as＋比較對象》可以婉轉地表達。

He is as hard-working as an ant.
他像螞蟻一樣努力。

例句

1　Zack is as tall as an adult | 查克和一個成年人一樣高。

2　Linda is as beautiful as an angel. | 琳達和天使一樣美。

3　Kate is as confident as David. | 凱特和大衛一樣有自信。

4　She is as smart as Confucius. | 她和孔子一樣聰明。

105

七、現在完成式：1.現在完成式的用法—完了・結果（1）

CD1- 54

➡ 「現在完成式」是用來表示，到現在為止跟現在有關的動作或狀態。用《have+過去分詞》的形式。現在完成式含有「過去＋現在」的語意。常跟just（剛剛）連用，表示剛做完的動作，意思是「（現在）剛…」。

I have just finished my work.
我才剛完成我的工作。

➡ 例句

1 I have just left that store.　　　　　　　我才剛離開那家店。

2 She has just finished her icecream.　　　她剛吃完她的冰淇淋。

3 Mary has just gone to the church.　　　　瑪莉剛剛才去教堂。

4 Have you just mopped the floor?　　　　　你剛拖了地板嗎？

2.現在完成式的用法—完了・結果（2）

➡ 現在完成式還表示動作結束了，而其結果現在還留的狀態。意思是「（已經）…了」。

I have lost my pen.
我丟了筆。

➡ 例句

1 I have got a cold.　　　　　　　　　　　我著涼了。

2 I have got a new job.　　　　　　　　　　我找到一份新工作。

3 My mother has taught me a new word.　　我媽媽教了我一個新單字。

4 He has saved a million dollars　　　　　他已經存了一百萬元。

● 3.現在完成式的用法──完了‧結果（3）

➲ 表示動作「完了」、「結果」用法的否定句，常用副詞 yet，表示動作還沒有完成，意思是「還沒…」。

I have not seen the movie yet.
我還沒去看那部電影。

➲ 例句

1 The waiter has not come yet. | 服務生還沒來。

2 I have not spoken to Mr. Lin yet. | 我尚未和林先生說話。

3 I have not found my workbook yet. | 我還沒找到我的習作簿。

4 I haven't found the way to the gym yet. | 我還沒找到去體育館的路。

初級
Level

● 4.現在完成式的用法──完了‧結果（4）　CD1-55

➲ 動作「完了、結果」用法的疑問句，常用副詞 yet，來詢問動作完成了沒有。意思是「（已經）做了…沒？」。

Have you finished your part yet?
你完成你的那部份了嗎？

➲ 例句

1 Has it stopped raining yet? | 雨停了沒有？

2 Has he called the police yet? | 他打電話給警察了沒有？

3 Have the workers finished yet? | 工人做完了沒有？

4 Have they fixed the computer yet? | 他們修理電腦了沒？

107

● 5.現在完成式的用法—繼續（1）

➡ 現在完成式，用來表示從過去繼續到現在的動作或狀態。意思是「（現在仍然）…著」。這時候常跟表示過去已結束的某一期間的 for（…之久），或表示從過去某時起，直到說話現在時的 since（自…以來）連用。

She has lived in Taiwan, the R.O.C, for six years.
她住在中華民國已經六年了。

➡ 例句

1 We have worked on this case for many years. | 我們處理這件案子已經很多年了。

2 We have dated for three years. | 我們交往已經有三年了。

3 I have been worried about you since then. | 我從那時以來就一直很擔心你。

4 She has repeated the same thing for ten minutes. | 她已經重複同樣的東西有十分鐘了。

● 6.現在完成式的用法—繼續（2）

➡ 表示「繼續」的用法時，be動詞也可以成為現在完成式。be動詞的過去分詞是 been。

I've been busy since yesterday.
從昨天開始我就很忙了。

➡ 例句

1 I've been standing beside you for ten minutes. | 我站在妳旁邊十分鐘了。

2 I've been making pizza since noon. | 我從中午就一直在做披薩。

3 What's he been doing since then? | 從那時到現在，他都在幹什麼？

4 Why have you been knocking at the door? | 你剛剛為何一直在敲門？

7.現在完成式的用法—繼續（3）　　CD1- 56

➡ 現在完成式的疑問句可以用 How long開頭，來詢問繼續的「期間」。這時候要用 For…或 Since…來回答。

How long have you been studying history?
你讀歷史讀多久了？

初級
Level

➡ 例句

1 How long have you been cheating on me? | 你欺騙了我多久了？

2 How long have you been building this house? | 你這房子蓋多久了？

3 —For ten years. | 已經十年了。

4 —Since February, 1987. | 從1987年二月開始就住這裡了。

8.現在完成式的用法—繼續（4）

➡ 「繼續」用法的否定句，表示「（現在仍然）沒有…」的意思。

I haven't seen him since last October.
我從去年十月起就沒看到他了。

➡ 例句

1 You haven't taken the medicine yet? ｜ 你還沒吃藥？

2 I haven't been to this place before. ｜ 我以前沒來過這個地方。

3 They haven't found the island yet. ｜ 他們還沒找到那座島。

4 We haven't finished the movie. It's not over. ｜ 我們還沒看完電影，它還沒結束。

● 9.現在完成式的用法──經驗（1）

➡ 表示從過去直到現在為止的經驗，意思是「（到現在為止）曾經…」。這時候常跟twice（兩次）, once（一次）, before（從前）, often（時常）, …times（次）等副詞連用。

I've missed the show twice.
我已經錯過這節目兩次了。

➡ 例句

1 I've been there once. ｜ 我曾經去過那裡一次。

2 He has been to that lake before. ｜ 他之前就去過那座湖了。

3 John has gone to Japan often. ｜ 約翰常去日本。

4 Jane has tried giving up that bad habit many times. ｜ 珍試著戒除那壞習慣很多次了。

● 10.現在完成式的用法──經驗（2）　CD1- 57

➡ 「經驗」用法的否定句，常用 never（從未…，從不…）。

I have never said that.
我從來沒有說過（那些話）。

➲ 例句

1 I have never been to China. | 我從來沒有去過中國。

2 He has never ridden a bike. | 他從來沒有騎過腳踏車。

3 I've never met any movie stars before. | 我以前從來沒有遇見過電影明星。

4 Laura has never forgotten a thing. | 蘿拉從來沒有忘記任何事情。

● 11現在完成式的用法─經驗（3）

➲ 詢問「經驗」的現在完成式疑問句，常用副詞 ever（曾經）。ever要放在過去分詞的前面。

Have you ever heard him sing?
你聽過他唱歌嗎？

➲ 例句

1 Have you ever visited Nara? | 你參觀過奈良嗎？

2 Have you ever practiced English with an American? | 你曾經和美國人練習英文過嗎？

3 Have you ever seen snow? | 你看過雪嗎？

4 Has he ever played this game? | 他玩過這遊戲嗎？

12 現在完成式的用法—經驗（4）

可以用 How many times 或 How often 做開頭，成為現在完成式的疑問句，來詢問「曾經做過幾次」。

How many times have you lent him money?
你借過他幾次錢了？

例句

1　How many times have I told you? Do your homework! | 我跟你說過幾次了？做你的作業！

2　How many times has he come along with you? | 他和你一起來幾次了？

3　How often has he cleaned his room? | 他多常清理他的房間？

4　How often have we washed the bottom of the sink? | 我們多常清洗水槽的底部？

八、前置詞：1.介系詞的功能及意思（1）　CD1-58

介系詞是放在名詞或名詞相當詞之前，來表示該名詞等和句中其他詞之間的關係的詞。at用在表示時間上的一點，如時刻等；in表示較長的時間，用在上下午、週、月、季節及年等；on用在日或某日上下午等。

He was born in 1865.
他是1865年生的。

例句

1　We can meet in the morning. How about 9:00 a.m.? | 我們可以下午見面。九點如何？

2　It is hard to find wild animals in winter. | 冬天很難找到野生動物。

3 The TV program begins at eight o'clock. | 這電視節目八點開始。

4 We play jokes on our friends on April 1st.. | 我們四月一號都會開朋友玩笑。

● 2.介系詞的功能及意思（2）

➡ 下面這些片語，要記住喔！

Ann turns on the machine in the morning.
安在早上把機器打開。

➡ 例句

1 Patty came here in November. | 派蒂十一月到這裡的。

2 Don't burn the midnight oil too often. | 別太常熬夜。

3 He cleans the living room on Sunday morning. | 他星期天早上打掃客廳。

4 I want to go to the square on Friday. | 星期五我想去廣場。

● 3.介系詞的功能及意思（3）

➡ 區分下列這些介系詞的不同：表示動作完成的期限by（最遲在…以前），表示動作繼續的終點 until（直到）；表示期間 for，表示某狀態繼續的期間 during。

I'll finish my plan by the fifth of July.
我會在七月五號以前完成我的計畫。

➡ 例句

1 We watched TV until ten o'clock. | 我們看電視看到十點。

2 She went deep into the forest and stayed for a month.

她深入森林裡並且停留了一個月。

3 She spoke in a low voice during the speech.

在演講時她很小聲說話。

4 We played basketball till noon.

我們打籃球打到中午。

● 4.介系詞的功能及意思（4）　　CD1-59

➡ 用在一地點或比較小的地方 at（在），用在較大的地方 in（在）；緊貼在上面 on（在上面），中間有距離的在上面 above（在上）。under（在下面）在正下方。

The truck turned right at the corner.
卡車在轉角處右轉。

➡ **例句**

1 They are digging a hole in the backyard.

他們正在後院挖洞。

2 Your apple pie is on the table.

你的蘋果派在桌上。

3 Our plane is flying above the clouds.

我們的飛機正飛翔在雲端。

4 The cat is under the desk.

貓在書桌底下。

● 5.介系詞的功能及意思（5）

➡ 各種介系詞的位置關係。

He is in the bedroom.
他在臥房裡。

➡ 例句

1 My notes are on my desk. | 我的筆記在書桌上。
2 The ball is beside the box. | 球在箱子旁邊。
3 I put the ball under the box. | 我把球放在箱子下。
4 The ball is behind the box. | 球在箱子後面。

● 6.By以外的介系詞

➡ 除了可以用by來說明是誰做的動作，不同的介係詞和動詞組成慣用的片語，還有其他不同的意思，像是：「be interested in+有興趣的對象」、「be excited about+感到興奮的對象」、「be surprised at+感到驚訝的事物」…。

My brother is interested in music.
我弟弟對音樂很有興趣。

➡ 例句

1 We are all excited about this big business. | 我們都對這筆大生意感到興奮。
2 I am surprised at the scientific fact. | 我對那個科學證實感到驚訝。
3 All tickets were sold out in thirteen minutes | 所有票都在十三分鐘內賣完。
4 This bowl is made of glass. | 這個碗是用玻璃做的。

九、被動式：1.用by來表示動作者　CD1-60

➜ 被動式就是「被…」的意思，主要的結構是《主詞＋be動詞＋過去分詞》，若是想要特別說明是「被誰…」，那就要主要結構後面加上《by+動作者》。

The grass is eaten by the cow.
草被母牛吃掉了。

➜ 例句

1	Those new gloves are made by the designer.	這些新手套是那位設計師做的。
2	John is hit by a ball.	約翰被球打到。
3	Mr. Brown is loved by his students.	伯朗先生受學生喜愛。
4	I'm very sure that this e-mail was not written by her.	我很確定這封電子郵件不是她寫的。

2.行為者不明

➜ 被動式中，不清楚是誰做的動作時，可以不用加上「被誰…」來說明做動作的人。只要講出《主詞＋be動詞＋過去分詞》來說明「接收動作的人，接受到怎樣的動作」就可以了。

What he said was written down.
他說的話被寫下來了。

➜ 例句

1	The church was built many years ago.	這座教堂是好幾年前建造的。
2	My wallet was stolen in a public restroom.	我的錢包在公共廁所被偷了。

3 Many of us were invited to Lisa's party. | 我們之中很多人受邀參加麗沙的派對。

4 This novel is written in different languages. | 這本小說是用不同語言寫的。

● 3.疑問用法

➔ 被動式的疑問句,是把直述句主要結構中的be動詞移到句首,變成《be動詞＋主詞＋過去分詞?》這樣的問句結構。

Is this seat taken?
這個位子有人坐嗎?

➔ 例句

1 Is it the year two-thousand-eight? | 是西元兩千零八年嗎?

2 Was the man killed? | 那男人被殺了嗎?

3 Is this meeting finished? | 這場會議結束了嗎?

4 Is the land sold? | 那塊土地被賣掉了嗎?

● 十、不定詞:1.名詞的用法　　CD1- 61

➔ 不定詞主要的功能是讓一個句子裡,不會同時出現兩個動詞,而造成錯誤文法。舉例來說:want (to go) 的用法,可避免want和go兩個動詞同時存在,這時,不定詞具有名詞的性質。

I want to cross the street.
我想過馬路。

➡ 例句

1 They started to count from one to a hundred.	他們開始從一數到一百。
2 I would like to leave within fifteen minutes.	我想要再十五分鐘以內離開。
3 My father wanted to leave the hospital.	我爸爸想要離開醫院。
4 I need to keep my body in shape.	我需要保持我的身材。

● 2.副詞的用法（1）

➡ 不定詞也可以當作副詞來使用，舉例來說：I use this notebook.（我用這本筆記本）已經是句完整的句子，若想要詳細說明筆記本的用途，就加上to keep a diary（寫日記），當作副詞來修飾use的用途（目的）。

I use this to protect my knees.
我用這個來保護我的膝蓋。

➡ 例句

1 My father asked me to stay away from the snake.	我爸爸叫我離那條蛇遠一點。
2 His dog bites the toys to sharpen its teeth.	他的狗啃咬玩具來磨牙。
3 The Lins borrowed some money to buy a house.	林家人借了一些錢來買房子。
4 I turned on the stove to heat up the soup.	我把爐子打開，把湯加熱。

3.副詞的用法（2）

不定詞當副詞使用時，除了修飾動詞、也可以修飾形容詞，主要的結構是《主詞＋be動詞＋形容詞＋不定詞》，其中的不定詞用來修飾形容詞，表示其原因。

I am glad to have a sunny day after a horrible typhoon.
我很高興在可怕的颱風後看到一個晴朗的天氣。

例句

1	I am sorry to hear about the matter.	聽說了這件事情我感到遺憾。
2	He is nervous about seeing the medical report about his stomach.	他因為要看自己的胃部醫療報告而感到緊張。
3	Judy is happy to receive a dozen roses.	茱蒂收到一打的玫瑰花很開心。
4	Larry is proud to win the prize.	賴瑞很得意能得獎。

初級
Level

4.形容詞的用法　　　　CD1- 62

不定詞也可以當作形容詞來使用，位置是接在名詞後面，修飾及補充說明名詞，舉例來說：work to do就是用不定詞該去完成（to do）形容前面的work，指該完成的工作。

I have a few messages to listen to.
我有一些留言要聽。

例句

1	My ninety-year-old grandpa has many stories to tell.	我九十歲的爺爺有很多故事可以講。
2	Do you want me to dry the towel for you?	你想要我幫你把毛巾弄乾嗎？

119

3 I have seventy five cents left to spend. | 我剩七毛五的錢可以花用。

4 They still have three miles to go. | 他們還有三英里的路程。

● 5.疑問詞 "to"

➡ 不定詞也可以放在疑問詞後面,來形容疑問詞,表示你不知道有關於那個不定詞的訊息,舉例來說:what to do後面的不定詞（to do）用來修飾前面的疑問詞（what）,表示不知道要做什麼。

I don't need to tell him when to say good-bye.
我不需要告訴他何時說再見。

➡ 例句

1 They have no idea how to cook the meat. | 他們完全不知道該怎麼料理肉。

2 She didn't tell me where to find the pair of gloves. | 她沒跟我說該去哪裡找那雙手套。

3 Excuse me. Do you know how to use the computer? | 不好意思,你知道怎麼使用這台電腦嗎?

4 My sister doesn't know how to blow up a balloon. | 我妹妹不知道如何吹氣球。

● 6.不定詞的否定

➡ 不定詞的否定和一般否定一樣,若是句中的動詞是一般動詞,就在動詞前面依照時態和人稱,加上否定助動詞don't、didn't、doesn't,若句中是be動詞,就在be動詞後面接上not。

I don't want to know if he's coming.
我不想知道他是否要來。

➡ 例句

1 The mailman doesn't have any mail to give us. | 郵差沒有任何信件要給我們。

2 Jack is not happy to lose his new kite | 傑克很不開心他弄丟了新風箏。

3 Half of us don't want to accept the challenge. | 我們之中有一半的人不想接受挑戰。

4 Don't you want hot coffee to drink? | 你不想要喝些熱咖啡嗎?

● 7.不定詞當主詞　　　　　　CD1- 63

➡ 要跟朋友聊聊做某件事情的甘苦談,可以用不定詞當主詞,針對不定詞引導的那件事發表意見。句子的結構和一般的句子相同《不定詞＋動詞＋受詞》,用來描述不定詞所說明的那件事。

To paint the walls is a lot of work.
粉刷牆壁是件大工程。

➡ 例句

1 To take the MRT is very convenient. | 搭捷運很方便。

2 To hurt other people is bad. | 傷害別人是不好的。

3 To fight for your dream is really cool! | 為夢想奮鬥很酷!

4 To deal with fourteen kids at a time is exhausting. | 一次面對十四個小朋友很累人。

英語文法・句型詳解

8.It is…to

要針對不定詞指的那件事發表意見時，可以用句型《It is+形容詞＋不定詞》。It在這裡是虛主詞，也就是沒有實質意義的主詞，真正的主詞是不定詞。這樣的句型也可以轉換成《不定詞＋is＋形容詞》的形式。

It is urgent to find my child.
找到我的小孩是很緊急的。

例句

1 It is comfortable to sit on that chair. | 坐在那張椅子上很舒服。

2 It is common to own pets in the U.S.A.. | 在美國養寵物很普遍。

3 It was fun to go fishing. | 釣魚很好玩。

4 It is important to eat less and exercise more. | 少吃多動很重要。

9.It is…for人to

和前面的句型相同，只是在句中加入《for＋人》，就可以表達出「對某人而言」這個概念，所以《It is＋形容詞＋for＋人＋不定詞》就表示「不定詞這件事對某人來說是…」的意思。

It isn't hard for me to climb to the top.
對我來說爬到山頂並不困難。

例句

1 It is lucky for him to have an excellent partner. | 對他來說有個出色的夥伴是很幸運的。

2 It is pleasing for Jack to hear his friends cheering for him. | 對傑克來說聽到朋友為為他喝采是很開心的。

3 It is bad for you to chat with a stranger. | 對你來說和陌生人聊天是不好的。

4 It is dangerous for the elderly to fall off the chair. | 對年長者來說從椅子上摔下是很危險的。

● 10.Too⋯to

➡ 無法答應別人的要求、邀請時，可以用《Too＋形容詞＋不定詞》就是「太⋯而不能⋯」，委婉地說出自己的苦衷，來請對方諒解。在句子中加入《for＋人》表示針對某人而言。

I am too tired to push the door open.
我太累了，而沒辦法推開門。

初級
Level

➡ 例句

1 He is too fat to hide inside the closet. | 他太胖了，無法藏身在衣櫥裡。

2 It is never too late to acquire new knowledge. | 學習新知永遠不嫌晚。

3 This sheet is too small to cover the whole bed. | 這件床單太小了，無法蓋住整張床。

4 Is she too busy to celebrate Nancy's seventh birthday? | 她太忙了，無法慶祝南西的七歲生日嗎？

● 十一、連接詞：1.And　　　CD1- 64

➡ And是對等連接詞，左右兩邊所連接的事物要對稱，要是左邊的是單字，那麼and右邊也必須是單字，若是左邊是動詞片語右邊也必須相同，而且詞性也必須對稱喔，像是名詞對名詞、形容詞對形容詞。

George and Mary nodded to each other.
喬治跟瑪莉對彼此點頭。

→ 例句

1 Relax your shoulders and your arms. | 把你的肩膀和手臂都放鬆下來。

2 The dog and the cat belong to me. | 那狗跟貓都是我的。

3 I went home and took a shower because I was too tired. | 因為我太累了，所以回家然後洗澡。

4 Release the girl and drop your weapons! | 放開那女孩，放下你的武器！

● 2.But

→ 當事情有了變化，語氣有轉折，像是中文裡的「但是、不過、可是」，都可以使用but這個轉折連接詞。和前面的連接詞一樣，but左右所連接的事物要對稱，詞性和類型都要相同，規定和and相似。

The shape of the cookie is weird but creative.
那餅乾的形狀很奇怪但很有創意。

→ 例句

1 Fifty kilograms is an OK weight for me but not OK for a model. | 五十公斤對我而言很OK，但對模特兒來說不是。

2 She wanted to cheer up Sam but he felt bored. | 她想要取悅山姆，但他覺得很無聊。

3 I tried to kick the ball but missed it. | 我試著踢那顆球但卻失了準頭。

4 There are twenty minutes left but I have five pages still unread. | 剩下二十分鐘，我卻還有五頁還沒讀。

● 3.Or

➡ 選擇餐點、選要買哪件衣服、選擇要唸的科系…，生活上常會面臨大大小小的選擇，Or就是給人選擇的連接詞，左右連接的是對稱的兩個選擇。兩邊的類型、詞性都要相同。

He doesn't care whether we win or lose.
他不在乎是輸還是贏。

➡ 例句

1 I have no idea which team's better, the Lakers or the Sixers. | 我完全不知道湖人隊和七六人隊哪個比較好。

2 Please give me a medium size or a small size. | 請給我中號的或是小號的。

3 Is the bag full or empty? | 那袋子是滿的還是空的？

4 Is the wind cold or warm? | 風是冷的還是溫暖的？

初級
Level

● 4.Because放在句中　　　　　CD1-65

➡ 要說明原因、解釋狀況的時候，用Because連接主要子句和附屬子句，形成這樣《主要子句＋because＋附屬子句》的結構，其中附屬子句是用來解釋原因，無法跟主要子句分開自成一句。

The line wasn't straight because she didn't use a ruler.
這條線不直是因為她沒有用尺（畫）。

➡ 例句

1 The girls like Jason because he is handsome and friendly. | 女孩們喜歡傑森，因為他長得帥又很友善。

2 The markets here confuse me because they sell things by the pound. | 這裡的市場讓我很困惑，因為它們都按磅來賣東西。

3 The post office is closed today because it's Sunday.

因為今天是星期天所以郵局休息。

4 I was late because I turned left instead of right at that corner.

我遲到是因為在那個轉角左轉了而沒有右轉。

5.Because放在句首

➡ Because也可以放在句子的開頭，形成這樣《Because＋附屬子句＋ ,主要子句》的結構，其中because所引導的附屬子句是用來解釋主要子句的原因，而且，要注意用逗點分開兩個句子喔。

Because their hobbies were similar, they became friends.
因為他們興趣相近，所以成為朋友。

➡ 例句

1 Because I pointed in the wrong direction, she was lost.

因為我指錯方向，所以她迷路了。

2 Because he's standing in front of me, I can't see anything!

因為他站在我前面，所以我什麼也看不見！

3 Because it's the tenth visit to the zoo, he felt bored.

因為這是第十次來動物園了，所以他覺得很無聊。

4 Because the office is on the eighth floor, I took the elevator.

因為辦公室在八樓，所以我搭了電梯。

6.So

➡ 有因就有果，So就是用來說明結果。so可以放在句子中間，連接主要子句和附屬子句，形成《主要子句＋so＋附屬子句》的結構，其中附屬子句用來說明結果；也可以放在句子的開頭，但要注意用逗點分開兩個句子喔。

The price was low so I bought it.
價格很低廉所以我就買了。

➡ 例句

1	There are seventy days left before the wedding so he is nervous.	還有七十天就是婚禮了，所以他很緊張。
2	They'll spend nineteen days in Europe so they are packing up.	他們要去歐洲十九天，所以正在打包。
3	The sandwich costs forty dollars, so I bought something else.	那三明治要四十塊錢，所以我就買別的了（太貴）。
4	Lydia just took an eleven-hour flight so she wants to rest.	莉蒂亞剛結束十一小時的航程，所以她想要休息一下。

初級
Level

● 7.Before

➡ Before是說明時間先後的連接詞，可以放在句子的中間，形成這樣《主要子句＋before＋附屬子句》的結構（其中附屬子句是用來敘述較早發生的事件），或是放在句子的開頭，只是要注意用逗點分開兩個句子喔。

Think twice before you spend that money.
花那筆錢之前要三思。

➡ 例句

1	I covered my ears before she started to talk.	在她開始講話之前我就把耳朵蓋起來了。
2	We should finish the report before August.	我們應該在八月前完成報告。
3	Before you sell used computers, you should sheck them.	賣二手電腦前你應該要檢查。

4 Before I tell you the answer, why don't you make a guess? | 在我告訴你答案之前，何不猜猜看呢？

● 8.After   CD1- 66

➜ After是說明時間的先後的連接詞，可以放在句子的中間，形成這樣《主要子句＋after＋附屬子句》的結構，（其中附屬子句是用來敘述較晚發生的事件），也可以放在句子的開頭，但注意要用逗點分開兩個句子喔。

What happened after I left?
我離開後發生了什麼事?

➜ 例句

1 Fill the pot with water after you clean it. | 清洗完鍋子後在裡面裝水。

2 Should I go home or go swimming after school? | 放學之後，我該回家還是去游泳呢？

3 I will not be here after six o'clock. | 六點之後我不會在這裡。

4 After dinner, we said bye-bye to each other and returned home. | 晚餐結束之後，我們對彼此說再見然後回家。

● 9.If

➜ If是說明條件和限制的連接詞，可以放在句子的中間，代表著「如果…，就…」，形成這樣《主要子句＋if＋附屬子句》的結構。（其中附屬子句是用來敘述可能的狀況或要求的條件），也可放在句子開頭，但要用逗點分開兩個句子。

If your dad's also coming, please let me know.
如果你父親也要來，請先告訴我。

➡ 例句

1 If that's the wrong answer, I will fail the test. | 如果那是錯的答案，我考試就會不及格。

2 You are welcome if you want to come to my house. | 如果你想來我家的話，我很歡迎。

3 If he's not going, I am not going either. | 如果他不去，我也不會去。

4 I usually go jogging in the morning if it doesn't rain. | 如果沒下雨的話，我通常會去晨跑。

● 10.Whether   CD1- 67

➡ Whether有著義無反顧的精神，代表著「不論如何…」。可以放在句子的中間，形成這樣《主要子句＋whether＋附屬子句》的結構，其中附屬子句是可能的情況，等於「是否…」的意思。

I can't tell whether this dog is sick (or not).
我無法分辨這狗是否生病了。

➡ 例句

1 She is not sure whether she will go abroad (or not). | 她不確定是否要出國。

2 I still won't buy it whether it's less than fifty dollars (or not). | 不管它是否在五十元以下我都不會買。

3 The result depends on whether we win (or not). | 結果得看我們有沒有贏。

4 You can't fall asleep whether you're tired (or not). | 不論你是否疲倦，都不能睡著。

初級 Level　英語文法・句型詳解

● **11.when**

➡ When用來連接兩件同時發生的事情。左右都是現在式時，代表著「當…，就…」，是一種普遍的狀況。放在句中是《主要子句＋when＋附屬子句》的結構。When也可以放在句子的開頭，但要用逗點分開兩個句子。

Listen when somebody gives you advice.
有人給你意見的時候要聽。

➡ **例句**

1 You should be careful when you make a decision.	你在做決定的時候應該要小心。
2 Stay calm when you're in danger.	當你身在危險中時要保持冷靜。
3 When things are delayed, David becomes nervous.	事情延誤的時候大衛會變得緊張。
4 When Bob talks to other girls, Anna gets jealous.	鮑柏和其他女生說話時，安娜會吃醋。

● **12.when動詞過去式**

➡ When的左右兩個事件都是過去式時，代表「當…，就發生了…」，描述過去同時發生的事件。放在句子中形成《主要子句＋when＋附屬子句》的結構。When也可放在句子開頭，但要用逗點分開兩個句子喔。

I was shocked when I saw that car accident.
看到那場車禍時我感到很震撼。

➡ **例句**

1 His face turned red when he described that girl to me.	他向我形容那女孩的時候臉都紅了。

2 There was trash everywhere when I arrived home. | 我回到家時到處都是垃圾。

3 When I talked to the class, I especially mentioned that problem. | 我對全班說話的時候，特別提到這個問題。

4 When the camera was invented, nobody was interested in it. | 當相機被發明出來時，沒有人對它感興趣。

● 13.when動詞現在式　　　CD1- 68

➡ When引導現在式的附屬子句，連接未來式的主要子句，表達出動作先後的銜接，也就是「現在一完成…，就馬上…」。放在句中形成《主要子句＋when＋附屬子句》的結構。另外，when放在句子的開頭時，要注意用逗點分開兩個句子喔！

初級 Level

We will have a barbecue together when my dad returns.
等我爸回來，我們會一起烤肉。

➡ 例句

1 Connie will print the page when the computer is on. | 電腦打開後康尼會列印那一頁。

2 When the audience is ready, the show will begin. | 當觀眾準備好時，表演就會開始。

3 When the data is ready, I'll take it to your office. | 資料準備好時，我會把它送到你的辦公室。

4 I will start to talk when you stop shouting. | 等你們停止大聲喊叫，我就會開始說話。

初級 Level 英語文法・句型詳解

● 14.While

➡ While是說明同時發生的連接詞，強調持續了一段時間，可以放在句子的中間作連接，形成這樣《主要子句＋while＋附屬子句》的結構。while放在句子開頭時，要注意用逗點分開兩個句子喔。

He looked at me while explaining what had happened.
他看著我，當他在向我解釋發生什麼事情的時候。

➡ 例句

1	The guests arrived while I was baking cookies.	當我在烤餅干時，客人就到了。
2	The phone rang while I was watching the soccer game.	我看足球賽的時候電話響了。
3	While Penny thinks of the old memories, she feels happy.	佩妮想著以前的回憶會很快樂。
4	While she apologized, I saw tears in her eyes.	她道歉的時候，我看見她眼裡有淚光。

● 15.Not…but

➡ 想要澄清誤會、或解釋說明事實時，可以用《Not…but》兩個連接詞組成的組合連接詞，代表「不是…而是…」的意思，同樣的not和but後面接的詞必須詞性和類型都要對稱。

This is not a practice but a quiz..
這不是練習，而是測驗。

➡ 例句

1	We realized that she's not angry but upset.	我們發現她沒有生氣，只是沮喪。

132

2 He is not just nice but super nice.

他不只是人好,而是超級好。

3 He received not a hat but a cup.

他收到的不是帽子,而是個杯子。

4 It is not rainy but snowy.

現在不是下雨,而是下雪。

● 16.both A and B   CD1- 69

➡ 《both A and B》是由兩個連接詞組成的組合連接詞,代表「A和B都」的意思,其實就是and的句型,加上了both來加強語氣,意思用法還是很類似,both和and後面接的詞語需要對稱。

Both you and I have the ability to do that.
你跟我都有能力可以做那件事。

➡ 例句

1 Both Thanksgiving and Christmas are important holidays.

感恩節和聖誕節都是重要的節日。

2 I am both intelligent and athletic.

我不但聰明也很有運動細胞。

3 She bought both the shoes and the wallet.

她買了鞋子也買了皮夾。

4 I ran into Jack both in the library and on the subway

我在圖書館跟體育館都遇到傑克。

● 17.Not only…, but also…

➡ 要誇讚某人能力很好,可以用《Not only…, but also…》這個組合連接詞,代表「不只…,還…」的意思,後面都要接對稱的語詞,另外,also可以省略。

The scandals are not only terrible, but also shameful.
那些醜聞不只是糟糕，也很丟臉。

➡ 例句

1 Louis is not only smart, but also brave.
> 路易士不只聰明，也很勇敢。

2 Paris not only lied, but also stole.
> 芭莉絲不只撒謊，還偷了東西。

3 I not only took him to dinner, but also paid the bill.
> 我不只帶他去吃晚餐，還付了帳單。

4 They cooked not only potatoes but also turkey.
> 他們不只煮了馬鈴薯，還有火雞。

● 18.So…that

➡ 要說明原因和結果的關係時，可以用《So…that》這個組合連接詞，是「太…，以致於…」的意思，其中，so後面可以接上形容詞或副詞，用來表示原因；而that則是引導了一個句子，表示結果。

His mother was so mad that she hit him with a stick.
他母親很生氣，（以致於）用棍子打他。

➡ 例句

1 His beard was so long that he looked like an old man.
> 他的鬍子太長了，（以致於）看起來像個老人。

2 She was so embarrassesd that she left immediately.
> 她覺得很尷尬，（以致於）立刻就離開了。

3 The storm was so scary that we all stayed home.
> 暴風雨太嚇人了，（以致於）我們全部待在家裡。

4 The total price was so high that she couldn't afford it.
> 總金額太高了，（以致於）她負擔不起。

● 19.So am I   CD1- 70

想要表示同感時，除了可以用also、too表示「也…」，還可以用《So＋be
動詞＋人》來表示，其中的so就是代替了主要子句，使用方法是《主要子
句＋and＋(So+ be動詞+人)》。

Jack was absent yesterday and so was I.
傑克昨天缺席，而我也是。

● 例句

1 I am against this idea and so are they.

我反對這個想法，而他們
也是。

2 Linda is a Taiwanese singer and so is Jack.

琳達是一位台灣歌手，而
傑克也是。

3 Kate is used to eating brunch and so is the boss.

凱特習慣吃早午餐，而老
闆也是。

4 Dolly is afraid of the sharks, and so is she.

桃莉怕鯊魚，而她也是。

● 20.So do I

想要告訴對方自己也有同感時，除了可以用also、too表示「也…」，還可
以用《主要子句＋and＋(So+ do+人)》來表示，就等於（主要子句＋and＋
人＋do, too），其中，若是人是單數就要把do改成does。

He accepted my apology and so did she.
他接受了我的道歉，而她也是。

● 例句

1 Jerry believes that all men are equal and so do we.

傑瑞相信人都是平等的，
而我們也這麼想。

2 Emily needs more energy and so do I. | 艾蜜莉需要更多的精力，而我也是。

3 Alice loves toast with butter and so does Jason. | 艾莉絲很喜歡奶油吐司，而傑森也是。

4 I prefer small villages to big cities, and so does she. | 我喜歡小鎮勝過大城市，而她也是。

● 21.So can I

➡ 想要告訴對方自己也可以做得到，除了可以用also、too表示「也能…」，還可以用《主要子句＋and＋(So+ can+人)》來表示，，其中的so就是代替了主要子句，所以等於（主要子句＋and＋人＋can, too）。

Larry can survive the war and so can I.
賴瑞能在戰爭中活下來，而我也能。

➡ 例句

1 You can deal with it and so can he. | 你能處理這件事，而他也能。

2 Patty can play volleyball well and so can you. | 派蒂排球打得很好，而你也能。

3 They can support you and so can we. | 他們可以支持你，而我們也可以。

4 Ricky can make yummy muffins and so can Lily. | 瑞奇會做好吃的杯子蛋糕，而莉莉也能。

● 22.Neither　　　　　　　　CD1- 71

➡ 想要告訴對方自己也有同樣負面、否定的感覺時，可以用Neither，代表「也不」的意思，句子結構是《主要子句＋and＋(neither…人)》，和《so…人》的用法相同，只是意思完全相反。

Neither Sally nor Jane wanted to share their cooking tips.
莎莉和珍都不想分享她們烹飪的小秘訣。

➡ 例句

1	He didn't like that design and neither did Jack.	他不喜歡那個設計，而傑克也不喜歡。
2	That jar is not empty, and neither is the one next to it.	這罐子不是空的，而它旁邊的（罐子）也不是。
3	Wendy never wastes money, and neither do I.	溫蒂絕不浪費錢，而我也不。
4	Dad hasn't had supper and neither has Mom.	爸爸還沒吃晚餐，而媽媽也還沒。

初級
Level

● 23.Too

➡ Too是「也是」的意思，句子結構是《主要子句＋and＋（人＋助動詞/ be 動詞）＋,too》，口語中常用的Me, too.（我也是），雖不符合文法，但卻常被掛在嘴邊。

Lucy likes koalas, and Kim does, too.
露西喜歡無尾熊，而金也喜歡。

➡ 例句

1	He knows a lot of magic tricks, and I do, too.	他知道很多魔術技法，而我也是。
2	Mathew is homesick, and Lisa is, too.	馬修想家，而麗莎也是。
3	She is a lovely girl, and you are, too.	她是個可人的女孩，而妳也是。
4	She is busy during weekdays, and Diana is, too	她在平日都很忙，而黛安娜也是。

● 24.Either

➡ 想要告訴對方自己也有同樣負面、否定的感覺、或說到彼此同樣沒做到…，Either是「也不是」的意思，意義和too完全相反，但用法和too完全相同。

I don't use a Walkman anymore, and Patrick doesn't either.
我不再用隨身聽了，而派翠克也不用。

➡ 例句

1 Tiffany doesn't have a secretary, and Oliver doesn't either. | 蒂芬妮沒有秘書，而奧立弗也沒有。

2 They didn't decorate the Christmas tree, and we didn't either. | 他們沒有裝飾聖誕樹，而我們也沒有。

3 She wasn't downstairs, and he wasn't either. | 她當時不在樓下，而他也不在。

4 Cathy is not a selfish person, and Frank isn't either. | 凱希不是個自私的人，而法蘭克也不是。

● 25.either…or…   CD1- 72

➡ 想法不確定時，就用《either…or…》這組合連接詞，說出「不是…就是…」代表自己有隱約的記憶。和前面連接詞相同，either和or後面接的詞語必須對稱，詞性和類型必須相同。

I suggest you play either basketball or tennis.
我建議你不是打籃球，就是打網球。

➡ 例句

1 The wedding will be either this month or next. | 婚禮不是這個月舉行，就是下個月。

2 You may choose either jam or honey. | 你有果醬和蜂蜜可以二選一。

3 Either Jack or I will take her to the dentist. | 不是傑克就是我將帶她去看牙醫。

4 Either you or he suits our needs. | 不是你就是他符合我們的需求。

26.neither…nor…

➔ 一時忘記正確答案，可以用刪去法，把不對的選項去掉，《neither…nor…》這組合連接詞，有著「既不…也不…」的刪去概念。而neither和or後面接的詞語同樣必須對稱，詞性和類型也必須相同。

I don't see any whales nor dolphins here.
這裡我看不到有任何鯨魚或是海豚。

➔ 例句

1 Joy likes neither pumpkin pie nor apple pie. | 喬依不想要南瓜派，也不想要蘋果派。

2 I want neither chicken nor duck. | 我既不想要雞肉，也不想要鴨肉。

3 Neither Lily nor I have been to Europe. | 莉莉和我都沒去過歐洲。

4 Neither you nor he knows the right direction. | 你和他都不知道正確的方向。

● 十二、介系詞：1.With後接名詞（1） CD1- 73

➔ 出去遊玩、旅行最重要的就是隨行的伙伴了，可以用with說說自己是跟誰一夥的。With是「和」的意思，後面可以接名詞，《with＋一起行動的人或物》就變成「和某人或某物一起」。

He suddenly showed up with the boss.
他和老闆忽然一起現身。

➡ 例句

1 Lisa is reading magazines with Mark. | 麗莎正和馬克一起看雜誌。

2 Patty moved to Russia with her husband. | 派蒂和她丈夫一起搬到俄國住。

3 Dolly had dinner with Miller on Valentine's Day. | 情人節那天桃莉和米勒一起吃晚餐。

4 Rita climbed onto the roof with her little brother. | 麗塔和弟弟一起爬上屋頂。

● 2.without後接名詞（2）

➡ Without是「沒有…」的意思，後面可以接名詞，《with＋人或物》就變成「沒有和某人或某物一起」。

This family is not whole without you.
這個家沒有你是不完整的。

➡ 例句

1 Kate can handle the report without any partners. | 凱特沒有任何夥伴就可以處理這個報告。

2 I told the truth without personal emotion. | 我不帶私人感情地說出真相。

3 Wendy made some egg rolls without sugar. | 溫蒂做了些沒放糖的蛋捲。

4 You can't lose weight without exercise. | 你不能不運動就減重。

● 3.without後接名詞（3）

➡ Without是「沒有」的意思，後面若是要接動作時，要把動詞變成動名詞的型態，《without＋沒有發生的事》就變成「沒有…」。

Jack made the decision without discussing it with his wife.
傑克沒有和他妻子討論就做了決定。

➡ 例句

1 You can't go to school without wearing underwear!	妳不能不穿內衣就去學校！
2 We went to Korea without telling our parents.	我們沒跟父母說就去了韓國。
3 It is very likely that he left home without closing the door.	他很可能沒有關門就離開家了。
4 You can't run a business without understanding customers.	做生意不能不了解顧客。

● 十三、附加問句：1.一般動詞用法　CD1- 74

➡ 附加問句是在直述句後，接上簡短的問句並用逗號隔開。若直述句是肯定的，後面問句就是否定的。否定助動詞要用縮寫形式，如：doesn't、can't…；直述句是否定的，後面附加問句是肯定的。

You keep a diary, don't you?
你有寫日記（的習慣），對吧？

➡ 例句

1 She has great power, doesn't she? | 她有很大的權力，對吧？

2 The judge believes me, doesn't he?｜法官相信我，對吧？

3 We have to celebrate Halloween, don't we?｜我們一定得慶祝萬聖節，對吧？

4 Jack needs a haircut, doesn't he?｜傑克需要剪頭髮，對吧？

2.Be動詞用法

➡ be動詞的附加問句，如果直述句是肯定的，那麼後面要加上否定的附加問句（否定be動詞＋人），否定be動詞都要用縮寫形式，如：aren't、isn't、wasn't…；如果直述句是否定的，那麼後面加上的附加問句就是肯定的（be動詞＋人）。

They are on a diet, aren't they?
他們在節食，是嗎？

➡ 例句

1 This semester is finished, isn't it?｜這學期已經結束了，對吧？

2 The level of this book is too difficult, isn't it?｜這本書的程度太困難了，是吧？

3 They are kindergarten teachers, aren't they?｜他們是幼稚園老師，是吧？

4 It's a long distance, isn't it?｜距離很遠，是嗎？

十四、現在分詞形容詞：1.現在分詞形容詞—放在名詞後

CD1- 75

➡ 靈活使用動詞轉變成的形容詞，可以讓描述的人事物更多了一分生動。現在分詞當作形容詞使用時，位置可以放在名詞後面，用來修飾形容名詞。表示「正在…就是…」。

The dog running over here is huge!
跑過來的那隻狗好大啊!

➔ 例句

1 The movie playing now is horrible. | 現在正在播放的電影很可怕。

2 The day after tomorrow is Teacher's Day. | 明天過後到來的是教師節。

3 The boy sitting there seems to be curious about us. | 坐在那裡的男孩似乎對我們很好奇。

4 Hi! Is the cell phone ringing yours? | 嗨!是你的手機在響嗎?

● 2.現在分詞形容詞—放在名詞前

➔ 靈活使用動詞轉變成的形容詞,可以讓描述的人事物更多了一分生動。現在分詞當作形容詞使用時,位置也可以在名詞前面,用來修飾形容名詞。表示「正在…就是…」。

We like those falling leaves.
我們很喜歡那些正落下的葉子。

➔ 例句

1 It's impossible for her to see the flying bird. | 她不可能看得到在飛的鳥兒。

2 I can't stand the plane shaking. | 我受不了飛機一直搖晃。

3 They can't catch the running thief | 她們抓不到那個逃跑的小偷。

英語文法・句型詳解

● 3.過去分詞形容詞－放在名詞後

靈活使用動詞轉變成的形容詞，讓描述的對象更生動。現在分詞當作形容詞使用時，位置也可以在名詞後面，而要形容的名詞不是自己進行動作，而是被動地接受那個動作。表示「被…就是…」。

This is the girl protected by the police.
這個女孩是警方在保護的。

● 例句

1 The crowd was gathered by the speaker. | 那群眾是由演講者招集的。

2 These are the bottles that are recycled. | 這些是回收的瓶子。

3 These are the cars provided by Ford. | 這些是福特提供的車子。

4 This is the gift chosen by Sarah. | 這是莎拉挑選的禮物。

● 4.過去分詞形容詞－放在名詞前

靈活使用動詞轉變成的形容詞，可以讓描述的對象更生動。現在分詞當作形容詞使用時，位置也可以在名詞後面，而要形容的名詞不是自己進行動作，而是被動地接受那個動作。表示「被…就是…」。

Try some sliced melon.
來試試切片的香瓜。

● 例句

1 Let's see the newly invented robot. | 我們來瞧瞧這新發明的機器人吧。

2 We're talking about the robbed gold. | 我們正在討論被搶走的金子。

3 Don't use that broken toothbrush. | 別用那支壞掉的牙刷。

4 The newly opened store is across the street. | 那家新開的店面位在對街。

● 十五、未來式：1.未來式　　CD1- 76

➡ be going to後面接上動詞原型，可以用來表示未來將要發生的動作、行為，屬於比較輕鬆、不一定會達成的未來計畫，語氣沒有will那麼堅決。

We are going to visit our grandparents in France.
我們將要去拜訪在法國的祖父母。

➡ 例句

1 I am going to move forward. | 我要往前移動。

2 Mary is going to win the big prize! | 瑪莉要拿到那個大獎了！

3 You are going to be a prince in the future. | 你將來會是個王子。

4 He is going to the mall after lunch. | 他在午餐過後要去購物商場。

● 2.未來式疑問句（1）

➡ be going to的疑問句，就是把直述句中的be動詞移到句首，其餘的都不變，變成《be動詞＋人＋going to＋未來將要做的事》，用來詢問未來的計畫。回答是用yes、no來開頭。

Are they going to go skating together?
他們要一起去溜冰嗎？

初級
Level

➔ 例句

1 Is he going to sign the contract tomorrow? | 他明天會簽合約嗎？

2 Are you going to wear slippers? | 你打算要穿拖鞋嗎？

3 Is he going to fool the professor? | 他打算要欺騙教授嗎？

4 Are they going to apologize to me? | 他們要向我道歉嗎？

● 3.未來式疑問句（2）

➔ be going to的疑問句，可以針對想問的是：什麼人、用什麼方法、什麼時候⋯，來加上疑問詞who、how、when⋯。句型《疑問詞＋be＋人＋going to＋未來的計畫》，可詢問未來將要發生的事。

What are you going to do with the poster?
你要怎麼處理那張海報？

➔ 例句

1 What's going to be popular in the next century? | 下個世紀會流行什麼？

2 How are you going to prove it? | 你要怎麼證明？

3 Are these going to be mine? | 這些會成為我的東西嗎？

4 Who is going to see that tiny mistake? | 誰會看到那極小的錯誤呢？

● 4.未來式否定句

➔ Be going to的否定句，是在be和going to中間，加上否定詞not，變成《人＋be動詞＋not＋going to＋未來沒要做的事》，用來表達未來沒有要做的事。

We are not going to buy the diamond.
我們不會買那個鑽石。

➡ 例句

1 I am not going to be a salesman. | 我不會成為一個業務員。

2 I am not going to live in Japan. | 我不是要住在日本。

3 He is not going to plant a tree in the backyard. | 他不是要在後院種樹。

4 We are not going to shut up. | 我們沒有要閉嘴。

● 十六、助動詞：1.Will you　　CD1- 77

➡ 想要委婉地請對方幫忙、或提出邀請，可以使用《Will you＋請求事項？》這樣的句型，其中的you可以依照對象的不同而更改。而請求事項裡的動詞，一定要使用原型。

Will you stop arguing with me?—Sure.
你可以停止和我爭辯嗎？一好阿。

➡ 例句

1 Will you call me later?—Certainly. | 你可以等一下打給我嗎？一沒問題。

2 Will you please keep silent?—Sorry. | 你可以保持安靜嗎？一抱歉。

3 Will you pass me the dessert?—OK. | 你可以把甜點傳給我嗎？一好。

4 Will you please leave me alone?—All right. | 你可以讓我一個人靜一靜嗎？一好吧。

● 2.Shall I

➡ 想要開口詢問對方需不需要幫忙、或是客氣的詢問自己能不能做某件事時，可以使用《Shall I＋詢問事項？》這樣的句型，其中詢問事項裡一定要使用原型動詞。

Shall I pass you the rope?—Yes, please.
要不要我把繩子傳給你嗎？—好啊，麻煩你。

➡ 例句

1	Shall I help you clean the toilet?—No, thank you.	要不要我幫你一起打掃廁所？—不了，謝謝。
2	Shall I start from the beginning?—Yes, thank you.	要不要我重頭開始？—謝謝。
3	Shall I find more tools for you?—Yes, please.	要不要現在幫你找其他工具？好啊。
4	Shall I get a little bit of wine for you?—No, thank you.	要不要我幫你拿一些酒來？—不了，謝謝。

● 3.Shall we

➡ 想要提出邀請、要求對方一起時，可以說《Shall we＋邀請內容》。在 shall we 前面加上疑問詞，例如：《When shall we…?》（我們什麼時候…？），來詢問對方各式各樣關於「我們…」的話題。

Shall we meet in that area?
我們要在那塊地方會面嗎？

➡ 例句

1	How shall we get to Asia?	我們要怎麼到亞洲去？
2	Which tie shall I wear?	我要戴哪條領帶？

3 What shall I leave in the basement?　　我要在地下室留下什麼東西？

4 When shall we change the topic?　　我們什麼時候換個話題？

● 十七、動名詞：1.動名詞一當補語　　CD1- 78

➜ 一個句子裡只能有一個動詞，所以當出現了兩個動作時，後面的動詞要變成動名詞，當作前面動詞的補語，才不會造成兩動詞同時出現的文法錯誤。

He stopped playing chess.
他停止下棋了。

初級
Level

➜ 例句

1 The dog started chasing its own tail.　　那隻狗開始追自己的尾巴。

2 Try paying attention, please.　　請專心點。

3 I like playing with the puppy.　　我喜歡和小狗玩。

4 He enjoys talking about his childhood.　　他很喜歡談他的童年。

● 2.動名詞一當主詞

➜ 動名詞因為具有名詞的性質，所以也可以放在句首當作主詞，《動名詞＋be動詞＋形容語句》，用這樣的句型就可以形容說明某項行為。

Meeting new friends is the main reason (why) he came.
認識新朋友是他來這裡的主要原因。

➜ 例句

1 Standing in rows would be better.　　站成一排一排的會比較好。

2 Writing a poem is difficult for me. 寫詩對我來說很困難。

3 Respecting one another is necessary. 尊重他人是十分必要的。

4 Burning the midnight oil is bad for your health. 熬夜對身體不好。

十八、人 或 事 物 中 的 全 部 或 部 份： 1.Both放句首，在動詞前面

CD1- 79

➡ 想要描述兩個有相同狀況的對象時，可以用both，一次針對兩者同時說明：《Both of＋複數受格＋敘述內容》或《Both＋對象1 and對象2＋敘述內容》，而既然是兩個對象，後面動詞當然是複數型囉！

Both of the dogs are alive.
兩隻狗都活著的。

➡ 例句

1 Both of the teams were beaten. 兩支隊伍都被打敗了。

2 Both of these CDs are available. 這兩片CD都還買得到。

3 Both of the twins are beginners. 兩個雙胞胎都是初學者。

4 Both of them are famous throughout the world. 他們兩個都是世界知名的。

2. Both放句中，在動詞後面

➡ both用來描述的是兩個有相同狀況的對象時，也可以放在動詞後面：《對象1 and對象2＋動詞＋both＋敘述內容》，現在式時動詞用are或動詞原型即可。

Ricky and I are both fond of badminton.
瑞奇和我都喜歡打羽毛球。

➡ 例句

1 Sam and Lisa both sat on the bench. | 山姆和麗莎都坐在長凳上。

2 They both have AIDS. | 他們兩人都有愛滋病。

3 We both studied in advance. | 我們兩個都事先讀過了。

4 You both should stop bothering me. | 你們兩個都該停止打擾我了。

● 3.Both的否定（部分否定）

➡ 要注意喔！Both的否定是部分否定，只是針對其中之一做否定「其中有一個不是」，《both…not…》這樣的用法可以不明講地縮小範圍到兩者之間，隱約而模糊地透露出否定的對象。

初級 Level

They both are not under control.
他們兩個都不在控制之下。

➡ 例句

1 Not both of my ankles are hurt. | 我的其中一邊腳踝受傷了。

2 I do not like both of the advertisements. | 那兩個廣告其中之一我不喜歡。

3 Not both of the girls went to Canada. | 並不是兩個女孩都去了加拿大。

4 Not both of the bombs are found. | 並不是兩個炸彈都找到了。

初級 Level **英語文法・句型詳解**

● 3.全部可數—All

➡ 當要說明的對象是三者以上的全體時，就會用all來涵蓋全部的範圍。用法和both很像：《All of＋對象＋敘述內容》。既然是三者以上，後面動詞當然也是複數型囉！

All of the cities were attacked.
所有的城市都被攻擊了。

➡ 例句

1 All of the players are active. 　所有的選手都很積極。

2 All of the bats are broken. 　所有的棒子都斷了。

3 All of the birds are in the cage. 　所有的鳥都在籠子裡。

4 All of the members attended the meeting. 　所有的成員都出席了會議。

● 4.全部不可數—All　　　　　　CD1- 80

➡ all用來涵蓋全部的範圍，句型和前面一樣，但要注意動詞用法喔！當對象是不可數名詞時，Be動詞和一般動詞都要做《第三人稱・單數》的變化，例如：walk→walks、are→is。

All of the information is gone.
所有的情報都不見了。

➡ 例句

1 All of the furniture is hand-made. 　所有的傢俱都是手工打造。

2 All of the work was canceled. 　所有的工作都取消了。

3 All of the food in this cafeteria is delicious. 　這家自助餐廳的所有食物都很好吃。

4 The generous man took out all of his money.

那慷慨的男士拿出了他所有的錢。

● 5.人或事物中的一部份

➡ 當描述的對象是人或事物中的一部份時，會用《數量＋of＋對象＋描述內容》的句型。描述部分的範圍，依照數量的不同有大有小，例如：one（之一）、some（其中有些）、most（其中大部分）…。

One of the articles is mine.
文章之中有一篇是我的。

➡ 例句

1 Some of the girls came from Australia.

有些女孩是從澳洲來的。

2 Many of the buttons are red.

有好幾個紐扣是紅色的。

3 Several of the bones heve to be checked.

有很多骨頭要被檢查。

4 Most of us want to avoid rush hour.

我們之中大部分的人都想避開尖峰時間。

● 6.兩者之一——One of

➡ 沒有要給予確定的選擇時，可以用one of來將想說的對象限定在二選一的範圍內。要注意喔！因為one of是指兩者之一，所指對象是單數的一人，所以，後面接的動詞要用《第三人稱‧單數》喔！

One of us was aware of his madness.
我們其中之一有人察覺到他的忿怒。

➡ 例句

1 One of the blood samples is type B.

兩（個）血液樣本有一個是B型。

153

2 One of the boys is gentle.

> 兩個男孩其中的一位很溫和。

3 One of the bags will be taken later.

> 其中的一個包包晚一點會被拿走。

4 She purchased one of the books.

> 她買了其中一本書。

● 十九、動詞：1.使役動詞—後接形容詞　CD1- 81

➡ 使役動詞就是「某人使另外一人…」，最常見的使役動詞就是make（讓），如果是讓某人心情改變的話，就可以直接用《人1＋make＋人2＋心情的形容詞》，其中人1若是單數，make加s。

The gentleman wished us luck.
那位紳士祝福我們好運。

➡ 例句

1 The greedy kids made their parents crazy.

> 貪吃的孩子們讓他們的父母快抓狂。

2 The director asked the actor to be angry.

> 導演要求演員生氣。

3 That genius makes me envious.

> 那個天才讓我感到忌妒。

4 "I wish the citizens were happy!" said the mayor.

> 「我希望市民都快樂！」市長說。

● 2.使役動詞—後接動詞原型

➡ 使役動詞也可以用在命令、要求，《人1＋使役動詞＋人2＋動詞》，像是：「某人要求另外一人做…」、「某人叫另外一人去…」，要注意喔！這時後面接的是原型動詞。

Mom let him have cereal with milk.
母親讓他吃麥片配牛奶。

➡ 例句

1	My sister helped me clean the carpet.	我姐姐幫我清理地毯。
2	Nicky has his brother change the channel.	尼奇叫他弟弟轉台。
3	Mom made me finish the carrots.	母親叫我吃完那些胡蘿蔔。
4	The teacher had her read the whole chapter.	老師叫她朗讀一整個章節。

● 3.感官（知覺）動詞後接原型動詞＜表示事實、狀態＞

➡ 感官動詞就是用「五覺」感受的動作，像是：視覺（see）、聽覺（hear）、嗅覺（smell）、體覺（feel）…等，形成《感官動詞＋人或物＋動作》的句型。注意喔！要用原型動詞來表示你感覺到的事實或存在的狀態。

初級 Level

I saw my dad hanging up the calendar.
我看見我父親在掛日曆。

➡ 例句

1	She heard the audience clap.	她聽見觀眾在鼓掌。
2	I listened to the grandpa talk to his granddaughter.	我聽到祖父在跟他孫女說話。
3	He felt a ghost touching him	他感覺到一個鬼魂在觸碰他。
4	They saw water dropping from the ceiling.	他們看到水從天花板滴下來。

初級 Level 英語文法・句型詳解

● 4.感官（知覺）動詞後接動名詞<表示動作正在進行>

CD1- 82

➡ 想要生動地傳達出你的體驗，讓你的朋友也有身歷其境的臨場真實感，可以使用動名詞，當作感官動詞後的動作，用來強調動態的進行，如此一來，可以讓你描述的動作就像是栩栩如生地正在進行著喔！

I saw Jack lighting the candles.
我看見傑克正點燃蠟燭。

➡ 例句

1 Patty looked at the speaking captain. ｜ 派蒂看著領隊正在發言。

2 We are watching a goose flying away. ｜ 我們正在看著一隻鵝飛走。

3 Pat felt the monster touching his shoulder. ｜ 派特感覺到那怪物碰他的肩膀。

4 They listen to Jack complaining. ｜ 她們聽著傑克在抱怨。

● 5.其他動詞—Spend

➡ Spend是花費時間或是金錢的意思，兩者用法略有不同：花費金錢是《人＋spend＋價錢＋on/for＋買的東西》或《spend＋價錢＋buying＋買的東西》；花費時間則是《spend＋價錢＋動名詞、地點》。

They spent a lot of money building the castle.
他們花了很多錢蓋這個城堡。

➡ 例句

1 She spent two hundred dollars on handling charges. ｜ 她花了兩佰元付手續費用。

2 I spent two hours curing the cat. | 我花了兩小時在給那隻貓治病。

3 We spent one week looking for the best grapes. | 我們花了一星期尋找最上等的葡萄。

4 Helen spends ten minutes greeting every guest. | 海倫花十分鐘跟每位客人問候。

● 6.其他動詞—take

➔ Take只能表達花費時間，用法如下：《虛主詞it＋takes＋人＋時間＋動作》其中動作要用不定詞，也可以把動作搬到句首《動作＋takes＋人＋時間》，其中的動作可以是不定詞或動名詞。

It takes me ten minutes to hike up the mountain.
我爬上山需要十分鐘。

➔ 例句

1 How long does it take to become the chief manager? | 成為總經理要花多久的時間？

2 It takes us five days to get out of the desert. | 我們需要花五天的時間離開沙漠。

3 To develop a relationship took him years. | 發展一段關係花了他好幾年的時間。

4 Finding his granddaughter took him thiry minutes. | 他找他的孫女花了三十分鐘。

● 7.有助動詞功能的Have to　　CD1- 83

➔ Have to是必須的意思，和助動詞must的意思相近，後面要接上原型動詞，《人＋have to＋必須完成的事》，就表達出一定要做到的決心和使命。

I have to stay awake until dawn.
我必須保持清醒直到天亮。

➡ 例句

1 You have to find a gasoline station. | 你一定要找個加油站。

2 We had to find a guide yesterday. | 我們昨天就必須找個嚮導。

3 We had to leave Germany in three days. | 我們必須在三天之內離開德國。

4 You have to set a goal. | 你必須建立一個目標。

● 8.有助動詞功能的 Have to 疑問句用法

➡ 想要得知必須完成的事情、或反問對方有沒有必要⋯時，可以用疑問句《Do/Does＋人＋have to＋動詞原型》，當人是《第三人稱・單數》時，前面的助動詞用Does，其餘情況，用Do開頭。

Do I have to comment?
我非得要評論嗎？

➡ 例句

1 Do they have to chase after me? | 他們非得追著我跑嗎？

2 Do we have to prepare crabs? | 我們一定要準備螃蟹嗎？

3 Do we have to care about a difference of just one gram ? | 我們有必要在意那絲毫的差別嗎？

4 Does he have to learn German? | 他有必要要學德文嗎？

● 9.有助動詞功能的Have to否定句用法

➡ 要說明「不用…」、「沒必要…」時，可以用have to的否定句《人＋don＇t＋have to＋動詞原型》，當人是《第三人稱・單數》時，則要把don＇t改成doesn＇t。

I don't have to make myself a hero.
我沒必要把自己弄成個英雄。

➡ 例句

1 She doesn't have to do it herself. | 她不需要自己親手做這件事。

2 You didn't have to use a gun. | （那時）你沒必要用槍的。

3 I don't have to imagine; I know! | 我沒必要想像，因為我知道。

4 You don't have to use the hanger. | 你沒必要用衣架。

● 10.接動名詞的動詞   CD1- 84

➡ 一個句子裡不可以同時出現兩個動詞，所以，若有兩個動詞的狀況發生，要把後面的動詞改成動名詞或不定詞。有些動詞後面只能接動名詞，像是這裡的所舉的例子。

He gave up using the glue.
他放棄使用那膠水了。

➡ 例句

1 Joy avoids driving over the holes in the road. | 喬伊避免開車駛過路上的坑洞。

2 They kept looking for gold. | 他們不停地尋找黃金。

3 The thieves avoid running into the guards. | 小偷們避免遇見警衛們。

4 She enjoys having guests in her house. | 她很喜歡家裡有客人。

● 11.接不定詞的動詞

➡ 一個句子裡不可以同時出現兩個動詞,所以,若有兩個動詞的狀況發生,要把後面的動詞改成動名詞或不定詞。有些動詞後面只能接不定詞,像是這裡的所舉的例子。

I hope to see you in college.
我希望能在大學裡見到你。

➡ 例句

1 She hopes to work for the government. | 她希望能為政府工作。

2 I promise to finish the work for certain. | 我保證一定完成工作。

3 She tried to get to the central bank. | 她嘗試著到中央銀行去。

4 I need to get to the concert hall. | 我得到音樂廳那裡去。

● 12.可接動名詞或不定詞的動詞

➡ 同一個動詞接上不定詞或動名詞,可能會有不同意義。動名詞通常代表過去已經做過的,例如:《remember+動作》表示記得做過…;不定詞通常代表未來將要進行,例如:《remember+動作》表示記得要去做…。

They remembered to turn off the heater.
他們記得要關掉暖氣。

➡ 例句

1 They hardly remembered washing the dishes. | 他們幾乎不記得洗過盤子了。

2 We like to say "hey!" when we meet people. | 我們喜歡在跟人見面的時候說 " 嘿！" 。

3 We love playing golf. | 我們喜歡打高爾夫球。

4 The waiter forgot to give us some napkins. | 服務生忘了給我們一些餐巾了。

● 二十、形容詞：1.-ing　　　CD1- 85

➡ 用現在分詞當形容詞，可以讓對方更能想像、體會你所形容的人事物。形容的對象通常是無生命的事或物，因為本身的條件而引起別人的情緒感覺，是「讓人覺得…的」。屬於外界的想法。

Ben is a boring guy.
班是個無聊的傢伙。

➡ 例句

1 The story is confusing. | 這故事很令人疑惑。

2 It was a surprising movement. | 那是個驚人的動作。

3 I read an interesting report. | 我讀了一個有趣的報告。

4 Repairing cars is a tiring job. | 修車是個累人的工作。

● 2.-ed

➡ 想讓對方能想像體會你所形容的人事物，也可以用過去分詞當形容詞，而形容的對象，因為外在的條件而造成自身的情緒感受，是「感到…」，屬於每個人自己內在的感受、體會。

I am bored of making charts.
我對於製作圖表感到很無聊。

英語文法 · 句型詳解

⇒ 例句

1 He is surprised to see his son's growth.

他看到他兒子的成長很驚喜。

2 Mandy is tired of the humid weather.

曼蒂對潮濕的天氣感到厭煩。

3 She is excited about hosting the party.

她對主辦派對感到興奮。

4 Laura is interested in visiting Hong Kong.

萊拉對於去香港很有興趣。

● 二十一、關係代名詞：1.關係代名詞是主格／受格

CD1- 86

⇒ 把兩句併做一句，就可以俐落地表達所有想說的訊息，用《對象＋形容話題…》補充說明。若對象是人，用who當關係代名詞；對象是事或物，用which或that。關係代名詞是主格時，不可省略，但作受詞時，是可以省略的

The chairman is Lucy's dad. He is nice.

→The chairman who is nice is Lucy's dad.

那位主席是露西的父親。他很和善。
→ 那位和善的主席是露西的父親。

例句

1 She bought a purse. It was expensive.

→The purse that she bought is expensive.

她買了個錢包。那錢包很貴。
→她買的錢包很貴。

2 I have a classmate. She is very childish.

→I have a classmate who is very childish.

我有個同學。她非常幼稚。
→我有個非常幼稚的同學。

3 The rabbit is hopping around. It is David's.

→The rabbit (that is) hopping around is David's.

那隻兔子跳來跳去的。他是大衛的。
→那隻跳來跳去的兔子是大衛的。

4 The insects were alive. We saw them.

→The insects we saw were alive.

那些昆蟲是活的。我們看見了它們。
→我們看見的那些昆蟲是活的。

● 2.關係代名詞是所有格

➜ 《對象＋形容話題…》形容話題是用關係代名詞引導的句子，當對象是另一句話裡面的所有格時，不論是人或物都要用whose（…的）當作關係代名詞。whose不可省略。

They saw the hunter. His hair was brown.

→They saw the hunter whose hair was brown.

他們看見一個獵人。他的頭髮是棕色的。
→ 他們看見一位頭髮是棕色的獵人。

例句

1 I went to the sea. Its color was deep blue.

　→I went to the sea whose color was deep blue.

我去了海（邊）。海的顏色是深藍色。
→我去了一片深藍色的海（邊）。

2 Peter has a brother. His height is 180cm.
　→Peter has a brother whose height is 180cm.

彼得有個弟弟。他身高一百八十公分。
→彼得有個身高一百八十公分的弟弟。

3 Phoebe showed me a hat. Its design was fashionable.
　→Phoebe showed me a hat whose design was fashionable.

菲比給我看了一頂帽子。帽子的設計很時尚。
→菲比給我看了一頂設計很時尚的帽子。

4 We brought a hammer. Its handle was yellow.
　→We brought a hammer whose handle was yellow.

我們帶了一支鐵鎚。鐵鎚的把柄是黃色的。
→我們帶了一支把柄是黃色的鐵鎚。

初級 Level 英語文法 · 句型詳解

● 3.that的省略用法

➡ 在某些特定動詞後面所接的that子句,可以省去關係代名詞that,至於是哪些動詞,則只能多學多熟悉囉!

She hopes (that) her grandson can come.
她希望她的孫子可以來。

➡ 例句

1 They realized (that) she feels ill. | 她們發現她感覺病了。

2 I think (that) the purse is hers. | 我認為這錢包是她的。

3 We feel (that) God is listenning. | 我們感覺到上帝在傾聽。

4 He said (that) he won't go hunting. | 他說他部會去打獵。

● 4.what的用法　　　　　CD1- 87

➡ 間接疑問就是《what+對象+動作》,配合上間接疑問前的動作《人+動作+間接疑問》,就可以用來說明某人做了什麼、說了什麼。

I don't have what you require.
我沒有你需要的(東西)。

➡ 例句

1 She doesn't know what his favorite dish is. | 她不知道他的最喜歡的菜是什麼。

2 They don't remember what he replied. | 他們不記得他回覆了什麼。

3 We catch what the musician is saying. | 我們懂那位音樂家說的話。

4 She shows me what she painted with the brush.

她給我看她用刷子畫了什麼。

● 5.why的用法

有時候用直接用問句詢問原因，會有一種質疑別人的感覺，想要避免這種咄咄逼人的口氣時，可以用間接問句《why＋對象＋動作》，這樣就可以溫柔、平和的問出想要的答案。

I know why he marked my name.
我知道為什麼他要標記我的名字。

● 例句

1 They wonder why he is standing.

他們在想他為什麼站著。

2 I want to know why she has so much mud on her shoes.

我想知道她鞋子上怎麼會這麼多泥土。

3 I forgot why I brought the ball.

我忘了為什麼我要帶著球來。

4 I understand why she's always at the gym.

我了解她為什麼總是在健身房了。

● 二十、補充：1.表因為… / 若是… / 即使…

要解釋原因、設定條件限制等情況下，都可以用省略式的句型《連接詞＋動名詞, 主要子句》，當前後兩個句子裡的主詞是同一人時，可以省略附屬子句中的主詞，並把動詞改成動名詞。

Because he was in a hurry, he took the highway.

→Being in a hurry, he took the highway.

因為趕時間，所以他走高速公路。

例句

1 As he is a giant, he can see very far.
→Being a giant, he can see very far.

因為是個巨人，他可以看得很遠。

2 If you don't hide from Mom, you will regret it.

→You will regret not hiding from Mon.

如果不躲著媽媽，你將會後悔。

3 Though Ana knows the reason, she still felt angry.

→Though knowing the reason, Ana still felt angry.

即使知道原因，安娜還是感到很生氣。

4 After I lost the coat, I saw it somewhere else.

→After losing the coat, I saw it somewhere else.

遺失外套之後，我在某個地方看到一樣的。

2.假設法

➡ 要說明一個假設的情境下，會採取怎樣的手段，會用這樣的假設法《If＋主詞＋現在式動詞…, 主詞＋will＋原型》，前面做假設情況的說明，後面則是用未來式解釋將會採取的手段。

If you pay in cash, the price will be lower.
如果你付現金，價格會變得比較低。

➡ **例句**

1 If the students look at the examples, they will understand.

如果學生看那些例子，他們就會懂了。

2 If the bell rings, he will answer it.

如果電鈴響了，他會去應答。

中級
LEVEL

一、時態

英文文法中存在著許多不同的時態用法，分別適用於不同的時間點、不同的含意上。英文時態除了有現在、過去、未來的差別外，大致又分為簡單式、進行式、完成式等型態。瞭解不同的句法的真正意思，才能確切地描寫出想表達的事物喔！

● 1. 現在簡單式　　　　　　　　　　　　　CD2- 1

➡ 直接使用現在式動詞，就是現在簡單式。雖然叫做現在式，但其實是用來表示「普遍的情況」，而不是「現在」正發生的事情喔！所以常常需要配合頻率副詞，才能點明動作真正發生的時機。

He is sometimes passive.
他有時候很消極。

➡ 例句

1 We seldom go to concerts. ｜ 我們很少去聽音樂會。

2 My family goes fishing once a month. ｜ 我們全家一個月去釣一次魚。

3 Penguins live in cold areas like Antarctica. ｜ 企鵝住在如南極一般寒冷的地區。

4 Her readers express their admiration through her online blog. ｜ 她的讀者透過她線上的部落格，表示對她的讚賞。

167

2. 過去簡單式

➡ 直接使用過去式動詞，就是過去簡單式。可能是字尾加上-ed的規則動詞，或是沒有定律的不規則動詞。我們用它來說明過去發生的事件。

I took some sleeping pills last night.
我昨晚吃了一些安眠藥。

➡ 例句

1 Chiu-Fen prospered quickly during that time. | 那段期間，九份快速地繁榮起來。
2 The landlord came this morning to collect the rent. | 今早房東來收房租。
3 A plane crashed into the Twin Towers in New York City. | 一架飛機撞上了紐約市的雙子星大樓。
4 The Japanese occupied Taiwan during the first half of the 20th century. | 在二十世紀上半期，日本人曾經侵占過台灣。

3. 未來簡單式

➡ 使用《will＋原形動詞》的句形，就是未來簡單式，也可以用《be going to＋原形動詞》的句型來代替，用來說明未來即將要發生的事，或是計畫要去做的事情。

Do you think there will be a miracle?
你覺得奇蹟會出現嗎？

➡ 例句

1 I will write an essay on Shakespeare. | 我將會寫一篇關於莎士比亞的論文。

2 You will find him to be a very reliable person.

你會發現他是個很可靠的人。

3 We will proceed after a ten-minute break.

休息十分鐘之後，我們將繼續。

4 We're going to stay in a cheap hostel tonight.

今晚我們會住進一家便宜的旅社。

● 4. 包含助動詞的簡單式（1）　　CD2- 2

➜ 用《助動詞＋原形動詞》的結構可以「改變動詞的語氣」。每個助動詞都有各自的意思，像是should（應該）、must（一定）、may（可能）、can（可以）…等。如果要加上否定詞not，要放在助動詞和動詞之間喔！

Your computer may be infected with a virus.
你的電腦可能被病毒感染了。

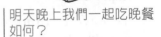

➜ 例句

1 Shall we dine together tomorrow night?

明天晚上我們一起吃晚餐如何？

2 We should think of something more practical.

我們應該想一些更實際點的東西。

3 You can be sexy as long as you want to be sexy.

只要你想變性感，你就可以性感的。

4 You must be more concise in writing summaries.

你撰寫摘要一定要再更精簡些。

5. 包含助動詞的簡單式（2）

有些片語所表達的意思是和某些助動詞很相近的，例如should（應該）
→ought to、will（將）→be going to、must（必須）→have to等。其中have
to變成否定語氣的don't have to時，表示「可以不必」的意思，和must not
「絕不可以」的意思不一樣喔！

I'm going to contact the embassy for help.
我要聯絡大使館以尋求協助。

例句

1	You really don't have to dash around all day like this.	你大可不必整天這樣跑來跑去的。
2	You ought to visit that gallery before you leave the city.	在離開這個城市以前，你應該去參觀那間畫廊。
3	You ought not to miss the landmark of Taipei–Taipei 101.	你不該錯過台北的地標：台北101大樓。
4	We have to think of another way to accommodate more people here.	我們得另外想個辦法，來讓這裡容納更多的人。

6. 包含助動詞的簡單式（3）

雖然助動詞後面要接原形動詞，但還是有別的方法可以表現過去的事
件的！用have to（必須）→「had to」、can（可以）→「could」、will→
「would」或是「was(were) going to」等。

They had to do whatever they could to ensure their survival.
當時他們為了生存什麼事都得做。

➡ 例句

1 I thought he was going to become a surgeon. | 當時我以為他會成為一個外科醫生。

2 He realized that he would live in shame for the rest of his life. | 當時他發現，自己將會含辱度過餘生。

3 They had to follow the standard procedure to apply for probate. | 他們當時必須遵照標準程序，來申請遺囑檢驗。

4 We thought we could do some research on some endangered species. | 當時我們認為可以對某些瀕臨絕種的物種進行研究。

● 7. 現在、過去進行式　　CD2- 3

中級 Level

➡ 進行式的標準句型就是《be動詞＋V-ing》，由前面的be動詞來決定動作是「過去」還是「現在」進行中的事情。

The interpreter is translating what he just said.
翻譯員正在翻譯他剛剛所說的話。

➡ 例句

1 Something is dripping from the ceiling. | 有東西正從天花板上滴下來。

2 The clumsy boy is trying to repair his bicycle. | 那個笨拙的男孩，正試著修理自己的腳踏車。

3 The soldiers were fighting to defend our country. | 當時士兵們正奮鬥著保衛我們的國家。

4 She was looking for the right definition of his words. | 當時她正在為他的話，找出正確的定義。

8. 包含助動詞的進行式

➡️ 助動詞後面要接原形動詞，這個規定在進行式的結構中也是不變的，所以綜合起來就變成《助動詞＋be＋V-ing》的句型啦！也就是說，be動詞在這個句型裡面是固定不變的。

They can't be boycotting our products!
他們不可能抵制我們的產品吧！

➡️ 例句

1 You shouldn't be yawning like that during class. | 在課堂上你不應該那樣打呵欠的。

2 They may still be looking for additional volunteers. | 他們有可能還在尋找額外的志工。

3 Mr. Fox must be working in his clinic at this moment. | 這時候福克斯先生一定是在他的診所工作。

4 The committee would be discussing some universal issues. | 委員會將會討論一些全球性的議題。

9. 未來進行式

➡️ 已知「明天早上會是在上班」，或是「下禮拜會是在度假」等未來的情形，就可以用《will be＋V-ing》的句型了，也就是未來進行式，表示未來的某個時刻將會在進行某件事情。

They will be competing against each other tonight.
他們今晚將要一決勝負。

➡️ 例句

1 The author will be introducing his new book on a TV show. | 那位作者將會在電視節目上介紹他的新書。

2 The newlyweds will be enjoying their honeymoon next week.

下個禮拜，這對新人將會享受他們的蜜月假期。

3 Will you be watching the Olympic Games in London in 2012?

2012年的時候，你會在倫敦觀賞奧運競賽嗎？

4 The students will be interacting in this class instead of just listening.

在這堂課中，學生們將會有所互動，而不只是聽課。

● 10. 不能用進行式的動詞　　CD2- 4

➡ 沒聽過有人說「我正在認識你」或是「我正在同意你」這類的話吧？聽起來多奇怪啊！有些動作是沒辦法用進行式來表現的，像是「感情」、「想法」、「知覺」等非動態的動詞。

中級
Level

I don't think anyone could ignore our discipline.
我不認為有誰可以漠視我們的紀律。

➡ 例句

1 We all know that this is not acceptable behavior.

我們都知道這是不被允許的行為。

2 I agree with the opinion that Hugh is a charming man.

我同意休是個有魅力的男人這個說法。

3 Some people don't believe in the existence of God.

有些人並不相信上帝的存在。

4 What you see now is the ancient palace of the Incas.

你現在所看到的是印加民族的古老宮殿。

英語文法・句型詳解

● 11. 現在完成式

→ 《have/ has＋過去分詞》就是現在完成式的句型，第一、二人稱或是複數形主詞用have，第三人稱或是單數形主詞則用has。現在完成式表示「從過去某時間點起的動作，一直持續到現在這一刻」，表示橫跨過去與現在的事件。常常搭配的詞有for（有多久）、since（自從）、ever（曾經）、never（從未）、yet（目前）、so far（目前），其中yet只用在問句和否定句中。

We have not found a single sponsor yet.
到目前為止，我們都還沒有找到贊助廠商。

➡ 例句

1	Have you ever heard of that phrase before?	你以前有聽過那句成語嗎？
2	The writer has written many imaginary stories.	那位作家已經寫了許多虛構的故事。
3	The Parkers have lived in the suburbs for years.	派克一家已經住在郊區好幾年了。
4	The students have split into six groups.	學生們已經分成了六組。

● 12. 現在完成進行式

→ 現在完成進行式的句型就是《have/ has＋been＋V-ing》，其中been是固定不變的，也就是《have/ has＋p.p.》和《be動詞＋V-ing》的結合。完成進行式的重點放在持續一段時間的「動作本身」，而不是到目前為止的結果。

I've been having a terrible ache in my back.
（從之前某個時候開始）我的背部就一直感到劇烈的疼痛。

➡ 例句

1 They have been negotiating for a better result. | 為了有個更好的結果，他們仍持續地進行談判。

2 She has been practicing her violin skills since an early age. | 她小時候就開始練習她的小提琴技巧了。

3 The lady has been saying prayers since her husband's accident. | 那位女士從她丈夫的那場意外開始，就一直念著禱告文。

4 My professor has been studying ancient Egyptian civilization. | 我的教授一直在研究埃及的古文明。

● 13. 過去完成式　　CD2- 5

中級 Level

➡ 過去完成式的句型是《had＋過去分詞》，沒有主詞人稱上的差異。它是用來凸顯兩個過去事件中，較「早」發生的那一個，因此都是和另一個過去式的句子一起出現的。所以要記住它的使用時機其實很簡單，就是靠口訣：「過去的過去」。

A murder had happened before we arrived.
在我們到達之前，已經發生了一場謀殺案。

➡ 例句

1 I read the folk tale that he had told me about. | 我讀了他之前跟我提過的那個民間故事。

2 They demonstrated the machine that they had invented. | 他們展示了他們發明的機器。

3 She found the receipt that she had lost a few days ago. | 她找到了前幾天弄丟了的收據。

4 The police arrested the legislator after he had taken bribes. | 警察逮捕了先前收取賄賂的立法委員。

● 14. 未來完成式

➡ 未來完成式的用法比較少見，用來表示「某個動作，在未來某個時間點將會完成」，使用的公式是《will have＋過去分詞》。由於will是助動詞，所以have固定是原形的狀態，不隨人稱而改變。

The exhibition will have ended by tomorrow.
到了明天展覽就已經結束了。

➡ 例句

1 We will have reached an agreement tonight.	今晚我們就會達成一個共識了。
2 The employees will have gotten off work by then.	到了那時候，員工們都已經下班了。
3 The price of petrol will have skyrocketed 30% by then.	到了那時候，石油價格就會漲足百分之三十了。
4 Your lungs will have been destroyed by the time you quit smoking.	等到你戒菸的時候，你的肺就已經被毀啦。

● 15.「與事實相反」的助動詞完成式

➡ 很不幸地，助動詞後面不能用過去式動詞，所以我們得繞個路，用《助動詞＋have＋過去分詞》的句型，來表達過去已經完成的事情。特別的是，這個句型同時會表達出「與既定事實相反」的意思，所以常常是表示「惋惜」、「懊悔」等意思。

You should have gone surfing with us!
你當時真應該和我們去衝浪的！（但你沒去）

⮕ 例句

1 I might have found more references if I had had time.

如果有時間的話，我也許可以找到更多參考資料的。（但當時沒有時間）

2 We could have gotten a sufficient amount of money.

當時我們或許能得到充裕的資金的。（但是沒得到）

3 Mom might have sued the manufacturer if I hadn't stopped her.

如果當時我沒有阻止，媽媽可能就會去告那個製造商的。（我阻止了她）

4 They would have rebuilt the memorial if the government had supported them.

當時如果政府有支持的話，他們就會重建紀念碑了。（但沒有）

● 16. 現在進行式的其它用法　　CD2- 6

中級
Level

⮕ 現在進行式還可以用來表示「近期的狀態」，像是最近正著手於什麼事情、最近正在學什麼才藝等；另外，它也可以表示未來的意思，說明「已經安排好要做」的事情。

I'm presently looking for new recipes .
我最近在尋找新的食譜。

⮕ 例句

1 Their company is being pretty conservative these days.

他們公司最近還滿保守的。

2 Cecilia is thinking about attending medical school.

西莉雅正在考慮去讀醫學院。

3 That fatal disease is spreading quickly throughout the country.

那個致命的疾病正快速地在國內蔓延開來。

4 The two parties are debating over racial discrimination these days.

這陣子，兩政黨進行著有關種族歧視的爭辯。

17. 比較：過去進行式與過去簡單式

→ 過去進行式和過去簡單式時常一起連用，用簡單式來敘述事件一，用進行式來說明事件二。這時候整個句子會變成這樣的意思：「在事件一發生時，事件二已經持續發生了一段時間」。

I was bleeding when the rescue team arrived.
當救援小組抵達時，我正在流血。

→ **例句**

1	We were having dinner when the TV news reported the tragedy.	當電視新聞播報那場悲劇時，我們正在吃晚餐。
2	The phone rang when we were discussing visions for the future.	當我們正針對未來的見解進行討論時，電話響了。
3	The rebels were attacking whomever they saw when we arrived.	我們到的時候，叛軍們正在攻擊每一個他們所看到的人。
4	The professor was making an announcement when we entered the classroom.	當時我們進入教室時，教授正在宣布一件事情。

18. 比較：現在完成式與過去簡單式

→ 舉例來說，完成式可以表達「我到現在為止已經讀了三小時的英文」，有可能還繼續要讀，或是現在剛好讀完；而簡單式則可以表達「昨晚我讀了三小時的英文，現在在做別的事情」。現在完成式的動作和現在有關聯（所以才叫「現在」嘛！），過去簡單式則沒有。因此，當動作確切發生的時間點已經點明時，我們會使用過去簡單式，並且是已經完全結束的事。

Have you ever been to India?
你（從出生以來）有去過印度嗎？

178

➡ 例句

1 Frank has seen countless comedies.

法蘭克（從以前到現在）看過無數場的喜劇片。

2 The communists took over their country 50 years ago.

五十年前，共產黨接手（統治）了他們的國家。（現在沒有）

3 I haven't finished the multiple choice questions yet.

我目前還沒完成多選題。

4 He delivered a very well-organized presentation this morning.

今早他做了一場條理清晰的簡報。（現在沒有在做簡報）

中級
Level

● 19. 比較：現在完成式與現在完成進行式

➡ 現在完成式的焦點是動作所產生的「結果」，完成進行式則是強調「動作本身」。靈活地運用兩種不同的句法，可以使句子更加生動喔！

The king's thoughts have never been liberal.
國王的想法從未是開明自由的。

➡ 例句

1 The civilians have been suffering under his dictatorship.

一直以來他的獨裁讓百姓們苦不堪言。

2 Their support has been a continual encouragement to us.

他們的支持，（一直）是對我們持續的鼓勵。

3 The jury has been discussing but has not yet reached a verdict.

陪審團一直討論著，還沒有作出判決。（未有結果）

4 He has been looking for his true self that seemed to have disappeared.

他一直在尋找那似乎（結果）已經消失了的真正的自己。

二、被動語態

反過來以「接受動作的那一方」來出發,換個觀點敘述事情,就是所謂的被動語態。然而『我愛你』並不等於『你愛我』,所以要熟悉被動語態的各種寫法,才能寫出與主動語態意義相符合的被動句喔!

另外,英文主動和被動的語法邏輯中,有一些和中文是剛好相反的,所以要細讀本章,趕快揪出藏在腦袋裡的「中式英文」吧!

● 1. 簡單式   CD2- 7

➔ 《be動詞＋過去分詞》 是被動語態的基本句型,此時be動詞要隨著主詞人稱來變化,過去分詞則是固定不變的。如果是未來的被動式,則要用《will be＋過去分詞》,固定使用be動詞即可。

My digital camera was stolen!
我的數位相機被偷了!

➔ 例句

1 Drunk driving is strictly prohibited. | 酒後駕車是嚴格禁止的。

2 Bamboo is used to make chopsticks. | 竹子被拿來製造筷子。

3 All of the expenses are listed on this paper. | 所有的花費都列在這張紙上。

4 His new theory is supported by many scientific facts. | 他的新理論是有許多科學根據支持的。

● 2. 進行式

➔ 進行式的被動並沒有未來的用法,所以只要考慮現在和過去式兩種就好啦!句型是《be動詞＋being＋過去分詞》,表示「在現在或是過去的某時候,正在承受某個動作」的狀態,而其中being是固定不變的。別忘了be動詞中,is / am / are是現在式,was / were是過去式喔!

The medals are being awarded to the winners.
正在頒發獎牌給獲勝者。

➡ 例句

1 His luxurious house is being furnished right now. | 他的豪宅正在給人安置家具。

2 The speech was being disturbed by a naughty child. | 當時一個頑皮的小孩正在擾亂演講。

3 The lobster I bought is being cooked by my mother. | 我媽媽正在煮我買的那隻龍蝦。

4 The young pianist was being introduced to the royal family. | 那位年輕的鋼琴家當時正被介紹給皇室。

中級
Level

● 3. 現在、過去完成式

➡ 現在完成式的被動句型是《have/has＋been＋過去分詞》，其中been是固定不變的。和一般的完成式一樣，如果要表現過去完成式，只要把have/has改成had就可以了，變成《had＋been＋過去分詞》。

Her accent has been corrected.
她的口音已經被矯正了。

➡ 例句

1 Mom has been persuaded by my words. | 媽媽已經被我的話給說服了。

2 The meadow has been tended to by our gardener. | 草地已經被我們的園丁修剪過了。

3 The lost children's location has been identified. | 已經找到失蹤孩子們的所在位置了。

4 The access road I used to take has been closed. | 那個以前我走過的入口，已經被關閉了。

4. 與助動詞連用

CD2- 8

被動語態中,助動詞只能用在現在簡單式和現在完成式中,變成《助動詞+be+p.p.》和《助動詞+have been+p.p.》。同樣地,因為是接在助動詞後面,be動詞和have been都是固定不變的喔!而因為will也是助動詞的一種,所以未來完成式的用法,也包含在這個類別裡面。

All the refugees will have been rescued by then.
到了那時,難民們已經全數被救出來了。

例句

1 The operator might have been fired for our complaints.	那個接線生可能已經因為我們的抱怨而被解雇了。
2 Those pirates should have been captured and executed.	那些海盜應該要被抓並處決了。(但卻沒有)
3 Elizabeth might have been awarded the scholarship and gone abroad.	伊莉莎白本來可能已經拿到獎學金,而且出國了。(但沒有)
4 They could have been surrounded by their enemies.	他們本來可能被敵人給包圍了。(但沒有)

5. 情意動詞 (1)

表示驚訝、疑惑、喜悅…等的情意動詞,跟中文的邏輯恰好相反。以interest(使…感興趣)這個動詞來說,是「有趣的事物→interest(s)→感興趣的對象」的關係,所以有感覺的人是受詞而不是主詞喔!

Did that horror film scare you?
那部恐怖片嚇到你了嗎?

➡ 例句

1 His fluent Spanish impressed us all. | 他流利的西班牙文讓我們印象深刻。

2 His great progress in math amazed me. | 他在數學方面進步神速，令我大為驚嘆。

3 Your actions have really disappointed me. | 你的舉動真叫我大為失望。

4 Her newly released novel fascinates me a lot. | 她新發表的小說讓我非常著迷。

● 6. 情意動詞 (2)

➡ 因為有感覺的人其實是「受詞」的那一方，所以如果要表示中文的「某人對某物感興趣」這句話，就要用被動語態來說囉！比較要花時間的是，每個情意動詞搭配的不一樣的介系詞，例如be satisfied with、be interested in等。

We were astonished with his performance.
他的表演讓我們感到非常驚訝。

➡ 例句

1 Grandma is very pleased by his frequent visits. | 他經常來家裡，讓祖母很高興。

2 The girl was surprised by his passionate admiration. | 那女孩被他熱情的讚美給嚇到了。

3 I was fascinated by her immense knowledge on the subject. | 她在這主題上有如此豐富的知識，令我著迷不已。

4 The students are shocked at the announcement on the bulletin board. | 學生們對於布告欄上的告示感到非常震驚。

7. 情意動詞 (3)

CD2- 9

→ 現在分詞（-ing）表示「主動」，過去分詞表示「被動」、「完成」，兩個都可以用來當作形容詞。再度以interest為例，interesting是形容人或事物是「有趣的、令人感興趣的」，也就是說明主詞的那一方；interested是形容被動方的，所以就是「感到有興趣的」人啦。只要弄清楚誰是主詞、誰是受詞，就不會搞錯了！

Her improvements are quite astonishing.
她的進步叫人驚歎不已。

→ **例句**

1 I think Latin culture is really fascinating.

我覺得拉丁文化非常迷人。

2 Listening to his pointless lectures is tiring.

聽他毫無重點的演講真是累人。

3 The scenery in the national park was amazing.

國家公園的景色，讓人歎為觀止。

4 My awkward movements were embarrassing!

我那些笨拙的動作，真是叫人尷尬！

8. 被動意義的主動動詞：「看起來」、「聽起來」等

→ 明明在句意中是「承受動作的對象」，怎麼寫法卻是跟主動語態一樣呢？有一種感官類動詞就有這種特殊情形喔！也就是國中學過的連綴動詞用法：《動詞＋形容詞》，有look（看起來）、sound（聽起來）、smells（聞起來）…等用法。

His announcements sounded definite.
他的聲明聽起來很明確。（別人聽）

➡ 例句

1 Her Halloween costume looks a little scary.
她的萬聖節造型看起來有點恐怖。（別人看她）

2 The little girl's skin feels smooth and cool.
那個小女孩的皮膚（摸起來）感覺光滑而冰涼。（別人摸它）

3 The fish has rotted and now it smells disgusting!
那條魚腐爛了，現在聞起來真令人作嘔！（別人聞牠）

4 The suspect seemed nervous when the police asked him questions.
警察問問題的時候，那個嫌疑犯似乎很緊張。（別人看他）

● 9. 使役動詞的被動寫法

➡ Make、let、have等表示「令某人做某事」的使役動詞，在變成被動語態的時候，要將原本的動詞變成《to＋V》才行，是個特例。

The crew were made to abandon the ship.
當時船員們被迫要棄船。

➡ 例句

1 Billy was forced to resign for his grave error.
比利為了他嚴重的錯誤而被迫要辭職。

2 I was made to give her an additional discount.
我被強迫要給她額外的折扣。

3 The drunken man was told to show his identification.
那個酒醉的男人，被要求出示證件。

4 The guard was threatened to liberate the prisoners.
警衛被威脅要釋放囚犯。

中級
Level

中級 Level 英語文法 · 句型詳解

● 10. 常見被動語態句型

➡ 英文中有不少慣用語是固定使用被動語態的，下面列出一些常用的片語，要好好記住並活用喔！

Tobacco is believed to be a very profitable crop.
菸草被認為是一種高利潤的作物。

➡ 例句

1 Leon's suggestions are often considered constructive. | 里昂的建議常被認為是很有建設性的。

2 Jeff is thought of as the most promising boy in his family. | 傑夫被認為是他們家裡最有前途的男生。

3 Vivien Westwood is said to be the godmother of fashion. | 薇薇安衛斯伍德被稱為時尚界的教母。

4 Michael Jordan is regarded as one of the most admirable athletes. | 麥可喬登被視為是最值得敬佩的運動員之一。

三、代名詞

我們常用代名詞來避免重複提到某樣東西。除了最基本的人稱代名詞和只是代名詞，要挑戰高中程度的你更要熟悉其他的代名詞，才能寫出精簡又不失精確的句子！有些代名詞代表「前面提過的事物」，有些則代表「與前面事物的同一類別」，還有些甚至代表「句子中的子句」…種類繁多，快來瞧瞧吧！

● 1. this / that / these / those（1）　　CD2- 10

➡ This（這個）、that（那個）、these（這些）、those（那些）等四個代名詞，最基本的用法就是當作指示代名詞，指稱眼前的事物，或是較遠的事物。有時候這些代名詞也用來指代「前面出現過的事物」，甚至是前面的「句子」、「敘述」等較大範圍的東西。

中級
Level

That is the female dormitory.
那就是女生的宿舍。

➡ 例句

1	These are really comfortable linen pants.	這是很舒服的亞麻褲呢。
2	Is this the original version of that song?	這個是那首歌的原始版本嗎？
3	Are these pickled cucumbers?	這些是醃小黃瓜嗎？
4	The final rehearsal is tonight. That is for sure.	最終的採排時間是在今晚，那已是千真萬確的事了。

● 2. this / that / these / those（2）指「人」的those

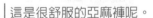

➡ Those常常被應用在關係子句上，指的是沒有特別對象的「任何人」，是這四個代名詞中，唯一有此用法的一個。

Prosperity will not come to those who are idle.
財富不會降臨在懶散的人身上。

⇒ 例句

1	Those who dislike others are often disliked, too.	那些不喜歡別人的人，通常也不會被喜歡。
2	Supplies were distributed to those who are homeless.	物資被分配給了那些無家可歸的人。
3	We erected a monument to honor those who died in the attack.	我們建立了一座紀念碑，來景仰那些在攻擊中喪生的人。
4	Those who have no sense of guilt are natural-born criminals.	沒有任何罪惡感的人，是天生的罪犯。

● 3. this / that / these / those（3）that與those

⇒ That以及those還有另一個特殊用法，就是用來代表前面提過的、某類型的事物。也就是說，它們指的並不是前面的同樣一件東西，而是「同類」的事物，例如要比較「A的眼睛」和「B的眼睛」時，有時候就會用those來指代「眼睛」這個重複的項目

Her potential is greater than that of her classmates.
她的潛力比她同學們的（潛力）要大。

⇒ 例句

1	The deadline for this project is earlier than that of the other one.	這個企畫的截止日，比另一個（企畫）要更早。
2	German grammar is much harder than that of English.	德文的文法比英文的文法要難多了。
3	The prospects of this company are much better than those of the other one.	這家公司未來的展望，比另一家公司的（展望）要好多了。

4 The age of this Egyptian tablet is older than those of all others discovered. | 這塊埃及面板的年齡比所有其他發現過的都要來得老。

4. It 的用法（1）天氣、時間、明暗等 CD2- 11

➡ 常用的代名詞it可以用來代替很多抽象、不具體的東西，像是天氣，或是跟單位測量有關的時間、距離、價格、重量等。

It is five dollars per gallon.
一加侖五塊錢。

➡ 例句

中級 Level

1 It is always blazing hot at midday. | 正午的天氣總是炎熱的。

2 It is late. Shall I accompany you home? | 很晚了，要不要我陪你回家？

3 It is about six miles away from the nearest volcano. | （這裡）離最近的火山大約有六英哩。

4 It's sunny today. We should do some outdoor activities! | 今天天氣晴朗，我們真該去做些戶外活動呢！

5. It 的用法（2）《It is/it was＋形容詞或名詞＋to V》

➡ 虛主詞 it 就等於後面的不定詞片語（to V…）。由於是當作「一件事情」來看待，所以be動詞一定是使用單數形的is/was，用來形容「這是件怎麼樣的事」。想要做些變化，變成「也許是」、「應該是」等語氣時，可以在be動詞前面加上助動詞。

It was a nightmare to hear him sing!
聽他唱歌真是一場惡夢啊！

➡ 例句

1 It is my greatest honor to receive this award.

得到這個獎是我最大的榮幸。

2 It might be a solution to buy insurance.

買個保險也許會是一個解決之道。

3 It could be dangerous to approach wild animals.

接近野生動物可能會很危險。

4 It is impolite to ask a woman about her actual age.

向一個女人詢問實際年齡很沒禮貌。

● 6. It 的用法（3）《It is/it was＋形容詞或名詞》與其他搭配

➡ 虛主詞 it 就等於後面的「某件事情」，所以只要是可以視作「一件事」的名詞子句（或片語），就可以放在後面。除了最常見的不定詞片語（to ＋原形動詞），另一個常用的就是「疑問詞開頭」的名詞子句：《疑問詞→S→V》。

It is surprising how fast Beijing has prospered!
北京的快速崛起，真是令人驚訝！

➡ 例句

1 It was impressive what an exceptional artist he was.

他是個如此優秀的藝術家，令人印象深刻。

2 It is an order to arrest anyone suspicious in this area.

逮捕這區域裡任何可疑的人物，這是命令。

3 It was amazing how music became part of the therapy.

音樂竟變成了治療的一環，這真令人驚訝。

4 It was disappointing to have canceled the trip.

旅行取消了，真令人失望。

● 7. It的用法（4）《It is/it was＋形容詞或名詞＋for或of＋人＋to V》

➡ For和of在這裡的差別是什麼呢？用for表示「對某人而言，這件事情是…的」；用of則表示「某人做這件事情是… 的」。換句話說，使用for時，形容詞所形容的是「事件」，但使用of時，形容的對象則是「人」。

It was a disaster for her to dress like that.
對她而言，穿成那樣真是一場災難啊！

➡ 例句

1 It is ridiculous of him to accuse me of stealing. | 他告我偷竊，真是太可笑了。

2 It is vital for you to apply for a new passport. | 申請新的護照對你來說是件很重要的事。

3 It is reasonable of him to change the original plan. | 他改變原訂的計畫是很合理的。

4 It is necessary for animals to absorb enough protein. | 對於動物而言，攝取足夠的蛋白質是很必要的。

● 8. It 的用法（5）It is...that...(should) 句型

➡ 有一種特殊的《It＋is/was＋adj.＋that one (should)＋原形動詞》句型公式，用來表示建議，把should當作「竟然」來使用，或是表達個人主觀的想法。其中，should通常是被省略的，因此看到原形動詞時，可不要覺得奇怪喔！

It is strange that they (should) eat raw food.
真奇怪，他們竟然吃生的食物。

➡ 例句

1 It is urgent that you quit abusing drugs. | 你得趕緊戒掉對藥物的濫用。

2 It is necessary that she (should) simplify her writing.

她必須簡化她的文章。

3 It is pathetic that many people (should) pursue only fame and money.

很可笑的是，很多人只追求名譽和金錢。

4 It is a pity that some players (should) skip the elementary training.

真遺憾！有些選手竟跳過了基礎的訓練。

● 9. It 的用法（6）強調

➡ 如果想要強調某個重點事物，也可以用it來表達喔！《It＋is/was＋名詞＋that…》的句型在這裡變成「（名詞）…才是…」的意思。當重點主題是人物的時候，that也可以換成另一個關係代名詞who喔。

It was distrust that destroyed their marriage.
是彼此的不信任，摧毀了他們的婚姻。

➡ 例句

1 It was the committee that made such a decision, not me.

是委員會做出那樣的決定的，不是我。

2 It is only your explanation that I want to hear.

我想要聽的就只是你的解釋。

3 It was actually Megan who joined the gang, not her brother.

其實是梅根加入了幫派，而不是她弟弟。

4 It was the Battle of Waterloo that shattered Napoleon's dream.

是滑鐵盧之戰，粉碎了拿破崙的夢。

● 10. It 的用法（7）其他慣用法　　CD2- 13

➡ 英文中有些慣用語是固定使用虛主詞 it 的，以下列出常見的一些 it 慣用語。

It is never too late to mend.
改進永遠也不嫌晚。

➡ 例句

1 It is no use crying over spilt milk. | 為了灑出來的牛奶哭泣，是沒有用的。（比喻覆水難收）

2 Rumor has it that Hannah and Jack are a couple. | 有謠言說漢娜和傑克是情侶。

3 It is (high) time (that) you revealed the truth. | 這是你該說出真相的時候了。（早該說了卻還沒有做）

4 It was not until the army received its orders did it retreat. | 軍隊一直等到收到命令之後才撤退的。

中級
Level

● 11. One的基本用法

➡ One在當作代名詞時可以表示與前面提過的事物「同類」的東西，而不是指同樣一件東西喔！除此之外，它還可以用來表示一個沒有確切對象的「人」，常用來敘述通則、真理等句子。

She has a beautiful gown. I wish I had one, too.
她有一件美麗的禮服，我真希望也有一件。

➡ 例句

1 Look at those tulips! Would you buy me one? | 看看那些鬱金香！你願意買一朵給我嗎？

2 One should never forget to reflect on oneself. | 絕不能忘記要反省自己。

3 One must not let hatred take over one's mind. | 人絕不能讓仇恨操控自己的心智。

4 My son wants a lantern for Lantern Festival, so I bought one.

我兒子想要一個燈籠過元宵節，所以我買了一個（燈籠）。

● 12. One、another和 others

➡ One、another和others分別表示「一個」、「另一個」、「其他的（複數）」的意思，三個常常放在一起連用，可以清楚地把團體中的不同事物，分別一件一件地娓娓道來。但注意喔，除了提到的這些事物之外，還是有其他這個團體的事物存在的，只是沒有提到罷了。

There are six drinks and one is poisonous.
這有六杯飲料，其中一杯是有毒的。

➡ 例句

1 While he spoke of his idea, others remained silent.

他訴說著自己的想法，而其他人則保持沈默。

2 She had two sons. One died, and the other is in jail.

她有兩個兒子，一個死了，另一個在坐牢。

3 To be elected is one thing, to actually govern the country is another.

當選是一回事，真正要治理國家又是另一回事。

4 Thomas Edison was a great inventor, and I'll become another.

湯瑪士愛迪生是個偉大的發明家，而我將是另一個（偉大的發明家）。

● 13. The others和the rest   CD2- 14

➡ 如果想要把一個團體中的東西通通談完，就可以用加上定冠詞the，表示是特定的對象。the others或是the rest來表示「（剩餘的）其他」，表示沒有別的了。注意another是不能夠和the一起使用的，因為它其實就是an（某一個）和other（其它的）組合啊！

Only three people stayed while the others had resigned.
只有三人留了下來，其他的都已經辭職了。

➡ 例句

1 Your job is to assemble the workers. I will worry about the rest. | 你的工作是召集員工們，剩下的（工作）由我來操心。

2 This state provides the rest of the country with a lot of timber. | 這一州大量地提供了其它州（國家其他地方）的木材。

3 I obeyed his order while the rest acted on their own judgment. | 我聽從他的命令，剩下的人則依自己的判斷行事。

4 While Tim expressed his thoughts, the others were too timid to speak. | 提姆表達了他的想法，而其他人則羞怯得不敢說話。

中級
Level

● 14. 複合代名詞（1）「some +...」

➡ 字根some-可以和其他的字組合成複合代名詞，變成「某個…」的意思，像是somebody（某人）、somewhere（某地）、someone（某人）、something（某個東西）等，還有相似的不定副詞somehow（某個方法）someday（某天）、sometime（某個時候）等。因為原理類似，所以放在這裡讓大家一起認識！

He will return for revenge someday.
有一天他會回來復仇的。

➡ 例句

1 The man says he has something to confess. | 那個男人說他要坦承某事情。

2 Somehow, my daughter copied my handwriting. | 我女兒不知道是怎麼模仿我的筆跡的。

3 I've seen a drawing similar to this somewhere.

我在某個地方看過跟這個類似的圖畫。

4 It is urgent to find someone to replace him.

要趕緊找人來取代他。

● 15. 複合代名詞（2）「any +...」

➡ 字根any-可以和其他的字組合成複合代名詞，變成「任何…」的意思，像是anybody（任何人）、anywhere（任何地方）、anyone（任何人）、anything（任何東西）等。這樣的代名詞也視作單數。

Anyone may become a future client of ours.
任何人都可能會成為我們未來客戶之一。

➡ 例句

1 Is there anything valuable in your suitcase?

你的行李箱裡有任何值錢的東西嗎？

2 Do you know anywhere I can find some aspirin?

你知道哪裡可以找到阿斯匹靈嗎？

3 Jamie's report was anything but satisfactory.

傑米的報告令人相當不滿意。

4 Can anybody here give me an accurate answer?

這裡有誰可以給我一個精確的答案嗎？

● 16. 複合代名詞（3）「no +...」　CD2- 15

➡ 字根no-可以和其他的字組合成複合代名詞，變成「沒有…」的意思，像是nobody（沒有人）、nowhere（沒有地方）、no one（沒有人）、nothing（沒有東西）等。其中的nowhere被歸類為副詞，不過因為原理相同，也放在這裡好方便記憶。

Nothing here is familiar to me.
這裡沒有任何東西是我所熟悉的。

➡ 例句

1 No one dares to speak of his mistress in public. | 沒有人敢在公開場合提到他的情婦。

2 The ambassador is going nowhere but to work tonight. | 今晚大使除了工作，哪兒也不會去。

3 Nothing but the king's mercy can save him now. | 現在除了國王的赦免之外，沒有東西救得了他。

4 Nobody has an extensive understanding of plants like Jack. | 沒有人能像傑克那樣，對植物的知識如此淵博。

中級
Level

● 17. 複合代名詞（4）「every＋…」

➡ 字根every-可以和其他的字組合成複合代名詞，變成「每個…」的意思，像是everybody（每個人）、everywhere（每個地方）、everyone（每個人）、everything（每個東西）等。這樣的代名詞也視作單數。

Everyone here has strong faith in you.
這裡的每個人都對你非常有信心。

➡ 例句

1 You must know that fame isn't everything. | 你必須瞭解，名聲並不是一切。

2 The police have inquired with everybody in the room. | 警方已經詢問過房間裡的所有人。

3 Everything in that museum was extremely beautiful. | 那間博物館裡，所有的東西都非常漂亮。

4 I've looked everywhere but still can't find my application form. | 我四處都找過了，但還是找不到我的申請表格。

英語文法・句型詳解

● 18. 所有格代名詞的強調用法

➡ 除了前面提到的《It＋is/was＋名詞＋that…》句型，可以用來說明強調的事物外，一般用來表示「某人的」的所有格形容詞，也可以發揮同樣功能喔！

George himself is in charge of the negotiations.
喬治本身是負責協商的。

➡ 例句

1 It was Sarah herself who decided to become a nun.

當時是莎拉自己決定要當修女的。

2 The melody itself is good enough to make this song a big hit.

旋律本身就足以讓這首歌成為暢銷金曲了。

3 I myself witnessed the murder with my own eyes.

我親眼目睹了兇殺案。

4 I was not depressed by the punishment but by the incident itself.

我並非因為處罰而感到失落，而是因為那件事本身。

四、不定代名詞

當我們只想討論很多事物中的其中一些時，就會使用不定代名詞。「不定代名詞」同時帶有「不確定的對象」和「代名詞」兩種特性。而不同情況下，不定代名詞又有單、複數的差別。要知道正確使用不定代名詞的方法，就往下看吧！

1. 數字＋of＋複數名詞　　　CD2- 16

➡ 只想討論很多事物之中的某幾個東西，並且也知道確切數字的話，就可以用《數字＋of＋複數名詞》的句型來表示。此時數字視作不定代名詞來看待，只知數量而不知確切的對象。通常複數名詞前都會加上the、所有格等指示詞，這是因為我們在針對某些特定的對象在做討論。

中級
Level

Two of the apples are rotten.
蘋果之中有兩個是腐爛的。（並非是所有的蘋果）

➡ 例句

1 Only one of you will be chosen as the representative.	你們之中只有一個會被選作代表。
2 Eight of the gamblers tonight were kicked out of the casino.	今晚的賭客裡，有八個被踢出了賭場。（專指今晚的賭客，不是其他賭客）
3 Hundreds of the buildings in that city have collapsed.	那城市中的幾百棟的建築都倒塌了。（專指某一個城市）
4 It's hard to believe that two of my classmates are already pregnant!	我的同學中已經有兩個懷孕了，真是叫人難以置信！（專指我的同學）

2. 表示「少（一些）」：(a)few與 (a)little

A few和a little的差別在於：前者用來描述可數名詞，後者用來描述不可數名詞，表示「一些」。如果去掉冠詞變成few或是little，則有負面的意思，表示「很少」喔！句型是《不定代名詞＋of＋複數名詞》。

They disagreed on few of the proposals.
他們對提議中的一部分有意見。

例句

1 Little of the evidence is actually useful. | 證據之中只有少部分是真的有用的。

2 A few of the chapters are still incomplete. | 還有一些章節是未完成的。

3 Few of the paintings here are masterpieces. | 這裡的畫作中，傑作很少。

4 The millionaire gave away a little of his money to charity. | 那個百萬富翁捐出了一些錢作慈善捐助。

3. 表示「多」：much、many、a lot

Much形容的對像是不可數名詞，many則是可數名詞，至於a lot則是兩者通吃，非常好用！

Many of the soldiers have surrendered.
士兵中有許多人都投降了。

例句

1 Much of the gossip about him is actually true. | 關於他的八卦，其中有不少是真的。

2 A lot of the icebergs in that area have melted. | 那個區域裡的冰山，很多都融掉了。

3 Many of the miners were trapped in the collapsed mine. | 很多的礦工被困在崩塌的礦坑裡。

4 Much of his money was transferred to his wife's account. | 他很多的錢都轉到他太太的帳戶裡去了。

● 4. 表示「部分」：some、most、part、half等　CD2- 17

➡ Some表示「一些」，most表示「大部分」，part表示「部分」，half則表示「一半」。這些不定代名詞同時可修飾可數和不可數名詞，但別忘記囉，不可數名詞一律都視為單數處理！

中級
Level

Most of the ice has melted already.
大部分的冰都已經融化了。

➡ 例句

1 Some of the goods in my shop are imported. | 我店裡的商品，有部分是進口的。

2 Part of the fund has been donated to NTU Hospital. | 部分的基金捐給了台大醫院。

3 Half of the participants made it to the top of the mountain. | 有一半的參與人員，成功地登上了山頂。

4 Most of the industrialized countries have pollution problems. | 大部分的工業國家，都有污染的問題。

● 5. 表示「全部」：all與both

➡ All與both都有「全部」的意思，不同的是，both是專門用來說明「兩者皆是」的情況的，也就是說，只要說明的對象多於兩個，就要用all而不能用both囉！

201

Both of the girls are attractive.
兩個女孩都很迷人。

➡ 例句

1 The old lady sold all of her jewels.

那位老太太把她所有的珠寶都賣掉了。

2 Both of these books have excellent illustrations.

這兩本書都有極為出色的插圖。

3 You should have listed out all of the ingredients.

你應該要把所有的成分都列出來的。

4 Both of the applicants were informed of a second interview.

兩個應徵者都收到第二次的面試通知。

● 6. 表示「擇一」：one與either

➡ One與either都表示「其中之一」的意思，但後者either則特別用在說明「兩者其一」的狀況。如果對象超過兩個，就得用one而不能用either了。而因為這兩個代名詞都帶有「數字」的意味在，所以不能用在不可數名詞上喔！

One of my credit cards is missing!
我少了一張信用卡！

➡ 例句

1 One of you will be promoted soon.

你們之中有一個會很快升職。

2 Either of the teams will be the champion.

兩隊之中，有一隊將成為冠軍。

3 Andy will be going to either of these academies.

安迪將會去（這兩所）其中一所學院上課。

4 Either of the candidates will become our next president.

兩個候選人之中，有一個會成為我們下一任總統。

● 7. 表示「無」：none與neither　　CD2- 18

➡ 同樣表示「沒有」的none和neither，其中特別用來說明「兩者皆沒有」的是neither。對象多於兩個時，要用none才可以。

Neither of us could resist his charm.
我們兩個都無法抗拒他的魅力。

➡ 例句

1 None of the victims survived the tsunami.

沒有一個受害者在海嘯之中逃過一劫。

中級
Level

2 Neither of these symbols is significant to me.

這兩個符號對我來說都沒有特別含意。

3 None of my men have ever hesitated on the battlefield.

在戰場上，我的弟兄們沒有人曾經猶豫過。

4 None of the applicants are qualified for the position.

沒有應徵者，資格符合這個職務。

● 8. 不定代名詞與動詞的一致性

➡ 別忘了，句子的主詞可是不定代名詞所指的「某部分」，而不是全體喔！所以可不見得是複數形動詞！如果後面的複數名詞是可數名詞，那麼就只有one才是單數形，其他皆為複數形；如果是不可數名詞，則一律視作單數喔！至於表示「沒有」的，則是單、複數皆可。

Some of the tombs in this area are lacking upkeep.
這一帶的墳墓，有些實在缺乏整理。

英語文法‧句型詳解

➔ 例句

1 Most of Dad's aged wine is stored in a specific room. | 爸爸的陳年酒,大部分都儲藏在一個特定的房間裡。

2 Some of the bread is made from wheat and some is not. | 這些麵包有的是小麥做的,有的不是。

3 More than half of the evidence was actually misleading. | 一半以上的證據,其實都具有誤導性。

4 Most of my friends are thinking of changing their occupations. | 我大部分的朋友都想要換工作。

五、比較的說法

不管是形容詞還是副詞,只要稍稍加以變化,都可以變成比較語氣的修飾法!除了從形容詞、副詞本身上做變化,本單元整理出英文文法裡用來比較不同事物的句型,比較型、最高級等通通不是問題!

● 1. 最高級(1)-est 和most   CD2- 19

➔ 形容詞和副詞基本的最高級用法,就是在字尾做-est的變化。碰到較長的單字,就在在原本的形容詞(副詞)前面加上most。又因為它們代表著獨一無二的、最高級的那個對象,所以前面要加上定冠詞the喔!

Leon is the mildest person I've ever met.
里昂是我遇過最溫和的人了。

➔ 例句

1 He sang the most perfectly in the competition. | 他在比賽中唱得最完美。

2 Kate behaves the most naturally of all those girls. | 凱特是那些女孩中，表現最自然的一個。

3 Those were the most enjoyable memories of my life. | 那些是我人生中最快樂的回憶。

4 The robbery was the most awful experience she has had. | 那次的搶劫是她遇過最糟糕的經驗了。

● 2. 最高級（2）用Other來表現最高級意義

➡ 除了基本的用法外，還有一些其他的說法，運用與其他事物比較的語氣，來達到表示最高級的效果。

No other ending could be as extraordinary as this one.
沒有任何結局可以比這個更棒了。

中級
Level

➡ 例句

1 Darren is more alert than all the other team members. | 達倫比其他的組員，都要有警戒心。

2 Chris has a stronger motivation than any of the other participants. | 克里斯比其他的參與者，都要有強烈的動機。

3 No other material is as suitable as copper for this product. | 沒有任何材料，能比銅更適合這樣的產品了。

4 Warren Buffet is more famous than any other investor in the world. | 華倫巴菲特比世界上任何投資者都要來得有名。

● 3. 最高級（3）帶有比較意味的詞語

➡ 除了特殊句型外，有些字彙本身就暗示著優、劣的意思，也可以達到同樣的比較效果。

Billy is the least able to concentrate in class.
比利是班上最沒辦法專心的一位。

➡ **例句**

1 As soldiers, his rank is superior to yours. | 以士兵來說，他的階級比你高。

2 Her contribution to our company is unparalleled. | 她對我們公司的貢獻，是無人可比的。（最有貢獻的）

3 Your project seems not as interesting as David's. | 你的企畫似乎沒有大衛的（企劃）來得有趣。

4 The racist man believes that other people are inferior to him. | 這個擁有種族歧視的男人，認為其他人都低他一等。

● 4. 表示「倍數」的句型   CD2- 20

➡ 無論是事物的數量或是特性，都可以用倍數的方式來做比較，基本句型是《倍數＋as＋adj./adv.＋as》，或是《倍數＋比較級＋than》。所謂的倍數詞，除了特殊的twice、half這些特殊的字外，其他都以《數字＋times》來表示。如果要用「項目」來做比較，像是size（大小）、length（長度）、price（價格）等，就要用《倍數＋the＋比較項目＋of》的結構。

This container is two times larger than the other one.
這個容器比另外一個要大上兩倍。

➡ **例句**

1 His pace is three times faster than everybody else's. | 他的步調是其他所有人的三倍快。

2 This pool is twice the depth of that at George's house. | 這個游泳池的深度比喬治家的要深兩倍。

3 My father is only half as protective as my mother toward me. | 爸爸對我的保護，只有媽媽對我的一半。

4 This capsule contains ten times as many nutrients as your lunch box. | 這一個膠囊含有你的便當十倍多的養份。

● 5. 比較句型的否定（1）

➡ 若是否定型的比較語氣，表示「不如」的意思，則要反過來用less (adj.) than的句型取代原本的more than或是 (adj.)-er than；若是要表達最高級的相反，也就是最低級的情況，則要把原本的most換成least。

That is the least probable thing that could happen.
那是最不可能發生的事情了。

➡ 例句

1 His judgements were made less fairly than mine. | 我的判決判得比他公平。

2 Monkeys are generally considered less logical than people. | 一般認為猴子沒有人類來得有邏輯性。

3 This is the least creative movie plot I've ever seen. | 這是我所看過最沒有創意的電影劇情。

4 The new procedure turns out to be less efficient than the old one. | 新的流程結果卻比舊的還沒效率。

● 6. 比較句型的否定（2）

➡ 用《not＋as (so)＋形容詞／副詞＋as…》的句型，就可以表示「不如…那麼樣地…」的意思，也就是常用句型《as…as…》（如同…一樣的…）的否定法。

Katherine is not as gracious as her kind mother.
凱薩琳沒有她和善的母親那麼親切。

➡ 例句

1 Henry didn't speak as honestly as the other kids.

亨利說話沒有其他孩子誠實。

2 I think Rachel is not as innocent as she seems to be.

我認為瑞秋似乎沒有像她外表那樣純真。

3 The experiment won't be as complicated as you think.

這實驗並不像你們想的那樣複雜。

4 It is actually not so extraordinary as what the media have said.

其實並沒有像媒體說的那樣了不起。

● 7. 延伸句型（1）：The more...the... CD2- 21

➡ 《The＋比較級（adj/adv），＋the＋比較級》的句型，暗示著前後兩個事件的因果關係喔！表示某個事物「越是…，（另一個事物）就越…」的意思！

Please join us! The more, the merrier.
敬請加入我們！人越多越開心哪！

➡ 例句

1 The older he gets, the more he cares about his reputation.

他活得越老，就越是在乎自己的名譽。

2 The stronger her opposition (is), the more insistent I am.

她的反對越是強烈，我就越是堅持。

3 The more you doubt yourself, the more unlikely it is you'll succeed.

越是懷疑自己，越是不可能成功。

4 The higher your expectations are, the greater your disappointment may be.

期待越高，失望可能就越大。

● 8. 延伸句型（2）：No more /No less …than…

➡ 從比較的語法延伸到別處，《no more /no less＋形容詞＋than…》的句型被用來形容某件事物「不比…要更（不）…」的意思。用邏輯推演一下，就不難了解，使用more時也就是說某個事物「和…是一樣的不…」，相反地，用less則表示某個事物「和…是一樣的…」。

Her mind is no more mature than her behavior.
她的思想和她的行為一樣不成熟。

➡ 例句

1	The portrait is no less beautiful than the princess herself.	這肖像畫跟公主本人一樣美麗。
2	Your response is no less cruel than John's refusal to help.	你的反應和約翰的拒絕幫忙一樣殘酷。
3	You, a grown-up, are no less dependent than your little sister.	你一個成年人，和你小妹一樣依賴人。
4	The outcome of this incident is no more wonderful than what I had thought.	這件事的結果和我料想的一樣不好。

中級
Level

● 9. 延伸句型（3）：No more /No less than…

➡ 《no more /no less＋than…》後面可以接上名詞、動詞、數量詞等不同用法。《no more than…》也就是only（只不過是）的意思，而《no less(fewer) than…》則等於as many as（多達）的意思喔！

She did no more than exaggerate the truth.
她做的只不過就是在誇大事實罷了。

⊃ 例句

1 To Ivy, his fawning over her is no more than a burden.	他的過度關心,對艾薇來說只是個負擔。
2 No less than a thousand people have quoted this information.	多達一千人引用過這個資訊。
3 To some employers, workers are nothing more than facilities.	對某些雇主來說,工人們就只是個設備罷了。
4 No fewer than a million visitors have visited the Museum of Contemporary Art.	多達一百萬人曾經參觀過現代美術館。

六、不定詞與動名詞

所謂的「不定詞」就是「to+原形動詞」,而「動名詞」就是「V-ing」的型態。它們長得雖像動詞,但卻不是真正的動詞,所以還有另一個名稱叫「準動詞」。也因為它們不能算是動詞,所以本身並不能顯示出「人稱」、「時態」這兩種重要的特性,而是得靠真正的動詞才行!

● 1. 不定詞的名詞用法 (1)　　CD2- 22

⊃ 不定詞片語為名詞片語的一種,也就是「當名詞使用的片語」。因此,把它當作一個長長的名詞來看待,當然也就可以把它放在不同的位置囉!其中一種就是用來當作主詞或是受詞的補語,對主詞、受詞加以說明。

My duty is to analyze the results of the experiment.
我的職責是要分析實驗的結果。

➡ 例句

1 My plan is to refresh myself with a hot bath after work.
我的計畫是，在下班後洗個熱水澡來提神。

2 It has been a blessing to know Sandy.
認識桑迪是我們的福氣。

3 His reason for doing that was to attract public attention.
他會那樣做，目的是要吸引社會大眾的注意。

4 The clerk is making an attempt to arouse customers' interest.
店員正試著引起顧客的興趣。

● 2. 不定詞的名詞用法 （2）疑問詞＋不定詞

中級
Level

➡ Who、how、when、where...等疑問詞，除了可以拿來提問，也可以用來當作不定詞片語前面的修飾詞，分別表示「人」、「方法」、「時間」、「地點」等項目。最後變成的《疑問詞＋to＋V》名詞片語，表示「該...」、「可以...」的意思，例如what to draw，就是指「該畫什麼東西」這件事情。

I'm not exactly sure about what to say.
我完全不知道該說什麼。

➡ 例句

1 It's a lecture about how to develop self-discipline.
這是個關於如何更具自律的演講。

2 The villagers are arguing about where to dump the trash.
村民們正在爭論著要在哪裡傾倒垃圾。

3 We'll talk about who to blame for this incident during the session.
在會議期間，我們會討論這次的事件該歸咎於誰。

4 Not knowing when to start the presentation, he shrugged at my question.
面對我的提問，他聳了聳肩，因為他也不知道要何時開始報告。

● 3. 不定詞的形容詞用法

➡ 不定詞片語還可以當作形容詞來使用，用一種動態的說明，來形容前面所提到的名詞有什麼「用途」。

I need a professional translator to help me.
我需要一個職業翻譯來幫我忙。

➡ 例句

1 (Are there) Any proposals for us to think about? | 有沒有什麼提議給我們大家參考的啊？

2 Repetition is one way to memorize vocabulary. | 反覆背誦是記單字的一種方法。

3 I don't have adequate time to produce a good paper. | 我沒有足夠的時間去寫一篇好論文。

4 Since he had nothing to lose, he decided to take the risk. | 既然沒什麼損失，他便決定冒這個險。

● 4. 不定詞的副詞用法（1）動作的目的　　CD2- 23

➡ 不定詞片語當作副詞使用時，常常是放在主要子句的後面，用來表示動作背後的「原因」、「目的」。因為是當副詞使用，所以不定詞也可以放在句子前面喔！只要在它之後加上逗點就可以了。

Combine water and flour to make dough.
將水跟麵粉和在一起，做生麵糰。

➡ 例句

1 You must carry an I.D. to prove your identity. | 你必須隨身攜帶身份證來證明你的身份。

2 To assure the essay's perfection, he revised it again.

他重新校過那篇文章，來確定它是完美的。

3 Kelly takes a hot bath in the evenings to relieve stress.

凱莉會在晚上泡個熱水澡以舒緩壓力。

4 I asked my teacher to give me an extension on my final paper.

我請求老師延長我交期末論文的期限。

● 5. 不定詞的副詞用法（2）修飾形容詞

➔ 副詞也可以用來修飾形容詞，所以不定詞片語也可以這樣用。以形容詞 good（好）為例，不定詞片語可以說明「哪方面好」、「如何的好法」等細節喔！

中級
Level

I find it hard to stick to my budget.
我發現要按照我的預算實在很困難。

➔ 例句

1 I was reluctant to believe him at first.

起先我不太願意相信他。

2 I've got a story to illustrate my point.

我用個故事來說明我的重點。

3 Emily is someone impossible to amuse.

愛蜜麗是個難以取悅的人。

4 My colleagues are easy to get along with.

我的同事都很好相處。

● 6. 不定詞的副詞用法（3）條件

➔ 為了要達到某個目的時，得做什麼事才行，這種情況就會用不定詞片語來表示「目的」，而由主要子句來說明「先決條件」。這樣的用法和前面所提到的「目的」用法相當接近，而不定詞片語也可以置前或是放在後面。

He's taking a course to get a teaching certificate.
他修了一堂課，以取得教師執照。

⊃ 例句

1 To blend the fruit well, you may slice it first. | 要讓水果好混在一起的話，可以先把它們切塊。

2 To make a quick reservation, please dial this number. | 要預先訂位的話，請撥這個號碼。

3 To be more energetic, take some vitamins in the morning. | 想要更有活力，早上就吃些維他命。

4 To keep a balanced diet, eat the right food at the right time. | 要保持均衡的飲食，就要在對的時間吃對的食物。

● 7. 類似不定詞慣用語：《to one's＋情緒名詞》

CD2- 24

⊃ 《to one's＋情緒名詞》的句型，表示「另某人感到...的，是...事情」，也就是在說明感情的原因，是相當常見的慣用語。注意這　要使用的是名詞，所以要和一般不定詞修飾形容詞的用法有所區別喔！

To her grief, her pet dog died in an accident.
令她悲痛的是，她的寵物狗意外地死了。

⊃ 例句

1 To my surprise, his reaction was quite positive. | 令我驚訝的是，他的反應還滿正面的。

2 To our disappointment, the celebration was canceled. | 令我們失望的是，慶典被取消了。

3 To their excitement, the story is reaching its climax. | 另他們感到興奮的是，故事正進入高潮。

4 To his satisfaction, his son was elected representative. | 令他感到滿意的是，他的兒子被選為代表。

● 8. 不定詞當準動詞

有些動詞的後面，必須要接上to+V或是V-ing才能表達完整的意思。有些動詞是規定要接不定詞的，此時的不定詞就算是「準動詞」，而不是句子裡真正的動詞。這種接不定詞的主要動詞，通常包含的是比較抽象的、不具體的意思，例如I want（想要）to talk這個句子裡，真正在做的事情是want，to talk則是想要做、當下實際上則沒有在做的事情。

We refuse to give in!
我們拒絕投降！

● 例句

1 She pretended to be a considerate person. | 她假裝是個體貼的人。

2 I want to express my gratitude by writing a card. | 我想要寫張卡片來表達我的謝意。

3 He clenched his fists and threatened to punch me. | 他握緊拳頭，威脅著要揍我。

4 My grandmother loves to knit sweaters and scarves. | 我祖母喜歡織毛衣和圍巾。

● 9. 進行式不定詞

當不定詞當其他動詞的準動詞用，而這兩個動詞的發生是同步進行時，就要用「進行式不定詞」，變成《動詞＋to be＋V-ing》的型式。此時「動詞」和「V-ing」兩個動作是同時進行的。

His company seems to be expanding.
他的公司似乎正在擴張。

Level 英語文法・句型詳解

➡ 例句

1 The rainfall is reported to be increasing this year. | 據報導今年的雨量正在上升。

2 Joseph is expected to be moving on to an advanced level. | 喬瑟夫被預期要進入高級班。

3 You are supposed to be feeling disappointed. Why aren't you? | 你現在應該要很沮喪的，為何你沒有？

4 One of my old friends is said to be writing a fashion column. | 據說我的老友中有一個在撰寫時尚專欄。

● 10. 完成式不定詞　　　CD2- 25

➡ 如果不定詞所敘述的動作，發生得比主要子句的動詞更早時，就要用完成式的不定詞，變成《動詞＋to have＋過去分詞》。

We're very fortunate to have met you.
我們很幸運能認識你。（「認識」早於「感覺幸運」）

➡ 例句

1 John seems to have conquered his fear. | 約翰似乎已經克服了他的恐懼。

2 The millionaire is said to have lived in luxury. | 傳說那位百萬富翁一直過著奢侈的生活。

3 Our ex-president is reported to have violated the law. | 報導說我們的前總統已經觸犯了法律。

4 Little John is said to have inherited Grandpa's property. | 據說小約翰已繼承了他祖父的財產。

216

● 11. 動名詞（1）

➡ 之所以叫做動名詞，就是因為它「引用動作當名詞」的特性，也就是說，動名詞就是當名詞來使用，表示「一件事」，也所以後面的動詞就要做單數形的變化。如果要寫出否定的不定詞，記得把not放在V-ing的前面喔！

Occasional gambling is acceptable to me.
對我來說，偶爾小賭是可以接受的。

➡ 例句

1 Thank you for gracing us with your presence. | 謝謝您的蒞臨，讓我們深感榮幸。

2 Not being tolerant is why you're always upset. | 你經常不高興的原因，就是你不夠包容他人。

3 Reprinting published books is a violation of the law. | 影印已出版的書籍是違法的。

4 We should take steps toward prevention instead of waiting to see what will happen. | 與其靜觀其變，我們應該採取預防措施。

● 12. 動名詞（2）與所有格連用

➡ 由於固定是V-ing的形式，動名詞本身並沒有「動作者」以及「時態」這兩個特性在裡面。幸好，動名詞可以跟真的名詞一樣，在前面冠上「所有格」，說明這個動名詞片語是「誰做的」事件。這個特性可是不定詞片語所沒有的喔！

His wife strongly forbids his drinking.
他老婆嚴禁他喝酒。

→ 例句

1 I just can't bear their quarreling in public.
我真的沒辦法忍受他們在公共場所吵架的樣子。

2 Frank asked his mother to permit his driving.
法蘭克要求他媽媽允許他開車。

3 Dad insists on my wearing a helmet for safety.
為了安全起見,爸爸堅持要我戴安全帽。

4 I made an apology for my interrupting the meeting.
為干擾會議一事,我道了歉。

● 13. 容易混淆的現在分詞　　CD2- 26

→ V-ing除了是動名詞外,也有可能是動詞的「現在分詞」,帶有動態的意味,而不像動名詞是當作名詞來使用。分詞放在主要子句後面,分詞和主要動詞的兩個動作是同時發生的,這也叫做「分詞構句」。

The poor hostage returned home crying.
可憐的人質哭著回到了家。

→ 例句

1 The designer went onto the stage smiling.
設計師笑著走到舞台上。

2 The lion walked around in the cage roaring.
那頭獅子在籠子裡走來走去,並咆哮著。

3 He ran and danced toward the sea stripping.
他一邊脫著衣服,一邊又跑又跳地朝海上跑去。

4 A maniac stood in the middle of the road cursing the government.
有個瘋子站在馬路中間咒罵著政府。

● 14. 動名詞的完成式

➡ 《having＋過去分詞》是動名詞的完成式結構。此時動名詞片語所敘述的事件，發生在主要子句之前喔！

Jessica recalled having seen him elsewhere.
潔西卡好像在哪裡看過他。（「see」發生在「recall」之前）

➡ 例句

1 Mario regrets having teased his sister like that.
馬力歐很後悔以前那樣欺負她妹妹。

2 The burglar admits having broken into my house.
那個小偷承認以前曾闖入我的房子。

3 Emily is in great sorrow after having ended a ten-year relationship.
愛蜜莉因為結束了一段十年的戀情而難過不已。

4 The man admitted (to) having spread the messages of terror on the Internet.
那名男子承認先前在網路散布過恐怖的訊息。

● 15. 接動名詞的動詞（1）

➡ 有些動詞是強制規定要接動名詞的，至於為什麼，通常沒有什麼道理可循，所以只好多看多背囉！一旦熟悉了，看到就知道要用什麼啦！

I don't mind reading science fiction.
我不介意看科幻小說。

➡ 例句

1 They kept criticizing a girl they don't even know.
他們一直在批評一個他們根本不認識的女孩。

2 She spent her whole life trying to atone for her sins.
她花了一輩子試著為自己贖罪。

3 Holly enjoys observing other people wherever she goes.

無論到哪裡，荷莉都很喜歡觀察別人。

4 You should avoid imposing your personal beliefs upon others.

你應該避免將個人的信仰，強加於他人之上。

● 16. 接動名詞的動詞（2）　　CD2- 27

➡ 感官動詞除了接原形動詞外，就只能接動名詞了。感官動詞包含了see、hear、listen to、watch、feel...等，接上動詞可說明，藉由感官發現了什麼事情。跟原形動詞比起來，接動名詞的感官句型，表示「感受到的那一刻，事件正在發生」。

I saw him buying souvenirs at that shop.
我看到他在那間店購買紀念品。

➡ 例句

1 She can feel the boy trembling in her arms.

她可以感覺到，小男孩在自己的臂彎裡顫抖著。

2 Did you hear the roosters crowing this morning?

你今天早上聽到公雞叫了嗎？

3 He watched the magician training the fierce beast.

他看著魔術師訓練那隻凶猛的野獸。

4 We listened to the orchestra playing inside the music hall.

我們在音樂廳裡，聽著管弦樂隊演奏。

● 17. 慣用動名詞的句型（1）介係詞或介係詞片語

➡ 除了獨立的介係詞，還有很多常用的片語都是以介係詞收尾的，它們後面接的不是名詞就是動名詞。當然，可別忘記to也是一個介係詞喔，所以並不是看到to，後面就要補上原形動詞來變成不定詞喔！

I am sick of enduring their constant quarrels.
我厭倦了忍受他們不斷地爭吵。

➡ 例句

1 The professor went on making his statement. | 教授繼續進行他的說明。

2 Don't you feel guilty about killing an innocent girl? | 殺了一個無辜的女孩，難道你不會有罪惡感嗎？

3 A financial adviser should be good at communicating. | 一個財務顧問，應該要擅於溝通。

4 In spite of being handicapped, Darren remained optimistic. | 儘管身體殘障，達倫還是很樂觀。

中級
Level

● 18. 慣用動名詞的句型（2）動詞＋介係詞＋動名詞

➡ 許多動詞都是以《動詞＋介係詞＋受詞》的型態出現的，此時的受詞除了名詞之外，也可代換成動名詞喔！這種句型常出現的介係詞包括：from、of、for、about...等。

I will not approve of playing cards in class!
我絕不贊成在課堂上打牌！

➡ 例句

1 Has he succeeded in convincing her to come? | 他有成功地去說服她來這裡嗎？

2 I don't feel like attending any religious ceremonies. | 我不想要參與任何宗教儀式。

3 The rebel party is planning on murdering the president. | 反叛黨正在策劃謀殺總統。

4 Kevin has always dreamed of establishing his own company. | 凱文一直夢想著要成立自己的公司。

英語文法・句型詳解

● 19. 慣用動名詞的句型（3）動詞＋受詞＋介係詞＋動名詞

CD2- 28

➡ 有些句子是以《動詞＋受詞＋介係詞＋動名詞》的形式出現，其中的動名詞是當作受詞補語來使用，對前面的動詞輔以說明。

He accused me of stealing his money.
他指控我偷了他的錢。

➡ 例句

1 Please forgive me for offending your friend. | 請原諒我冒犯了你的朋友。

2 There's no way to stop old memories from fading away. | 我們沒辦法去阻止記憶的消逝。

3 Her parents tried to prevent them from getting married. | 她的父母想要阻止他們倆結婚。

4 They're trying to keep the Mexicans from crossing the border. | 他們在試著不要讓墨西哥人越過邊界。

● 20. 慣用動名詞的句型（4）接在to後面

➡ 看到to就會想到不定詞嗎？別忘了，to本身也是個介係詞喔！也就是說，不見得看到to，後面就應該是原形動詞喔！有些動詞後面會接介係詞to，再來連接受詞，此時受詞便可以使用當作「名詞」看待的動名詞。

Tom is addicted to smoking cigarettes.
湯姆抽煙抽上癮了。

➡ 例句

1 She devoted herself to helping the poor. | 她致力於幫助窮人。

2 She is strongly opposed to amending the constitution. | 她強烈反對修改憲法。

3 The models are restricted to eating vegetables only. | 模特兒們被限制只能吃蔬菜。

4 I look forward to competing against you in the championship. | 我期待在冠軍賽中，跟你一決勝負。

21. 慣用動名詞的句型（5）Have fun/a good time/ trouble…＋ Ving

➡ 想要表示做某件事情是很開心的、很艱辛的，就可以用這個句型啦！《Have＋fun/a good time /trouble…＋Ving》的句型，可依不同情況而變換have後面的單字喔！表示「做…的期間是…的」意思。

The navy had a hard time winning the war.
海軍在經歷了一段艱苦的時期後，打贏了這場仗。

中級
Level

➡ 例句

1 Grandpa has trouble recalling the past. | 祖父就是想不起過去的事情。

2 I had a lot of fun playing a detective in this film. | 我在這部電影中扮演一個偵探，得到很多樂趣。

3 The old man has trouble walking in the chilly wind. | 那位老人在寒風中舉步艱難。

4 Chris had a difficult time becoming the governor of this state. | 克里斯經歷了一段艱苦的日子，才成為這州的州長。

22. 慣用動名詞的句型（6）其他慣用法　　CD2- 29

➡ 除了上述的用法外，在高中文法中還會學到一些慣用語是固定使用動名詞的，要好好記住喔！

Chinese prefer eating at a circular table.
中國人較喜歡在圓桌上吃飯。

⊃ 例句

1 There is no forecasting tomorrow's weather in a desert.

在沙漠中是不可能預測明天的天氣的。

2 There's no point being mad about other people's objections.

因為他人的反對而不高興，實在沒甚麼意義。

3 On seeing the emperor, the people knelt down on the ground.

一見到皇帝，人們就跪在地上。

4 She couldn't help weeping upon hearing the tragic story.

聽到那悲傷的故事，她不由自主地哭了。

● 23. 可接動名詞或不定詞的動詞

⊃ 有些動詞並不限制該接不定詞或是動名詞。不管使用哪一個，句子的意思都沒有太大差異，唯一的特別情況是，如果主要動詞以經是現在分詞（-ing），那麼準動詞便不會再接動名詞了。

New York continues to be a prosperous city.
紐約仍然是個繁榮的城市。

⊃ 例句

1 Will is now starting to seek a new profession.

威爾現在正開始找新工作。

2 Jerry began calculating this month's profits.

傑瑞開始計算這個月的利潤。

3 He loves watching traditional puppet shows.

他非常喜歡看傳統布袋戲。

4 I hate to discourage you, but isn't this too risky?

我實在不想潑你冷水，但這會不會太冒險了？

● 24. 用動名詞或不定詞表示不同意義

➡ 還有一種動詞是這樣的：接上不定詞或動名詞會產生兩種不同的意思。此時動名詞傾向表達已發生的事件，而不定詞則是尚未發生的事件。小心觀察下面的例句，就可以了解了！

I can't remember signing that treaty.
我不記得有簽下那份條約。

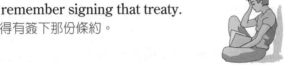

➡ 例句

1	Remember to leave some margins while you write.	寫作的時候，記得要稿子周圍要留點邊。
2	We stopped to check our baggage.	我們停下來（以便）檢查我們的行李。
3	Billy, a genius, just couldn't stop absorbing new information.	天才比利就是沒辦法停止吸收新資訊。
4	Let's go on to discuss the conclusion of this passage.	讓我們接著（下一個）來討論這篇文章的結論。

中級
Level

● 25. 容易混淆的句型（1）Be used to＋Ving和used to＋V

CD2- 30

➡ 這兩個是非常重要的句型！前者表示「習慣於某件事」，後者則表示「以前習慣於某件事，但現在已經不會了」的意思。如果要表示「變得習慣」的意思，可以將be動詞換成become、get等帶有「轉變」意義的動詞。另外，第一個句型中的動名詞也可以改成名詞。

He used to participate in the student committee.
他曾經參與學生會過。

225

例句

1 Betty still can't get used to the new regulations.	貝蒂還是無法適應新的規定。
2 Apparently, he hasn't gotten used to waking up so early.	顯然地,他還沒有習慣這麼早起床。
3 American students are used to doing group research.	美國學生很習慣集體做研究。
4 This new computer is superior to the one I used to have.	這台新電腦比我以前的那台高級。

● 26. 容易混淆的句型(2)worth、worthy、worthwhile

要表示事物或是人的價值時,就會用到這三個形容詞,但可得小心他們的不同用法喔!分別是《worth + N / Ving》、《worthy + 不定詞》或是《worthy of + N / Ving》以及《worthwhile + Ving / 不定詞》。

The boy's generous deeds is worth complimenting.
男孩慷慨的行為是值得稱讚的。

例句

1 The trip to this museum has really been worthwhile.	這間博物館真的值得一遊。
2 The magnificent job you've done is worthy of praise.	你做的大事值得讚揚。
3 The Bible is worth reading regardless of your religion.	無論你的宗教信仰為何,聖經都是值得一讀的。
4 His great achievements are worthy of being awarded the highest honor.	他卓越的成就,是值得被獎勵為最高榮譽的。

● 27. 容易混淆的句型（3）prefer

➡ Prefer表示「偏好」的意思，搭配動名詞和不定詞，分別是以下兩種句型：《prefer＋Ving/ N＋to＋Ving / N》以及《prefer＋to V＋rather than＋(V)...》。注意！在使用動名詞的句型裡，動名詞是不能省略的，只有在不定詞的句型裡，可以將第二次出現的動作省略。

Mom prefers fish soup with a lot of ginger.
媽媽喜歡多放薑的魚湯。

➡ 例句

中級
Level

1	I prefer to read science fiction rather than (read) romance.	和浪漫文學比起來，我比較喜歡讀科幻小說。
2	Terry preferred being engaged in work to going on a vacation.	和去渡假比起來，泰瑞比較喜歡投入工作。
3	I prefer to work with someone dynamic rather than someone passive.	我比較喜歡和有幹勁的人工作，而不是消極的人。
4	She prefers staying in an air-conditioned room to sweating under the sun.	和待在太陽下揮汗相比，她比較喜歡待在冷氣房裡。

● 28. 動名詞的被動式

➡ 動名詞的句子也和一般句子一樣，可以寫成被動語態的形式，公式是《being＋過去分詞》。若是這個被動句子是發生在主要動詞之前的事件，則可以用表示動名詞完成式的公式《having been＋過去分詞》喔！

You can't be a competitive player without being trained.
沒有接受訓練，是不可能成為一個有競爭力的選手的。

⇒ 例句

1 Sam became homeless after being suspended from his job.

山姆在被革職之後，變得無家可歸。

2 James is still upset about having been fooled by his friends.

詹姆斯還在為（之前）被朋友愚弄的事而不高興。

3 The judge regrets having been convinced to release the man.

法官為了（先前）被說服而釋放那名男子，而感到後悔。

4 Despite being deceived by her boyfriend, Amanda still can smile.

儘管被男友欺騙，亞曼達還是掛著笑容。

七、假設語氣

你是不是常常有著「如果A發生了，就會發生B了」的念頭呢？這些都是假設性的說法，叫做「假設語氣」。當然囉，有些假設可能成真，但也可能是無法扭轉的事實，這時就要用不同的句型來表現囉！

Should/would/could/might這四個助動詞，（以下簡稱s/w/c/m）是假設語氣必備的四大工具。不同情況時，可以用不一樣的助動詞來表現不同的語氣喔！

● 1. 有可能的假設　　　　　　　CD2- 31

⇒ 當事情還未定案，所以假設依然有可能成真時，就用現在式＋未來式來表現。標準句型是《If＋現在簡單式，＋will...》，也就是「如果...就會...」的意思。當然囉，如果要改變語氣，也可以把will換成其他助動詞喔！

If John gets drunk, he will act like a maniac.
如果約翰喝醉的話，他的行為會像個瘋子一樣。

⇒ 例句

1 If you boil the tomatoes first, you can peel them more easily.

如果你先把番茄煮滾，皮就會比較容易剝了。

2 If you plunge into the Dead Sea, you will end up floating. | 如果跳進死海裡，最後就會浮起來的。

3 If you all follow my instructions, everything will be just fine. | 如果你們都遵照我的指示，一切就不會有問題的。

4 If we enlarge this photo, the image may not be as clear as it is now. | 如果我們把這照片放大，圖像可能不會像現在這樣清楚。

● 2. 與現在事實相反的假設

如果事情已經定案了，那麼再假設些什麼也都不會改變現在的事實囉！這時候的假設句型是《If＋過去簡單式,＋s/w/c/m＋V...》，也就是「如果...就...」的意思。注意喔！假設語氣句型中，固定使用were這個be動詞，所以就不用擔心人稱的問題啦！

中級
Level

If I were the mayor, I would build more museums.
如果我是市長，我就會蓋更多的博物館。（但我不是）

● 例句

1 If I were invisible, I could go to the movies for free! | 如果我是隱形的，我就可以免費去看電影啦！（但我不是）

2 If she were a good consultant, I would not be so mad now. | 如果她是個好顧問，我現在就不會這麼生氣了。（但她不是）

3 If he won the lottery, he would be able to live a luxurious life. | 如果他中了樂透，他就可以奢侈過日子了。（但他沒有）

4 If you were enthusiastic about your job, you could learn more. | 如果你熱情投入工作，你可能會學到更多。（但你沒有）

● 3. 與過去事實相反的假設

➡ 如果是回想再久遠些的事情，表示「如果當時…那時候就會…」的意思，就要用《If＋過去完成式，＋s/w/c/m＋have p.p.》的句型囉！此時「假設條件」和「假設結果」都是過去的事情了，所以當然也是已經無法推翻的事實啦！

If she hadn't been so calm, we might have all panicked.
→She was so calm that we did not panic.
如果當時她沒那麼冷靜，我們可能全都會驚慌失措的。
→她當時很冷靜，因此我們並沒有驚慌失措。

➡ 例句

1 If Mike hadn't failed that subject, he would have graduated.
→Mike failed that subject, so he didn't graduate.

如果麥克那一科沒有不及格的話，他就會畢業了。
→麥克那一科被當了，所以他沒有畢業。

2 If he had tried harder, he might have accomplished the mission.
→He didn't try hard, so he didn't accomplish the mission.

如果當時他更努力些，那時就可以完成任務了。
→當時他沒有更努力，所以他沒有完成任務。

3 If we hadn't forgotten our life jackets, Tim would not have drowned.
→We forgot our life jackets, so Tim drowned.

如果我們沒有忘了（帶）救生衣，提姆就不會淹死了。
→我們忘了救生衣，所以提姆淹死了。

4 If I hadn't been unaware of his madness, we would not have broken up.
→I wasn't aware of his madness, so we broke up.

如果當時我有察覺到他的氣憤，我們就不會分手了。
→當時我沒有察覺他的氣憤，所以後來分手了。

● 4. 虛主詞it   CD2- 32

→ 好用的虛主詞it，也可以套用在假設句型裡面喔！搭配代表「原因」的介系詞for，虛主詞it同樣也可以表達假設的語氣。注意介系詞for後面要接名詞才行喔！

If it were not for her divorce, her child would not be so lonely.
如果不是因為她的離婚，她的小孩就不會這麼寂寞了。

→ 例句

1	Were it not for your proper manners, we would have all been kicked out.	如果不是你應對得體，我們就會全被趕出去啦。
2	If it hadn't been for fastening my seatbelt, I could have been killed.	如果當時不是因為我繫好的安全帶，我可能就已經死了。
3	Were it not for the short nap, I would be extremely tired now.	如果沒有那短暫的午睡，我現在會很疲倦。
4	If it hadn't been for the critic's praise, the book wouldn't be so famous.	當時如果不是評論家的稱讚，這本書就沒辦法這麼有名了。

中級 Level

● 5. 表示假設的句型（1）But for / but that / without / wish / hope

→ 即使不用假設語氣的標準句型，還是可以用其他的語法來表示相似的意義！其中wish傾向表達「可能性小的願望」，而hope則是純粹的「希望」，通常是敘述比較可能成真的事情。

You couldn't have arrived so soon without the Tube.
沒有地鐵，你當時就不會這麼早到的。

➡ 例句

1 I wish I hadn't sneezed in her face; she hates me now! | 我真希望當時沒有對著她的臉打噴嚏,她現在恨死我了!

2 It is (high) time that you corrected your pronounciation. | 應該是你矯正發音的時候了。

3 But for you constant support, I would have already failed. | 如果不是因為你不斷地支持,我早已經失敗了。

4 Jerry hopes that he can profit from the recent gains of the stock market. | 傑瑞希望他可以從近期的股票市場中獲利。

八、連接詞

連接詞(或連接詞片語)不僅可以當作子句、動詞、片語之間的連結以避免動詞重複,還扮演著語氣轉換、連結的角色,所以又被視作「轉承語」(Transitional Words),可以讓文章更加流暢喔!

◇對等連接詞:連接對稱的子句、動詞、片語等。

◇從屬連接詞:連接主要子句和從屬子句。注意從屬子句不能單獨存在。

◇準連接詞:接近副詞,用分號連接兩個對等句子或是直接分割成兩句。

● 1. 對等連接詞(1)and　　　　CD2-33

➡ And連接前後相關的、接續事物,可以是名詞、形容詞、副詞、子句...等,只要前後都是同種型態就可以囉!此外,它還可以用來表示事情「接著發生」的意思。

Martha became furious and impatient.
瑪莎變得又憤怒又不耐煩。

⮞ 例句

1 We encouraged him to be bold and (to) go for it! | 我們鼓勵他勇敢往前衝。

2 We stood on the bow and enjoyed the fresh air. | 我們站在船頭，並享受著新鮮的空氣。

3 Can you believe that they cook and eat beetles? | 你相信嗎？他們居然把甲蟲煮來吃！

4 How often do you babysit your niece and nephew? | 妳多久當一次妳姪子和姪女的保姆？

● 2. 對等連接詞（2）but

⮞ 和and不同，but是個帶有轉折語氣的詞，可以當作「但是」、「卻...」來解釋。後面連接的事物，和前面所提的常常會有些相反的意味在。

Justice is crucial but fragile.
正義雖然很重要，卻也很脆弱。

⮞ 例句

1 Why can grown-ups smoke but we teenagers can't? | 為什麼成年人可以抽煙，我們青少年就不行？

2 The things you've said are not facts but personal inferences. | 你說的並不是事實，而只是個人推論。

3 Duke was happy about his promotion but also nervous about it. | 杜克對自己的升遷感到很高興，但也因此感到很緊張。

4 The soldiers are extremely thirsty, but water is scarce on the battlefield. | 士兵們非常地渴，但在戰場上，水是很缺乏的。

● 3. 對等連接詞（3）or

➡ Or表示「或者」的意思，連接前後兩種可能的情況。另外它也可以表示「否則」的意思，表示可能的後果。

Which is more fatal, poverty or hatred?
貧窮與憎恨，哪一個比較致命？

➡ 例句

1 Will you seize the chance or just let it slip away? | 你是要抓住這機會，還是要讓它溜走？

2 You must keep the wound clean or it'll get infected. | 你必須保持傷口清潔，否則會被感染。

3 Is this your permanent address or just a temporary one? | 這是你的永久住址還是暫時的？

4 A product should meet consumers' needs, or they won't buy it. | 產品應該要符合消費者的需求，否則他們不會買的。

● 4. 對等連接詞（4）so   CD2- 34

➡ So也就是「所以...」的意思，後面連接原因、動機、事件等所造成的「結果」、「效用」等情境。

Helen is studying nursing so she can help others.
海倫為了助人在學習看護，。

➡ 例句

1 I'm grinding coffee beans so I can make some coffee. | 我為了煮咖啡在磨咖啡豆。

2 We built the memorial hall so people can remember him.

我們蓋了紀念堂，好讓人們可以記得他。

3 The escalator is broken so we'll have to take the stairs.

電扶梯壞了，所以我們要爬樓梯。

4 He's not very sociable, so he spends a lot of time in isolation.

他不是那麼愛交際，因此他大部分的時間都是孤單一人。

● 5. 對等連接詞（5）for

➡ 一般人最熟悉的for用法，大概就是介係詞了吧！但注意它也可以當作連接詞喔！當連接詞時，它表示「由於」、「因為」的意思，後面接上子句，來說明前面事件的源由。

中級
Level

Sarah succeeded for she's a very talented dancer.
因為莎拉是個極有天賦的舞者，所以她成功了。

➡ 例句

1 A substitute came in today for our regular math teacher is sick.

因為數學老師生病了，所以今天來了一個代課（老師）。

2 I doubt his betrayal for he's the most loyal person I know.

我之所以對他的背叛感到懷疑，是因為他是我所認識的人當中最忠誠的。

3 We won't buy the content of this report for it's obviously one-sided.

我們不會採信這篇報告的，因為它的內容明顯地很偏頗。

4 Sam doesn't date anymore for his previous girlfriend cheated on him.

山姆不再（和別人）約會，因為他的前女友欺騙了他。

中級 Level　英語文法・句型詳解

● 6. 對等連接詞（6）not only…but also…

➡ 從單字的字義，大概就可以猜到這個連接詞片語的用法了！就是「不止是…還是…」的意思。注意not only後面和but also後面的兩個部分，還是要符合連接詞對稱的原則喔！只要結構對稱，不管是名詞、動詞還是片語，都可以組合在一起。

They not only raised the boy but also cultivated his mind.
他們不只扶養小男孩長大，也陶冶了他的思想。

➡ 例句

1 Hurricanes are not only dangerous but also unpredictable. | 颶風不但危險，也是無法預測的。
2 The victims need not only sympathy but also real help. | 受害者需要的不只是同情，還有實際的援助。
3 Good writers require not only imagination but also prowess. | 好的作家不只要有想像力，還要有高超的技巧。
4 This novel has not only an English version but also a Spanish one. | 這本小說不只有英文譯本，還有西班牙文版。

● 7. 對等連接詞（7）both A and B　CD2- 35

➡ Both表示「兩者皆是」的意思，後面可以用「A＋B」的句型或是複數名詞。當然囉，如果是「A＋B」的形式，A和B兩者都要對稱喔！

The play was both dramatic and exciting.
那齣戲劇既生動又刺激。

➡ 例句

1 His anger resulted from both jealousy and depression. | 他的怒火源自於嫉妒和沮喪。

2 Both men are willing to give her lifelong commitments.

兩個男人都願意給她一輩子的承諾。

3 Both my parents teach philosophy in Cambridge University.

我的爸媽兩人都在劍橋大學教授哲學。

4 Both physical and mental intimacies are important in marriage.

對婚姻而言，身體和心靈上的親密都很重要。

● 8. 對等連接詞（8）Either…or…和neither…nor…

➲ Either…or…（不是…就是…）和neither…nor…（兩者皆非）所連接的事物也要維持對稱的原則，可以是詞、片語、句子等事物。

He is either very gifted or very hard-working.
他不是非常有天分，就是非常努力。

➲ 例句

1 What he has done is neither funny nor acceptable.

他所做的事，既不有趣也難以忍受。

2 You can either change the schedule or ignore him.

你可以變更行程表，或是根本不要理他。

3 Neither has he given his approval nor did he stand against it.

他既沒有表示答應，也沒有表示反對。

4 Either you will confess every detail of it or go to jail.

你要不就是對我坦白一切詳情，要不就是去坐牢。

● 9. 從屬連接詞（1）as long as和unless

➲ As long as可表示「只要…」的意思，unless則表示「除非…」的意思，意思有所不同，但都可以用來表示事情發生的條件。有一點要注意：雖然附屬子句（條件）部分可能是還沒發生的事情，但在寫的時候，卻不能用未來式喔！

英語文法・句型詳解

I would go anywhere as long as I stay outdoors.
只要我待在戶外，什麼地方我都願意去。

➡ 例句

1 As long as they are disciplined, kids will not be spoiled. | 只要有受管教，孩子們就不會被寵壞。

2 It's hard to become rich unless you make good investments. | 除非你做好投資，否則很難變有錢的。

3 The historians will be killed unless they portray the king as a hero. | 除非把國王描寫成英雄，否則歷史學家就會被殺。

4 You will feel happier as long as your life corresponds with your beliefs. | 只要你的生活與你的信念一致，就會比較快樂。

● 10. 從屬連接詞（2）after和before   CD2- 36

➡ After（在…之後）和before（在…之前）可以當作介係詞來使用，也可以當作連接詞喔！不同的是，介係詞後面只能接名詞或是動名詞，連接詞卻可以接較長的子句。

We shall have dinner after the fireworks.
我們（看完）煙火後，要去吃晚餐。

➡ 例句

1 Ray had been a professor before he became a carpenter. | 雷當木工之前，是個教授。

2 They will only stop fighting after they achieve true equality. | 唯有在獲得真正的平等後，他們才會停止奮鬥的。

3 I suggest you put some lotion on your skin after you bathe. | 我建議你洗完澡後，在皮膚上抹些乳液。

4 Sales of the product increased after the commercial was released. | 登廣告之後，這個產品的銷售量就增加了。

● 11. 從屬連接詞（3）while和as

● 除了表示「當...」的時間用詞之外，while和as兩個連接詞還有各自的其他用法喔！As可以暗示「因果」的關係，而while則是可以用來「對照」兩件不同、卻有些相關的事件，有「雖然」的意味在裡面。

As I can speak French, there was no need for translation.
因為我會說法文，所以當時並沒有翻譯的必要。

● 例句

1	He hoped to catch a fish as he cast his lure into the water.	他將誘餌丟到水中，希望能抓到魚.
2	We had to parachute many times while I was in the military.	我還是軍人時，常常要跳傘。
3	As time goes by, urban areas are becoming heavily populated.	隨著時間推移，市區的人口變得非常稠密。
4	While they achieved a glorious victory, there's still room for improvement.	（雖然）他們贏得了榮耀的勝利，還是有進步的空間。

中級 Level

● 12. 從屬連接詞（4）though (although) 和 in spite of (despite)

● 想要表示有點義無反顧的「儘管...，但還是...」的意思時，就可以用這樣的連接詞。注意！though (although)才是真正的連接詞，所以後面是接上有主詞、動詞的子句；可表示同樣意思的in spite of (despite)，卻是介系詞片語，所以後面要加上名詞而不是子句。此外，though也可以放在句末，作口語上的「不過」意思。

Although we are far apart, we are deeply in love.
雖然我們相距甚遠，卻依然深愛著彼此。

例句

1 James is a lazy person. His brother is hard-working though.

詹姆士是個懶人，不過他的兄弟倒是很勤奮。

2 They got married last week despite their parents' disapproval.

儘管家長們反對，他們還是在上禮拜結婚了。

3 Even though he luckily survived, his legs were severely damaged.

儘管他幸運地存活下來，他的雙腿仍受著嚴重的傷害。

4 In spite of my disappointment, I congratulated my opponent on his victory.

雖然我很失望，我還是向我的對手恭賀他的勝利。

13. 從屬連接詞（5）because和since　　CD2- 37

Since是表示「既然」或是「自從」的意思，because則表示「因為」的意思。

The man was arrested because he committed a crime.
那個男人因為犯罪，而遭到逮捕。

例句

1 Since you can't afford to make such payments, why did you rent it?

既然你無法負擔這樣的費用，你當時為什麼要租？

2 Since you've changed your hairstyle, I almost can't recognize you.

自從你換髮型後，我幾乎認不出你了。

3 We're going to use a different technique since plan A isn't working.

既然A計畫行不通，我們打算採用不同的方法。

4 She went to the doctor because she's been terribly depressed these days.

因為這陣子她一直都很憂鬱，所以去看了醫生。

14. 從屬連接詞（6）as soon as和no sooner than

➡ Soon這個單字原本就表示「立刻」的意思。《As soon as＋附屬子句，＋主要子句》可以說明「一...就...」的意思，《no sooner than＋附屬子句＋倒裝的主要子句》則表示「...發生沒多久就...了」的意思，說明兩件前後發生間距很短的事件。

No sooner than we returned home did it turn foggy.
我們一回到家就起霧了。

➡ 例句

1	The gardener started to tend to the lawn as soon as he arrived.	園丁一到，就馬上整理草皮。
2	My computer shut down as soon as I inserted this disc.	我一把這磁片放進去，我的電腦就關機了。
3	Everything will come to an end as soon as we settle this issue.	我們一旦解決了這件事，一切就會結束的。
4	No sooner than he made the announcement did the people begin to protest.	他才一發表聲明，人民就開始抗議了。

中級
Level

15. 從屬連接詞（7）as if (as though)和like

➡ As if 和as though是兩個可互換的連接詞片語，表示「彷彿」的意思，形容主要子句的事件就「彷彿是」如何如何，並且也可以用like來替換。不過呢，有時候也有假設語氣的意味在喔！例如as if後面使用過去式動詞時，有時也可能表示是「與現在事實相反的假設」。

She's talking as if selfishness were a virtue!
她講得好像自私是種美德似的。（但顯然事實上並不是）

➡ 例句

1 She's acting as if she were very good at cooking.
她表現得好像很擅長烹飪一樣。（但其實並不是）

2 It sounds like he's receiving great applause in there.
聽起來他好像在那裡獲得熱烈的掌聲。

3 He seems as though he is suffering from (major) depression.
他感覺像籠罩在極度的沮喪之下。

4 This place looks as if it's been attacked by a furious mob!
這地方看起來，簡直像是被憤怒的暴民攻擊過一樣！

● 16. 從屬連接詞（8）when和every (last/next) time

CD2- 38

➡ 《When＋附屬子句》的句型，是用另一事件的敘述來表示主要子句發生的「時機」。而《every/last/next＋time＋附屬子句》也有這樣的功能，只不過多了「每當」、「上一次」、「下一次」等三種不同的條件啦！

I will leave right away the next time you yell at me.
下次你再對我吼，我就馬上離開。

➡ 例句

1 Inspiration poured in when she wandered on the beach.
當她漫步在海邊時，靈感便接二連三地湧現。

2 I recall those vivid memories every time I look at the photographs.
每次我看著照片，就會想起那些鮮明的記憶。

3 When is the last time you enjoyed solitude somewhere distant?
你最後一次在遙遠的某處享受孤獨，是什麼時候？

4 When the bus fell off the cliff, he thought he would die for sure.
當公車墜落懸崖的時候，他以為自己死定了。

● 17. 從屬連接詞（9）that

➔ That最常被用在引導名詞子句，可以發揮主詞、受詞、補語等角色的功能，甚至還可以連接一個以上的名詞子句當作複數受詞喔！

The possibility that he will survive is almost zero.
他生還的可能性，幾乎等於零。

➔ 例句

1	The deal is that everyone should always be punctual.	約好大家都要準時的。
2	I suggest that you contact your agent and renew the contract.	我建議你聯絡你的代理商，然後跟他更新合約。
3	Kelly knows that she has to work on her reading comprehension.	凱莉知道她得加強自己的閱讀理解能力。
4	Ben said that he's an aggressive person and that I should stay away from him.	班說他是個有侵略性的人，還說我應該要跟他保持距離。

中級
Level

● 18. 準連接詞（1）therefore / thus / as a result(consequence)...等

➔ Therefore和thus都表示「因此」的意思，as a result(consequence)則是「結果...」，還可以加料變成《as a result(consequence)of＋原因》的句型呢！可以用來代換的還有副詞consequently、hence等。

Consequently, Mom will not give me a dime now.
結果，媽媽現在一毛錢都不願意給我。

➔ 例句

1	She keeps her feelings hidden. Therefore, no one really knows her.	她把自己的感情隱藏起來，所以沒有人能真正瞭解她。

2 As a result of her great talent, she became a professional performer.

因為她過人的天分，使她成了一個專業的表演者。

3 Jill lacks endurance. Thus, she always quits before things are done.

吉兒缺乏耐力，所以她常常在事情完成前就放棄了。

4 He's got a good coach. Thus, his skills have improved by leaps and bounds.

他有個好教練。因此，他的技巧突飛猛進。

● 19. 準連接詞（2）however / nevertheless　CD2- 39

➡ 帶有轉折語氣的however和nevertheless，都表示「然而」的意思，它們所連接的句子，通常都會和前面敘述的事物有相反的意味喔！

She's been honest with him. Nevertheless, he remains doubtful.
她對他一直都很誠實，但他依然疑心病很重。

➡ 例句

1 I love my teacher; however, it's hard to grasp the meaning of her words.

我很喜歡我的老師，但是她的話實在很難瞭解。

2 We enjoyed the climax; however, the rest of the story was a disaster.

我們很喜歡故事的高潮部分，但其餘的就糟透了。

3 The conductor was fabulous. However, the orchestra wasn't so great.

指揮者是很棒啦，但是管弦樂團就沒那麼出色了。

4 Fertilizers help increase productivity. Nevertheless, they're too expensive.

肥料是有助於增加產量啦，但是太貴了。

● 20. 準連接詞（3）moreover / besides / in addition

➡ 要對前面所敘述的事物加以補充、延續時，就要使用這些連接詞。它們都表示「除此之外，還有...」的意思，而其中besides可以補充變成《besides＋原本有的事物》，再接著說明補充的敘述。In addition也可以發揮同樣的作用，只不過得先加上介係詞to才可以喔！

Mary is a graceful woman. In addition, she's also bright.
瑪麗是個優雅的女人，此外她也很聰明。

➜ 例句

1 The style of this piece is rare. Besides, it's truly creative. | 這作品的風格罕見，而且也很有創意。

2 The virus was infectious; moreover, it was in an enclosed space there. | 那種病毒是會傳染的，更何況那裡還是密閉的空間。

3 Besides the products on display, the show girls were attractive, too! | 除了展示中的產品以外，秀場女郎們也很有吸引力呢！

4 In addition to the damp weather, there are also frequent earthquakes. | 除了潮濕的氣候以外，還有頻繁的地震。

中級
Level

● 21. 準連接詞（4）in other words / that is(to say)

➜ 這兩個連接詞分別是「換句話說」和「也就是說」的意思，都可以用來強調、解釋前面所敘述的事情喔！擔心對方不瞭解自己話中之意時，用這兩個連接詞是最恰當的了！

I'm always there for you. That is, you may call me anytime.
我隨時為你空出時間，也就是說，你隨時都可以打給我。

➜ 例句

1 Curiosity killed the cat. In other words, don't be too curious. | 好奇心殺死了貓。換句話說，好奇心別太過度了！

2 He is as cunning as a fox. That is to say, I do not trust him. | 他就像狐狸一樣地狡猾，也就是說，我不會相信他的。

3 You may refer to the booklet on the desk. That is, please don't ask me. | 你可以參考桌上的小冊子，也就是說，請不要來問我。

4 The juice is full of artificial flavoring. In other words, it's not pure. | 這果汁加了一堆人工香料。換句話說，它不是純的。

● 22. 準連接詞（5）on the contrary與in contrast

➡ 這兩個片語長得很像吧！小心它們的不同意思喔！On the contrary表示「相反的」的意思，與前面的敘述帶有相反的意味在。In contrast則單純地要說明「對照...」的意思，卻不見得是相反的喔！

In contrast to my work, yours is remarkable.
和我的作品比起來，你的相當出色。

➡ 例句

1 In contrast to a teacher, an engineer seems to have less leisure time.

跟教師比較起來，工程師的休閒時間，似乎比較少。

2 Bob thinks it's cool. On the contrary, it is pretty hot.

包伯以為天氣很涼爽，但相反地，天氣很熱。

3 We use a lot of sunblock; Americans, on the contrary, love sunbathing.

我們使用大量的防曬乳，相反地，美國人卻很喜歡做日光浴。

4 Sean wore long jeans plus a jacket; I, in contrast, wore shorts and a bikini.

西恩穿長牛仔褲配上外套，我卻穿了短褲和比基尼。

九、關係子句

把「句子」當作「形容詞」，就是關係子句的作用，當單一的字詞不足以形容要敘述的事物時，關係子句就派上用場了！但是子句和子句之間還是得有連結的，所以就出現了一個身兼「連接詞」和「代名詞」的角色：關係代名詞。關代所指代的對象，又稱作「先行詞」。

除了關係代名詞外，還有關係形容詞、關係副詞等用法，也都具有連接詞的功能。

● 1. 關係代名詞（1）：who與whom　CD2- 40

➜ 當句子的先行詞是「人」時，就要用who或是whom來當作關代囉。嚴格來說，當關代是關係子句中的受詞時，應該要用whom而不是who，但現今已經沒有那麼嚴格了，唯有在關代前面有介係詞時，才一定要使用whom。

中級
Level

He is someone who uses his wits.
他是個機智的人。

➜ 例句

1	She is the composer whom I told you about.	她就是那位我和你提過的作曲家。
2	That is the architect whom he admires the most.	那位就是他最崇拜的建築師。
3	The woman who had just lost her husband was sobbing.	那位才喪夫的婦人，在啜泣。
4	Ben is the one whom I consider the most productive of all.	班就是我認為所有人之中，生產力最高的一個。

2. 關係代名詞（2）：which

➡ 當句子的先行詞是「動物」、「事物」等人以外的東西時，要用which來當作關代。另外，如果是要對逗點以前敘述的句子加以說明，則一定要用which才行。

The animal which we saw is a leopard.
我們看到的那隻動物是隻豹。

➡ 例句

1 The part which impressed me the most was the speech.

最令我印象深刻的那部分是演講。

2 Leo forgot to do his laundry, which got him in big trouble.

李歐忘了洗自己的髒衣物，這可讓他麻煩大了。

3 The theory which Copernicus came up with was rejected during his lifetime.

哥白尼所提出的理論，在他有生之年是被否定的。

4 A severe earthquake occurred in China, which is heart-breaking.

中國發生了一場嚴重的地震，（而這件事）真令人痛心。

3. 關係代名詞（3）：that

➡ That跟which的用法非常接近，都可以用來表示人以外的其他事物。但是that有兩樣重要的規定：一是不能放在逗點之後，二是如果先行詞有only、every-、形容詞-est等表示「唯一」、「最高級」的用詞，則必須使用that而不是which。

What is it that you've been grieving for?
你一直在難過的，究竟是什麼事啊？

➡ 例句

1 Political benefit is the only thing that he cares about. | 政治利益是他唯一在乎的東西。

2 I'm touched by the poem that you recited in class. | 我對你在課堂上朗誦的那首詩，覺得很感動。

3 Every word that you write should have at least one vowel. | 你所寫的每一個字都至少要有一個母音。

4 The best sauce that I've ever tasted was made by Grandma. | 我所嚐過最棒的醬汁是祖母做的。

● 4. 關係副詞：where、when、why　CD2- 41

中級
Level

➡ 關係副詞是用來說明動作是在哪裡、何時、為何發生的。也就是說，關係副詞與先行詞的搭配應該是：「地點」→where，「時間」→when，「原因」→why。

This is the place where he committed suicide.
這就是他自殺的現場。

➡ 例句

1 This is the site where we found the fossils. | 這是我們發現化石的地點。

2 That is the reason why she made reading an everyday habit. | 那就是為什麼她把閱讀當作每天的習慣的原因。

3 His expertise and diligence are reasons why I recommended him. | 他的專業和勤奮，就是我之所以推薦他的原因。

4 I can never forget the day when Dad introduced me to my stepmother. | 我永遠忘不了，爸爸向我介紹繼母的那一天。

5. 關係形容詞：whose

➡ 當先行詞是人，但是關係子句的敘述卻是針對先行詞的「所有物」加以描述時，就要用whose而不是who了。

There's a student whose muscles are flexible.
有位學生的筋骨很柔軟。

➡ 例句

1 He named a patient whose recovery was surprisingly fast. | 他提到了一位復原速度驚人的病患。

2 It's my job to comfort people whose marriages have problems. | 我的工作就是要慰問婚姻有問題的人。

3 This is a man whose contributions were historically significant. | 這是個擁有歷史性的重大貢獻的人。

4 I find it hard to make friends with someone whose character is so defensive. | 我發現要和一個防衛性如此強的人交朋友，是件困難的事。

6. 非限定用法

➡ 當先行詞是獨一無二的對象時，關係子句其實並不能幫我們辨識出先行詞為誰，而只是一條補充的資訊。這時就要使用所謂的非限定用法（補述用法）了，也就是要用「兩個逗點」來把關係子句和主要子句隔開。非限定用法有幾個要注意的規定：一、關係詞不能省略，二、不能使用that。

Taiwan, which is located in East Asia, is my homeland.
位在東亞的台灣，是我的祖國。

➡ 例句

1 Hugh Jackman, who is known as an actor, is good at singing, too.

以演員身份著名的休傑克曼，也很會唱歌呢。

2 I'm going to New York, which is the financial center of the U.S.A.

我要去美國的金融中心—紐約。

3 Samantha, whose father is a politician, lives under heavy pressure.

父親是政治人物的莎曼莎，生活在極大壓力之下。

4 Arnold Schwarzenegger, who was a tough movie-hero, is now a governor.

曾經是螢幕硬漢的阿諾史瓦辛格，現在是個州長。

● 7. 關係詞的省略　　CD2- 42

中級 Level

➡ 當關係詞是關係子句中的「受詞」時，是可以將關係詞省略掉的；但有些東西不能省略：關係詞whose和《介係詞＋關係詞》的組合，以及前面提到的限定用法中的關係詞。

I found the grave in which they buried Kate.
我找到了當時他們埋葬凱特的墳墓。

➡ 例句

1 The lousy excuse (that) he gave me was quite stupid.

他給我的那個糟糕透頂的藉口，實在是滿愚蠢的。

2 What was the powder (which) had dissolved in the water?

那個在水中溶解的粉末，是甚麼啊？

3 Roger, who seems to be a dull person, is actually a scholar.

看起來像個呆瓜的羅傑，其實是個學者。

4 The girl (whom) I interviewed yesterday was filled with passion.

昨天我訪談的那個女孩，真是熱情洋溢。

● 8. 關係詞代換（1）：分詞

➡ 我們說關係子句是「當作形容詞用的句子」，而分詞也可以當作形容詞來使用，所以有時候兩者是可以互換的，而原始意義也不會因此改變。

I love a certain brand of chocolates (which is) called "See's".
我很喜歡一個特定的巧克力品牌，叫做「喜事」。

➡ 例句

1　I have a math tutor (who was) introduced to me by my uncle.　｜　我有一個舅舅介紹的數學家教老師。

2　The dinner (that was) prepared was delicious.　｜　準備好的餐點相當美味。

3　Everyone (that was) trapped in that building is safe and sound.　｜　困在那棟建築物裡的人，都很安全而且狀況良好。

4　Have you seen the list of products (which was) faxed this morning?　｜　你看到今早傳真過來的產品清單了嗎？

● 9. 關係詞代換（2）：介係詞＋關係詞

➡ 運用介係詞的不同用法，可以和關係詞一起搭配，藉此發揮和其他某些關係詞一樣的功能。但要小心介係詞的使用喔！看看先行詞平常都會搭配甚麼介係詞，關係子句就要用甚麼介係詞！

The day on which we were hijacked was a rainy day.
→ We were hijacked on a rainy day.
我們遭到搶劫的那天，是個下雨天。

➔ 例句

1 The company with which we worked was very cooperative.
→ We worked with a very cooperative company

我們之前合作的那家公司，非常好配合。

2 The lady to whom I was speaking was elegant and kind.
→ I was speaking to a lady who was elegant and kind.

之前我交談的那位女士，人不僅好也很優雅。

3 The reason for which he left was that he had lost his appetite.
→ He left for the reason that he had lost his appetite.

他之所以離開的理由，是他已經失去了食慾。

中級
Level

4 Digestion is the process by which your body breaks down food.
→ Your body breaks down food by the process of digestion.

消化是身體分解食物的過程。

● 10. 複合關係詞（1）關係代名詞兼形容詞　CD2- 43

➔ 與-ever合併後的whichever和whatever，就等於是no matter which(what)，也就是「無論什麼」和「無論哪個」的意思。當作形容詞的時候，後面要加上名詞，說明是「無論什麼東西」或是「無論哪個東西」。

Whatever is included in the box is yours.
不管這箱子裡裝有什麼東西，都是你的。

➔ 例句

1 Whatever gifts you have for me, I would be grateful.

不管你有什麼禮物要給我，我都會很感激的。

2 Whatever has been aroused in you, please don't show it now.

不管你心裡被激起了什麼感覺，現在請不要把它表現出來。

3 Whichever man you marry, be sure that he'll love you forever.

不管妳要嫁給哪個男人，要確定他會愛妳一輩子啊。

4 Whichever path I choose, my dog will always be my companion.

不管我選擇哪一條路，我的狗一直都會是我的同伴。

11. 複合關係詞（2）關係代名詞

➡ 等於No matter who/ whom的whoever和whomever，表示「無論是誰」的意思，與原始關係詞的用法類似，都是用來形容「人」的狀況。

Ana takes pity on whoever begs her for help.
安娜會同情任何懇求她幫助的人。

➡ 例句

1 Whoever inherits my wealth should use it wisely.

不管是誰繼承我的財富，都要善加利用它。

2 These inhabitants will attack whoever harms their homeland.

這些居民們會攻擊任何傷害他們家園的人。

3 Whoever wrote this letter must have great affection for you.

無論是誰寫了這封信，他一定對你有很深的情感。

4 You're now responsible for whomever you've guaranteed.

你現在得為你保證過的所有人負責。

12. 複合關係詞（3）關係副詞

➡ 說明「無論何處」的wherever、「無論何時」的whenever以及「無論如何」的however，都是複合關係副詞。

It rains whenever my family goes camping!
每次我們家去露營都會下雨！

➡ 例句

1 However frightened she is, she always remains calm.	不管她有多害怕，她總是保持冷靜。
2 Justin quickly adapts to the customs of wherever he travels.	無論去什麼地方，賈斯丁都能很快適應當地的風土民情。
3 Wherever there's a campaign, there is noise and garbage.	不管在哪裡，只要有選舉活動，就會有噪音和垃圾。
4 However hard I tried, I couldn't convince the student council.	無論我多麼努力地嘗試，都沒辦法說服學生會。

中級
Level

● 13. 類關係詞as / but / than　　CD2- 44

➡ 除了關係詞和關係子句之外，還有一些句型可以發揮和關係子句一樣的作用喔！這些詞因為很像關係詞，但又不是關係詞，所以又另有一個名稱叫做「類（準）關係詞」。

There are no soldier in this country but patriotic ones.
→ There are no soldiers in this country who aren't patriotic.
在這個國家沒有不愛國的軍人。

➡ 例句

1 As you all know, this is a very special occasion. → You all know the fact that this is a very special occasion.	如你們所知，這是個非常特別的場合。

2 Richard is being more considerate than I thought. 理查比我想的要來得更體貼。
→ Richard is being more considerate than how I had thought.

3 There was no one in the theater but applauded for the wonderful play. 劇院裡沒有人不為這齣美好的戲劇鼓掌。
→ There was no one in the theater who didn't applaud for the wonderful play.

4 This apartment costs a lot more than I could afford. 這棟公寓比我可以負擔的價格要貴多了。
→ This apartment costs a lot more than the price I could afford.

14.不定代名詞與關係代名詞

➡ 記得不定代名詞的用法嗎？我們用它來表示「...其中的某部分」。而因為關係代名詞有代名詞的效果，如果將兩者一起連用，就可以用來表示「前面提到的複數名詞中，某些部分是...」的意思，句型是《主要子句，＋不定代名詞＋of＋關代...》。

There are 30 students, few of whom have bad attitudes.
有三十個學生，其中有少數態度是差的。

➡ 例句

1 I have many acquaintances, none of whom is a true friend. 我認識很多人，其中沒有一個是真正的朋友。

2 Ben has two brothers, neither of whom could tolerate his selfishness. 班有兩個兄弟，兩個都沒辦法忍受他的自私。

3 This plan consists of four parts, one of which is my responsibility. 這項計畫由四個部分所組成，其中一部分是我負責的。

4 He donated 5 million dollars, most of which went to charity groups. | 他捐了五百萬元，其中大部分都給了慈善團體。

十、分詞

分詞又有「現在分詞」、「過去分詞」之分，一般熟悉的用法，都是和進行式以及簡單式一起使用。但它們其實也可以獨立出來作其他用途！

● 1. 現在分詞（1）形容詞的功能　　CD2- 45

➔ 現在分詞可用來當作有「主動意味」的形容詞，藉由事物在當下正在進行的動作，來對它做補充說明，將動作發揮形容詞的功能。

The dying victim was harmed in his lungs.
這瀕死的受害者，被傷到了肺部。

➔ 例句

1 She listened to her whining child with patience. | 她耐心地聽著她的孩子抱怨。

2 The shocking news was an absolute nightmare. | 這令人震驚的消息真是個惡夢。

3 That crying girl seems to be expressing her rage. | 那個哭泣著的女孩似乎是在表達她的怒氣。

4 I can foresee a lot of problems resulting from this. | 我能預知這件事會引起許多問題。

● 2. 現在分詞（2）分詞構句

➡ 當前後兩個動作的主角都是同一對象時，可以將其中一個省略，並將該子句的動詞變化成現在分詞。這樣的分詞構句除了表示「兩個動作同步進行」之外，也可以用來表示「原因」，而包含主詞的主要子句，就是「結果」了。

Being under construction, this restaurant is temporarily closed now.
（因為）正在施工中，這家餐廳目前暫時關閉。

➡ 例句

1 Having several symptoms of a cold, I took some pills.
（因為）有一些感冒的症狀，我服用了一些藥丸。

2 Walking through the hallway, I came across an old friend.
穿過走廊時我遇見了一位老朋友。

3 Nelly scooped out some ice cream to eat, cooling her down.
妮莉挖了一些冰淇淋來吃，好讓自己清涼一下。

4 Learning through experience, he's now a prominent leader.
從經驗中學習，他現在是個傑出的領導人了。

● 3. 過去分詞（1）表示「被動」的形容詞功能

➡ 過去分詞是動詞的另一種變化，被使用在被動語態的句子中。因此，它本身就帶有被動的意味在喔！變成表示「被...的」的意思的形容詞。

The man stabbed by a burglar was taken to the hospital.
那位被一個搶匪刺傷的男子，已經被送到醫院去了。

➡ 例句

1 The homework assigned to you is due next week.
指派給你的作業，完成期限在下周。

2 Her report is about the nuclear power plant built here.

她的報告寫的是關於興建在這裡的核能電廠。

3 The pilot tried to comfort the scared passengers.

機長試著安撫被嚇壞的乘客。

4 The ticket given to you was supposed to be a birthday gift.

給你的那張票，原本應該是生日禮物的。

4. 過去分詞（2）表示「完成」的形容詞功能　CD2- 46

➔ 過去分詞也常被應用在完成式的句型當中。只有過去分詞，其實也可以暗示動作「完成」的意思，進而變成一種形容詞喔！也就是「已經...的」意思。

中級
Level

A burnt child dreads fire.
被燒過的孩子會怕火。（喻「一朝被蛇咬，十年怕草繩」）

➔ **例句**

1 I assure you I will find the sunken ship.

我向你保證，我會找到那艘沉船的。

2 It is extremely dangerous to walk on a frozen lake.

在結冰的湖上行走是極度危險的。

3 The lost files are said to contain classified information.

傳說那遺失的檔案中有機密資訊。

4 The man is looking for scattered pieces of his map.

那男人在尋找他四散的地圖碎片。

5. 過去分詞（3）分詞構句

➔ 由過去分詞所組成的分詞構句，同樣也有「原因」、「同時間的事件」、「前提」等意味在。和現在分詞不同的是，過去分詞的分詞構句是持「被動」的語氣。

Captured after a year in exile, the man admitted his crime.
在一年的流浪之後被捕,男子承認了他的罪行。

➡ 例句

1 Defeated by the Celtics, the Lakers seem very depressed. | 被塞爾蒂克隊擊敗,湖人隊似乎很沮喪。

2 Buried in haste, the soldiers' bodies were piled up like rocks. | (因為)在倉促之中被埋葬,士兵們的屍體像石頭一樣被疊成一堆。

3 Given the other option, he decided to abandon the original plan. | (由於)被提供了另一個選擇,他決定要放棄原本的計畫。

4 Not (being) reformed yet, the educational system remains questionable. | 尚未經過改革的教育體系,還是令人質疑。

6. 分詞的完成式(1)主動

➡ 分詞也是有完成式的句型喔!公式是《having +過去分詞》,前面通常是必須接動名詞的動詞。它所暗示的意思是說,這件事情的發生比整個主要句子的動作要來得更早喔!

Having listened to my suggestions, Jerry changed his attitude a lot.
聽了我的建議,傑瑞的態度改變了不少。

➡ 例句

1 Having registered on this website, you may download free music and videos. | 你先前已經在這網頁上註冊了,所以可以下載免費的音樂和影片。

2 Having taken bribes, that politician is now on trial. | 由於先前收賄,那名政客現在正在接受審理。

3 Having finished the TV series, my daughter is starting on a new one.

看完了這齣電視連續劇，我女兒要開始看新的一齣了。

4 Having read your report, I say that its content is excellent.

我已經看完你的報告了，我認為內容很棒。

● 7. 分詞的完成式（2）被動　　CD2- 47

➔ 同樣要表示分詞動作的發生，比整個主要句子的動作要來得更早，句型《having＋been＋過去分詞》卻是帶有被動意味的分詞完成式呢！也就是說，分詞的動作，是以句子的主詞作為受詞喔！

Having been warned in advance, he escaped quickly.
（因為）事先被警告過，他很快地便逃走了。

中級
Level

➔ 例句

1 Having been sentenced to prison, he stopped arguing.

（因為）已經被判定入獄，他不再辯解了。

2 Having been annoyed by the boy, we shall help him no more.

（因為）已經被男孩給惹惱了，我們不會再幫他了。

3 Having been supported by the majority, she easily won the election.

（因為）受到多數人的支持，她很輕易地贏得了選舉。

4 Having been warned in advance, I examined everything carefully.

（因為）已經事先被警告過了，我很小心地檢查了全部的東西。

● 8. 複合形容詞（1）名詞＋分詞

➔ 當我們想要綜合名詞和分詞的兩種意思，變成一個形容詞來形容事物時，就在中間加上「-」的符號就行啦！除了一些常見的複合形容詞外，有時候還可以自己發明喔！

Who's the producer of this heart-wrenching movie?
誰是這部痛惻心扉的電影的製作人？

例句

1 It was a life-threatening infection that hit the village. | 侵襲小鎮的是個對生命具有威脅性的傳染病。

2 We're working on creating an energy-saving device. | 我們正著手於製造一個節約能源的設備。

3 The spectacular scenery of the Grand Canyon was breathtaking. | 大峽谷壯麗的美景真是令人嘆為觀止。

4 The kids scanned the mouth-watering delicacies with excitement. | 孩子們興奮地看著這些令人垂涎的美食。

9. 複合形容詞（2）形容詞（副詞）＋分詞

中間加上「-」的符號，還可以連接形容詞以及分詞喔！同樣地，這樣的複合形容詞也是綜合了兩種不同詞性、不同詞意的功能，必要時可以自行組合呢！而副詞和分詞的組合，除了特定的慣用法，一般並不加「-」。

I smell the fragrance from those flowers in full-bloom.
我聞到了那些盛開花朵的香味。

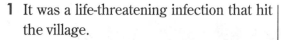

例句

1 Japan is renowned for its fully developed technology. | 日本因發展極致的技術而聞名。

2 That strange-looking man is said to have mental problems. | 那個看起來很奇怪的人，被說是精神有問題。

3 There are nearly a hundred cabins on this fast-moving train. | 這輛快速移動的火車有將近一百個客艙。

4 The nearly forgotten story was revealed as her journal was found. | 在她的日誌被發現後，那幾乎被遺忘的故事被揭開了。

● 10. 常用獨立分詞片語

➡ 下面列出幾個實用的分詞片語，習慣性地被獨立使用，放在句首來發揮
類似副詞的功能，修飾逗點之後的句子。

Honestly speaking, it was luck that saved you.
老實說，是運氣救了你的。

➡ 例句

1 Considering the unknown factors, a conclusion has not been reached yet.

考慮到未知（但會影響結果）的因素，目前還未下結論。

2 Judging from his response, he was a little irritated.

從他的反應來看，他有點被激怒喔。

3 Generally speaking, formal clothing is required on such occasions.

一般來說，在那種場合會要求（穿著）正式服裝。

4 Providing that my privacy is not to be questioned, I will accept the interview.

在不問及我的隱私的情況下，我願意接受採訪。

中級
Level

十一、主詞的各種型態

「主詞」就是句子要討論的、要敘述的主角。我們可能會討論人，或是某個現象、某個事件、某個計畫...等不同的主題。如何生動地描寫出討論的「主角」，又不違反英文文法的規定呢？趕快來看看吧！

● 1. 名詞、代名詞　　　　　CD2- 48

➡ 名詞和代名詞（包含不定代名詞）是最基本的主詞用法，表示各種人、事、物。這時候要多注意主詞與動詞的一致性喔！

His bad temper emerges under pressure.
他的壞脾氣在壓力下就會顯露出來。

➡ 例句

1 Elena is trying to eliminate junk food from her diet.　艾蓮娜正試著從她的日常飲食中剔除垃圾食物。

2 He elaborated on his proposal by giving some examples.　他用舉例的方式來詳述他的提議。

3 It takes a long time to heal when one's heart is so badly hurt.　如果心被傷得很深，會需要很長的時間來痊癒的。

4 Magnets can be used as tools to post messages on the blackboard.　磁鐵可以用來當作在黑板上張貼訊息的道具。

● 2. The＋分詞（形容詞）

➡ 《The＋形容詞》可以表示一個「統稱」，也就是「符合這個形容詞的所有對象」；《The＋分詞》表示「接受這個動作的所有對象」，兩種句型其實是差不多的，因為分詞原本就有形容詞的功能啊！另外，此時的主詞視作複數，所以動詞字尾不用加-s喔！

The educated may not always be reasonable.
受過教育的人不見得總是理性的。

➡ 例句

1 The needy are worthy of our attention and help.	貧困的人是值得我們的注意和幫助的。
2 The handicapped have special parking spaces.	殘障人士有特別的停車空間。
3 The elderly should have priority when it comes to using elevators.	老人家應該享有使用電梯的優先權。
4 The injured were taken to the nearest hospital immediately.	傷者立刻地被送往最近的醫院去了。

中級
Level

● 3. 動名詞（片語）

➡ 動名詞或是再長一些的動名詞片語，是可以當作名詞來使用的，所以當然也可以當作主詞囉！此時的主詞一律視作單數，因為不管片語之中有多少東西，整個片語都還是「一件事」，除非是有一個以上的動名詞片語做主詞，就變成不止一件事了，那麼當然就可以用複數型動詞囉。

Recycling plastic can reduce waste.
回收塑膠品可以減少浪費。

➡ 例句

1 Studying abroad may broaden your horizons.
在國外唸書也許可以讓你長長見識。

2 Singing a lullaby can help a baby fall asleep.
唱首搖籃曲可以幫助寶寶入睡。

3 Cooperating in class can be difficult for children.
在課堂上配合對孩子來說可能是很困難的。

4 Adding too many spices to your food does your health no good.
在你的食物中加太多香料，對你的健康沒有好處。

● 4. 不定詞（片語）　　　　CD2- 49

➡ 不定詞是可以當作名詞來使用的，所以當然也可以當作主詞囉！和動名詞一樣，不定詞片語都視作單數。

To develop enthusiasm takes time.
要培養熱情需要時間。

➡ 例句

1 To confront one's failure is not easy.
要面對自己的失敗，並不是件容易的事。

2 To fight global warming is everybody's responsibility.
對抗全球暖化是每個人的責任。

3 To stay in a dusty room is a nightmare for people with allergies.
對過敏的人來說，待在一個充滿灰塵的房間裡是一場噩夢。

4 To keep a family in harmony requires tolerance and patience.
要維持家庭的和諧，需要寬容和耐心。

● 5. That引導的子句

⟹ 通常that所帶領的子句都是放在句子中間，當作動詞的補語。不過因為它們也就等於「一件事情」，所以也可以放在開頭當作主詞，通常是表示一種說法或是事實。

That Kate became an accountant surprises us all.
凱特成為會計師的這件事，讓我們大家都很驚訝。

⟹ 例句

1 That astrological signs can explain one's personality is nonsense to me. | 星座可以解析一個人的人格特質，（這種事）對我來說是無稽之談。

2 That goodness lies in everyone doesn't make sense to me. | 人性本善，（這個說法）對我來說不怎麼有道理。

3 That his parents had divorced seemed to have a great impact on him. | 父母離婚這件事，似乎對他造成很大的衝擊。

4 That he asked me about my private life was done out of complete ignorance. | 他尋問我的私生活這件事根本就是無知。

中級
Level

● 6. 疑問詞＋S＋V

⟹ 《疑問詞＋S＋V...》又是個名詞片語的句型，可以放在句中，也可以放在句首當作主詞。此外，它也有另一個常見的名稱叫做「間接敘述（問句）」。

What he said was considered nonsense.
他說的話被當作是無稽之談。

⟹ 例句

1 How they built the pyramids remained a mystery. | 他們建造金字塔的方法依舊是個謎。

2 Which you should choose is quite obvious now. | 你該選哪一個了，現在已經很明顯了。

3 Why they postponed the ceremony is unknown. | 不知道他們為何把典禮延後了。

4 What he said during the meeting was quite persuasive. | 他在會議中說的話，還滿有說服力的。

十二、介係詞

小小的介係詞常常是高中生們的大困擾，它們可以用來表示「場所」、「時間」、「原因」、「對象」、「方法」…等意思，從具體到抽象都有！同一個介係詞可以表示很多種意思，所以要好好熟悉它們才行喔！

● 1. In
CD2- 50

➡ 表示「在…之中」的意思，除了表示具體的位置和時間（距離）範圍，又可以延伸至抽象的敘述，像是處境、狀態、動作或感情的對象、方法、屬性等。

Sam is an expert in computer engineering.
山姆是電腦工程方面的專家。

➡ 例句

1 Susie has put herself in a complicated situation. | 蘇西讓自己陷入了一個複雜的處境。

2 The mother of the child is in a desperate situation. | 那個小孩的母親情況相當危急。

3 Being identical means to be similar in every detail. | 所謂的一樣，意思是指在每個小細節上都相同。

4 In my opinion, society and people are continually evolving. | 我認為社會和人類都是一直在進化的。

● 2. On

➡ 表示「在...（平面）之上」的意思，可表示具體的位置、時間，也可延伸至抽象的敘述如：狀態、仰賴的對象、事物的主題、動作發生的時機等。

The bride has been on a diet for a month.
新娘已經減肥有一個月之久了。

➡ 例句

1 Rachel wrote an essay on English literature. | 瑞裘寫了一篇關於英國文學的論文。

2 You can't rely on others to do everything for you. | 你不能依賴別人替你做所有的事。

3 The government has decided to impose a tax on foreign tobacco. | 政府已決定要對國外煙草課稅。

4 On seeing the queen, the knights knelt down by their horses. | 一見到皇后，騎士們立刻在馬兒旁跪下。

● 3. At

➡ 表示「在...（點）上」的意思，可表示具體的位置、時間、動作的對象等，又延伸為抽象的敘述如：速率、狀態、回應、情感的原因等。

I was amazed at how well he could play football.
他的足球技術好的讓我感到吃驚。

英語文法・句型詳解

⇒ 例句

1 They assembled quickly at the commander's request.

因應指揮官的要求，他們很快地集合了起來。

2 I know he's at work, but I have some urgent news to tell him.

我知道他正在工作，但我有緊急的事要告訴他。

3 The high speed rail travels at a rate of about 300 km per hour.

高鐵以大約每小時三百公里的速度行進。

4 We were able to put our minds at ease after finishing the task.

完成任務之後我們終於可以鬆一口氣了。

● 4. Through和throughout　　CD2- 51

⇒ Through表示「穿透」的意思，抽象用法方面有：媒介（管道）、現象或動作的遍布、瀏覽、經歷等。另一個相似的介係詞throughout則用來表示「遍布」、「在整個事件期間...」的意思。

Innocent people suffered throughout the war.
無辜的人們在整場戰爭中飽受苦難。

⇒ 例句

1 We can observe new trends through public media.

我們可以透過大眾媒體來觀察新的趨勢。

2 Bill Gates's legendary success is known throughout the world.

比爾蓋茲傳奇性的成功廣為世人所知。

3 Let's go through the items on our memorandum quickly.

我們快速地討論一下備忘錄上的事項吧。

4 They've developed an intimate relationship after being through the war.

在經歷這場戰爭之後，他們發展出了一段親密的關係。

● 5. Outside和inside

➡ Outside（在...外部）和inside（在...內部）是用來說明事物的位置的。此外，outside也可以表示某事物的「範圍之外」、「除外」等意思，inside則可以延伸表示「時間以內」、「人或事物內部」的意思。

Outside of Jessica, all of the girls here are natives.
除了傑西卡之外，這裡所有的女孩都是本地人。

➡ 例句

1 Why is he always concealing his feelings inside? | 為什麼他總是要把自己的感受隱藏起來呢？

2 I would not interfere with anything you do outside work. | 我不會干預你在工作之外做的任何事情。

中級
Level

3 These duties are outside your range of responsibility. | 這些職務並不在你的責任範圍之中。

4 The popularity of hip-hop will not change inside the next decade. | 嘻哈的流行在未來十年之內是不會改變的。

● 6. Out of

➡ Out of除了表示「在...之外」、「離開」的意思，還有許多延伸的用法：行為的「動機」、挑選的「範圍」、「原料」、事物的「匱乏」、「狀況之外」等用法。

I think our truck is out of fuel.
我想我們卡車的燃料已經用完了。

➡ 例句

1 Always stay out of illegal business. | 永遠都別牽扯上非法的生意。

2 Ben did those favors out of generosity.

班幫的那些忙，是出自於寬大的胸懷。

3 We shall pick just one out of all the applicants.

我們會從所有的應徵者中，僅選出一位。

4 Lily makes toys out of recycled materials for recreation.

莉莉用回收的材料來做玩具，當作消遣。

7. Above和below

CD2- 52

➡ Above（在…上方）和below（在…下方）可以說是一組相反的介係詞。除了表示位置的高低、數字或水準的高低外，還有一些抽象的用法：above表示「排除」、「超出範圍」的意思，beyond則是可以表示「超出範圍」之意思。

The beauty of the sunset is beyond description.
日落之美真是難以形容。

➡ 例句

1 I believe I'm above doing such nasty things.

我相信自己不至於做那些陰險的事情。

2 Her loyalty to her husband is above suspicion.

她對她丈夫的忠誠是無庸置疑的。

3 James' scores have been below average this semester.

詹姆士這學期的分數一直都在平均值以下。

4 That arrogant girl is above adjusting herself to the environment.

那個驕傲的女孩是不會調整自己來適應環境的。

● 8. Over

➡ Over（越過…）除了表示「從上方越過」的動作、數量的「超過」以及「覆蓋…」的效果外，抽象的用法另有：「優越的情勢」、事物的「主題」或「原因」、「時間流逝」、「現象的遍布」等。

We rejoiced in our triumph over the opposing team.
我們因擊敗對手得到勝利而感到高興。

➡ 例句

1	The Spanish used to have control over many colonies.	西班牙人曾統治過許多殖民地。
2	I will be sailing near Phuket over the next few days.	接下來幾天，我都會在普吉島附近航行。
3	That strange disease has spread all over the country.	那個奇怪的疾病，已經蔓延至全國各地了。
4	An argument over money is possible even between close friends.	即便是和親近的朋友，也可能會有金錢上的糾紛。

中級
Level

● 9. For

➡ 介係詞for的用法有很多，除了表示原因、目標、用途、距離或時間的長度等意思外，還可以表示「代表」、「儘管」、「就…來說」、「相等的互換」、「贊成」等抽象的意思。

It's quite cool today here for a tropical island.
就一個熱帶島嶼來說，今天已經算很涼爽了。

➡ 例句

1	The man is speaking for the mistreated laborers in town.	這男人是代表鎮上被欺壓的勞工們發言的。

2 For all his efforts, he still failed to accomplish his work.

儘管他很努力，他還是沒辦法完成他的工作。

3 I'm for the idea of harsh punishments for drunk driving.

我支持對酒駕進行嚴厲懲處的看法。

4 Are they offering a reward for any information about the robbery?

他們提供獎賞給任何提供與該搶案相關訊息的人嗎？

10. From   CD2- 53

➡ From（從...）常常帶有「起點」的意味在，除了表示動作、時間、狀態的起始點，還可以表示事物的由來。進階的用法包括「預防」、「隔離」、「判斷的依據」、「區別」、「立場或觀點」等。

Most organic fruits are free from pesticides.
大部分的有機水果都沒有農藥。

➡ 例句

1 Dignity is definitely different from arrogance.

尊嚴和傲慢絕對是不同的。

2 Judging from his moves, I think he's an amateur.

從他的動作來看，我判斷他是個外行人。

3 We tried to stop that earthquake from destroying our homes.

我們試著不讓地震摧毀我們的家園。

4 From my point of view, it's necessary to give kids allowance.

我認為給小孩子零用錢是有必要的。

● 11. Against

➲ Against是表示「反」、「逆」的一個介係詞。除了表示「倚靠」外（因為物體和倚靠的對象為兩個相反的作用力），又可以表示「預防」、「違反」、「對照」的意思。

You must not act against your own will.
你做事絕不能違背自己的意願。

➲ 例句

1	Injections against rabies are necessary.	注射抗狂犬病的疫苗是必要的。
2	The lady leaned against the wall holding a drink.	那位女士拿著一杯飲料，倚靠在牆上。
3	Many people are against the death penalty.	很多人都反對死刑。
4	The dim light became bright against the darkness of night.	微光在黑夜的襯托之下變得明亮。

中級
Level

● 12. By

➲ By最常出現的地方，就是被動語態的句子（表示動作者），此外也常用來表示「工具」、「方法」、「鄰近」的意思。進階的用法包括「依據」、「接觸的身體部位」、「單位（速率）」，還可以當作四則運算的專用語喔！

I bought a fake by mistake.
我不小心買到了仿冒品。

➲ 例句

1	Multiply ten by two and you'll get twenty.	用二去乘十，就會得到二十。

2 The army must move forth by all means.

用盡一切方法，軍隊都一定要往前進。

3 The security guard grabbed the man by his arm.

警衛抓住了那個男人的手臂。

4 He plucked the petals off the flower one by one.

他把花瓣一片一片地摘下來。

13. Into和onto

CD2- 54

→ Into和onto其實就是in和on與「to」的組合，綜合了兩種介係詞的特性，比原來的用法更強調「動態」的感覺：into表示「進入到...之中」、「撞上」、「改變成...」、「使他人...」等意思，onto則表示「到...（平面）的上面」。

The fisherman dived into the water.
漁夫潛入了水中。

→ 例句

1 He was threatened into telling a lie.

他被威脅說了一個謊言。

2 How exactly did he bump into that van?

他到底是怎麼撞上那輛休旅車的呢？

3 The witch turned the princess into a statue.

女巫把公主變成了一座雕像。

4 I accidentally knocked the vase onto the floor.

我不小心把花瓶弄倒在地上了。

14. With和without

With帶有「一起」的意思,可用來表示「同伴」、「事物的特性」、「工具」、「動作的情緒」等意思。而with和without是兩個相反的介係詞,所以without主要表示的是「沒有一起」的意思,甚至可以用《without＋V-ing(或名詞)》的句型來表示「排除在外的狀況」。

I believe she did so with good intentions.
我相信她是出自好意才這麼做的。

➡ 例句

1	Billy was upset with Ana's offensive words.	比利對安娜無禮的言詞感到生氣。
2	Infants should not be left alone without any care.	嬰兒不該被丟下一個人,沒人照顧的。
3	He used my belongings without asking for my permission.	他沒有徵求我的同意,就使用我的東西。
4	With my professional assistance, there's nothing for you to worry about.	有我專業的協助,您沒有什麼好擔心的。

中級 Level

15. With的特殊用法

With除了上述的幾個用法外,還可以用來說明「附帶狀況」,此時會使用《with＋受詞＋受詞補語》的句型,表示在主詞做前面的動作時,同時又有什麼樣的狀況。

It was a neat bedroom with no dust at all.
那是一間一塵不染的乾淨房間。

➡ 例句

1	Kevin ran away with all his employees' salaries unpaid.	凱文逃跑了,所有的員工薪水都沒有支付。

2 The injured man is lying on the bed with his eyes shut.

那個受傷的男人正閉著雙眼躺在床上。

3 Grandma sat beside the fireplace with the fire burning.

祖母坐在火爐旁，火正燃燒著。

4 She talked about her miserable past with her eyes full of tears.

她訴說著自己悲慘的過去，眼中滿是淚水。

16. As

CD2- 55

➡ As同時具有連接詞、副詞、介係詞等三種特性。當作介係詞時，可表示「像是...」、「以...身份」、「因為是...身份」等意思。

Think of your rivals as your teachers.
把你的對手當作你的老師。

➡ 例句

1 There are still some people who treat Blacks as slaves.

還是有人會把黑人當作奴隸對待的。

2 I'm telling you as a friend that such luck won't last long.

我以一個朋友的身份告訴你，這樣的運氣不會持續太久的。

3 As someone with experience, you should not have neglected that.

以一個有經驗的人來說，你不應該忽略那點的。

4 As the executive director, Gary makes important decisions every day.

身為執行總監，蓋瑞每天都要做些重大的決策。

17. Of

➡ Of（屬於）這個介係詞常用來表示非生命體的所有格，另外也搭配數量形容詞或是不定代名詞，來說明事物的多寡。除此之外也可以表示「屬性」、「剝奪」、「主題」、「與...相關」、「原料」之意。

Prof. Roosevelt is a man of wisdom.
羅斯福教授是個有智慧的人。

➡ 例句

1 Do you think Dad will be proud of my achievements? | 你覺得爸爸會為我的成就感到驕傲嗎？

2 He was deprived of his freedom for a lifetime. | 他被剝奪了終生的自由。

3 I enjoyed a moment of clarity at dusk on a beach. | 我在黃昏的海邊享受神清氣爽的片刻。

4 The theme of tonight's party is "exotic elegance." | 今晚派對的主題是「優雅的異國風情」。

中級
Level

● 18. Beyond

➡ Beyond（到...之外）可以用來形容具體的位置，不過更常被使用的卻是它的抽象用法，就是「超出...的範圍」、「除了...以外」、「在...之後（時間）」等意義。

His ranch stretches beyond the hills.
他的莊園一直延伸到丘陵的另一邊。

➡ 例句

1 His loyalty to his wife is beyond suspicion. | 他對妻子的愛是無可懷疑的。（超出可懷疑的範圍）

2 The old man has nothing beyond some real estate. | 那個老人除了他的不動產之外，一無所有。

3 Those beautiful landscapes were beyond description. | 那些山水景觀的美麗，真非筆墨所能形容。

4 I'm planning to retire at sixty, but I haven't thought beyond that. | 我計畫在六十歲退休，不過還沒想到在那之後的事。

英語文法・句型詳解

● 19. 其他介係詞　　　　　　　CD2- 56

⇨ 除了前面提到的幾個用法較為多元的介系詞，還有不少好用的介系詞喔！配合例句，趕快把它們學起來吧！

She still has a lot more besides her modesty.
她除了謙虛之外，還有很多（優點）呢。

⇨ 例句

1 We managed to get some rest amid all the turmoil.	我們企圖在這場騷動之中，得到一些喘息空間。
2 The team has been a disaster during the coach's absence.	教練不在的時候，隊伍整個是一團糟。
3 Despite all of our efforts, we weren't able to fix the problem.	儘管我們已作出所有的努力，我們還是無法解決問題的。
4 They're having a private meeting regarding yesterday's events.	他們正針對昨天的活動舉行私人會議。

● 20. 實用介係詞片語

⇨ 顧名思義，所謂的介係詞片語，就是功能和介係詞一樣的片語囉！以下列出常見的幾個介係詞片語給讀者們參考。

According to the legend, the ship sank right here.
根據傳說，那艘船就是這在這裡沈沒的。

⇨ 例句

1 His cell phone rang loudly in the middle of the opera.	他的手機在歌劇進行中大聲響了。

2 You should respect your opponent instead of hating him.

你應該尊重而非是憎恨你的對手。

3 There's an oral presentation in addition to a written test.

除了一次筆試之外，還有一個口頭報告。

4 I shall marry him regardless of what everyone else says.

不管別人怎麼說，我都會嫁給他。

21. 補充用法（1）：形容詞與介系詞的搭配

➡ 有時候形容詞和介系詞的搭配，實在沒有什麼固定的邏輯去推敲，以下再補充一些高中常考的組合，要背起來喔！

Dan is capable of completing the assignment.
丹是有能力完成這個工作的。

中級
Level

➡ 例句

1 You shouldn't always be envious of other people.

你不應該總是忌妒別人。

2 This artist is world-famous for his sculptures.

這位藝術家以他的雕塑而聞名世界。

3 The customer exclaimed that he was unsatisfied with the product.

顧客大聲嚷著說他對產品感到不滿。

4 The aspect he focused on was different from mine.

他所關注的面向和我的並不相同。

22. 補充用法（2）：動詞與介系詞的搭配

➡ 如果不知道要使用哪個介系詞，有時候就算知道動詞是什麼也沒辦法運用自如。補充幾個動詞與介系詞搭配的組合，趕快記住吧！

Most people would associate basketball with the United States.
大部分的人都會把籃球和美國聯想在一起。

➡ 例句

1 Some scholars have warned us of a coming earthquake.

有些學者已經警告過我們，地震即將來臨。

2 I've never approved of your drinking alcohol.

我從沒允許過你喝酒。

3 Did he compliment you on your thorough analysis?

他有因為你透徹的分析而誇獎你嗎？

4 She succeeded in enhancing her presentation skills.

她成功地提升了自己的簡報技巧。

十三、倒裝

英文基本的語序是「主詞→動作（事件）→時間、地點、同伴等附加形容」。所謂倒裝就是顛覆這樣的順序，把本來放在後面的元素，移到句子的最前面。這樣的句法除了可以增加句子的變化性之外，通常也可以讓移到句首的部分受到注意。

● 1. Only... CD2- 57

➡ 表示「條件」的only，常常搭配副詞片語，倒裝在句子最前面，強調「只有...，才會...」的語氣。要注意主要句子的結構喔！在這樣倒裝的情況下，句子的結構和疑問句是一樣的，變成《Only＋條件＋疑問句結構》的形態。

Only by practicing can there be improvement.
只有靠練習，才有可能進步。

➡ 例句

1 Only with keen observation can you learn quickly.

只有靠敏銳的觀察力，你才可以學得更快。

2 Only when you find more proof can the case be clarified.

只有等你找到更多證據，案情才能被釐清。

3 Only for his daughter would he sacrifice his own benefits.

只有為了他女兒，他才會願意犧牲自己的利益。

4 Only through independence will our country gain true freedom.

唯有透過獨立，我們的國家才會獲得真正的自由。

● 2. 副詞置前（1）介副詞 → V → S

➡ 當主詞是一般的名詞而非代名詞時，句子可以從《S→V→介副詞》變成《介副詞→V→S》。相反地，如果不是代名詞，則可以不用倒裝。常見的介副詞包括up、down、out、away、here、there等，用來說明方位的變化。

The situation grew worse.
→Worse grew the situation.
情況變得更糟糕了。

➡ 例句

1 The girl plunged into the fountain.
→Into the fountain plunged the girl.

女孩跳進了噴泉裡。

2 They sent the boy out. He didn't behave properly..
→Out they sent the boy. He didn't behave properly.

他們把男孩叫出去了，他表現得很不得體。

3 The technician comes here. Let's ask him for advice.
→Here comes the technician. Let's ask him for advice.

技師來了，我們來問他的意見吧。

4 The bird flew away. I guess it's going somewhere remote.
→Away flew the bird. I guess it's going somewhere remote.

鳥兒飛走了。我想牠要飛到很遠的地方去吧。

● 3. 副詞置前（2）情態副詞 / 頻率副詞→S→V

➡ 副詞有分很多種類，其中，具體形容動作樣貌的副詞又稱作「情態副詞」，說明動作發生頻率的叫作「頻率副詞」。此時，句子可以從《S→V→adv.》變成《adv. →S→V》的順序。然而有一個頻率副詞事不能這樣倒裝的，就是always（總是）。

Obviously, you have made a huge mistake.
很顯然地，你已經犯了個天大的錯誤。

➡ 例句

1 Sometimes we go hiking on the weekend.

有時候我們會在周末去健行。

2 Immediately, the ice started to melt from the heat.

因為熱，冰塊立刻就開始融化了。

3 Hopefully I'll be able to come home for Christmas.

希望我可以回家過聖誕節。

4 Drastically, the invention of the computer changed the world.

電腦的發明徹底地改變了世界。

● 4. 有「儘管」意味的as　　CD2- 58

➡ As除了當作介系詞（表示「當作」）外，也可以當作連接詞，表示「當」、「因為」的意思。還有一種連接詞用法，則是和though/although一樣，表示「雖然」的意思，通常以倒裝的形式出現，變成《形容詞（副詞）＋as＋S＋V》的句型，再用逗點連接主要子句。

Tough as the meat is, we can turn it into a delicacy.
雖然肉很硬，但我們還是能將它變成美味的料理。

➡ 例句

1	Economical as I am, I spent a lot of money in Tokyo.	儘管我很省，我在東京還是花了很多錢。
2	Impatient as he is, they still made him wait for a long time.	儘管他很不耐煩，他們還是讓他等了很長的一段時間。
3	Shallow as the conversation was, I learned something from him.	雖然對話很膚淺，我還是從他那裡學到了東西。
4	Tiresome as the meeting was, we had to maintain clear thoughts.	雖然會議很累人，我們還是得保持清晰的思路。

中級
Level

● 5. 否定性質的副詞

➡ 副詞之中，有一些是特別用來表示否定的意味的，倒裝放在句首，更可以加強它們否定的語氣喔！

Never can you escape from reality.
你不能從現實中逃脫的。

➡ 例句

1	Little do I know about photography.	我對攝影的了解很少。

2 Seldom does she feel frustrated about life. | 她很少對人生感到沮喪。

3 Hardly can we detect the signal during a storm. | 在暴風雨中,我們幾乎偵測不到訊號。

4 Rarely have we got the opportunity to go on vacation. | 我們(這段時間以來)很少有機會去度假。

● 6. 包含否定詞的常用語

➡ 某些慣用語法會使用not(不)、no(沒有)等表示否定的字眼,並且常以倒裝的形式出現,以下列出常見的幾個句型喔!

Under no circumstances will I help you do this.
不管什麼情況,我都不會幫你做這種事的。

➡ 例句

1 Not only is he a good athlete but also a gentleman. | 他不只是個好運動員,還是個紳士。

2 By no means can she forget that frightening experience. | 她不可能忘記那次駭人的經驗。

3 Not that I don't want to trust her, but she's a habitual liar! | 並不是我不想相信她,而是她習慣撒謊。

4 Not until being invited to the funeral did he learn about her death. | 一直到被邀請參加喪禮,他才知道她的死訊。

● 7. 地方副詞片語　　　　　CD2- 59

➡ 配合介系詞來表現事物的「地點」的片語,就叫做地方副詞片語,可以倒裝到句子的最前面。這樣的句型有《S→V》和《V→S》的兩種順序,前者應用在「代名詞」的主詞上,後者則搭配「一般名詞」的主詞。

On the bed lies a sleeping beauty.
在床上正躺著一個睡著的美女。

➡ **例句**

1 Beneath the car we found a shivering cat.　｜　在車子底下，我們發現了一隻發抖的貓咪。

2 In the basement are the groceries.　｜　雜貨在地下室。

3 Behind the canvas they found a key and a note.　｜　在油畫後面，他們找到了一把鑰匙和一張便條。

4 Next to the railway is the house we used to live in.　｜　在鐵路旁的是我們以前住的房子。

● **8. 假設語的倒裝**

中級
Level

➡ 與現在（或過去）事實相反的假設語，都可以省略if，變成倒裝的句子，從《If＋S＋had (not)＋p.p.》變成《Had＋S (not)＋p.p.》，或是從《If it＋were not＋for＋名詞》變成《Were＋it＋not for＋名詞》。

Were it not for my wife's economy, we couldn't save so much money.
如果不是我老婆的節儉，我們現在沒辦法存這麼多錢。

➡ **例句**

1 Were it not for her immediate aid, I may have died from my injury.　｜　如果不是她的急救，我現在可能就因為我的傷勢而死了。

2 Had he not helped, our information would have been inadequate.　｜　當時若沒有他的幫忙，我們的資訊就會顯得不充足。

3 Had it not been for the queen's support, the explorers could not have made it.　｜　當初若沒有女王的支持，探險家們就不可能成功了。

4 Had she dared to speak in the meeting, the conclusion might have been different.　｜　當時如果她敢於在會議中發言，結論可能就不同了。

英語文法・句型詳解

● 9. So...that...

➡ 常用的《so...that...》（如此...以致於...）句型，也常常以倒裝的形式出現，將《S→be→so→形容詞》的順序變成《So→形容詞→be》的句法。其中so也可以換成such喔！只不過句子就要變成《Such→be→one's→名詞》的模式喔！

Such was her bravery that we all admired her.
她是如此的勇敢，以致於我們都很仰慕她。

➡ 例句

1 So gentle was the breeze that I began to feel sleepy.	風是如此的柔和，以致於我開始有點睡意了。
2 Such is his pessimistic attitude that he can't make himself happy.	他是如此的悲觀，以致於他無法讓自己快樂。
3 Such were his imitations that the audience laughed with big applause.	他的模仿是這麼地棒，以致於觀眾不但大笑，也大大地鼓掌。
4 So mysterious are the crop circles that some people are scared of going there.	作物圈是如此地神秘，以致於有些人會害怕去那裡。

十四、字首與字尾

英文的單字，常常是有跡可循的。許多字首、字尾都有他們固定的含意，因此即使是看到一個陌生的單字，也有可能根據他們的字首、字尾來推測出它們的意義！熟識常見的字首和字尾，不僅能更容易看懂句子，也可以幫助記憶喔！

● 1. 名詞字尾（1）- ism　　　CD2- 60

中級
Level

→ 常見的名詞字根-ism，常常是用來表示「主義」、「體系」等符合某些特定表徵和特質的群體，常常拿來討論的racism（種族主義）、heroism（英雄主義）等，都是典型的例子。

The Star of David symbolizes Judaism.
大衛之星象徵猶太民族。

● 例句

1 Today, more and more countries are adopting capitalism.	現在越來越多的國家接受了資本主義。
2 Constructive criticism should always be given to help people to improve.	給予有建設性的評語，應該是為了幫助他人進步。
3 The Americans have been haunted by the horror of terrorism.	美國人一直受恐怖主義的可怕所苦。
4 The tourism industry has really picked up in the last few years.	過去幾年觀光業的景氣的確有好轉。

英語文法・句型詳解

2. 名詞字尾（2）-ist

➡ 常用名詞字尾-ist代表的是「人」，也就是符合前半段字彙所描述的事物的「執行或信奉...者」、「相關人物」等。像是常見的scientist（科學家），不就是「研究科學（science）的人」嗎？

Taiwan is a capitalist country.
台灣是一個資本主義的國家。

➡ 例句

1 There are too many tourists here. | 這裡有太多觀光客了。

2 Lance Armstrong is a world-champion cyclist. | 蘭斯・阿姆斯壯是世界冠軍級的自行車手。

3 Jamie only eats organic foods because she's a naturalist. | 詹米只吃有機食物，因為她是自然主義者。

4 Jane Austin is considered one of the most important novelists ever. | 珍奧斯汀被認為是有史以來最重要的小說家之一。

3. 名詞字尾（3）-er、-or

➡ 想要表示「做...的人」的意思，就會常用到-er、-or這兩個字尾，前面總是搭配動詞，結合後成為「做此動作的人」的意思。例如teacher，不就是教書（teach）的人嗎？

Leo is a follower of Jesus Christ.
李奧是耶穌基督的追隨者（門徒）。

➡ 例句

1 My swimming instructor is very helpful. | 我的游泳教練對我幫助不少。

2 He is a supporter of the right to bear arms.

他是人民擁有攜帶武器權利的支持者。

3 My supervisor is a very reasonable man.
我的督導是個非常講理的人。

4 登山客在山區裡待了數週。

The hikers spent weeks in the mountains.

4. 名詞字尾（4）-

● ian CD2- 61

-ian身兼名詞字根和形容詞字根兩種角色。當名詞時，象徵「...的人」的意思，而當形容詞時，則表示「...的」之意。像是Brazil（巴西）→Brazilian（巴西人/巴西的），就是最簡單的例子。

Jim is a very devoted Christian.
吉姆是一位虔誠的基督教徒。

● 例句

1 Adam Sandler is my favorite comedian.

亞當山德勒是我最喜歡的喜劇演員。

2 The museum curator is a famous historian.

博物館館長是一位知名的歷史學家。

3 A guardian angel must be watching over me.

守護天使一定在看顧著我。

4 The electrician came over and installed a light.

電工來這裡安裝電燈。

● 5. 名詞字尾（5）-ness

只要看到-ness結尾，八九不離十就是一種「抽象名詞」，關括感情、關係、病痛等事物。

She died from a chronic illness.
她因為慢性病而死亡。

➡ 例句

1 We hiked around in the wilderness for weeks. | 我們在荒野長途跋涉了好幾個星期。

2 The sickness has caused him to feel tired all of the time. | 生病使他總是很疲倦。

3 The host family treated us with kindness and hospitality. | 接待家庭親切殷勤地招待我們。

4 The old man was overwhelmed with loneliness after the death of his dog. | 他的狗死後，老男人極為孤單。

● 6. 名詞字尾（6）-ship

➡ 別誤會，-ship這個字尾和「船隻」可沒有甚麼關係喔！而是表示「資格」、「關係」、「身分」等意思，例如championship（冠軍資格），就是champion結合-ship的結果呢。

There is a NT$5,000 membership fee to join the club.
加入社團要五千元台幣的會費。

➡ 例句

1 They are entering into a partnership to open a new business. | 他們合夥成立新公司。

2 It's important to have good sportsmanship when competing. | 比賽時有良好的運動精神是很重要的。

3 We have experienced many hardships over the past few years. | 我們在過去數年內經歷了許多苦難。

4 The landowners went to court to battle over ownership of the land. | 地主們去法院爭奪土地所有權。

● 7. 名詞字尾（7）-tion

CD2- 62

➜ 看到-tion結尾，差不多百分之百可以確定是名詞囉！配合前面的動詞，這樣的組合字通常象徵一種「總稱」。

I've entered the city-wide speech competition.
我晉級了全國性的演講比賽。

➜ 例句

1 This drink is a combination of different fruit juices. | 這杯飲料由各種不同的果汁混合而成的。

2 The neighbor's loud music keeps disturbing my concentration. | 鄰居大聲的音樂不斷地影響我的專注力。

3 We need to design a classification system to organize these papers. | 我們必須設計一套分類系統，來組織這些文件。

4 The Internet provides us with many convenient means of communication. | 網路提供了我們許多方便的聯絡及交流方法。

● 8. 名詞字尾（8）-sion

➜ 和-tion相當類似的-sion，在功能上也是一樣的，是象徵「總稱」、「概念」的一種名詞字尾。

He's got a silly expression on his face.
他臉上表現出愚蠢的表情。

➜ 例句

1 The highway expansion project took three years to complete. | 高速公路擴展計畫花了三年才完成。

2 In order to avoid confusion, everyone needs to read the handout. | 為了避免混淆，每個人都必須閱讀這份傳單。

3 The way she handled the situation left a deep impression upon me. | 我對她處理狀況的方法，留下深刻的印象。

4 There was a massive explosion that killed hundreds of people yesterday. | 昨天發生一場大爆炸，造成數百人死亡。

● 9. 名詞字尾（9）-ment

➡ 名詞字尾-ment表示「…的結果」、「…的方法或活動」的意思，像是 manage→management、require→requirement等變化。

The two sides finally reached a settlement.
雙方終於達成和解。

➡ **例句**

1 We are going to an amusement park this weekend. | 我們這個週末要去遊樂園玩。

2 I've made arrangements to be picked up at eight o'clock. | 我安排了一個要在八點整開始進行的計畫。

3 His new book reveals the importance of time management. | 他的新書闡述了時間管理的重要性。

4 You must make your requirements clear at the very beginning. | 你一定要在一開始就清楚說明你的要求。

● 10. 名詞字尾（10）-cy　　CD2- 63

➡ 常常與名詞或形容詞結合成名詞的-cy，象徵「狀態」、「性質」等意思。

He has a tendency to overwork himself.
他有工作過度的傾向。

➡ 例句

1	We are in a national state of emergency.	我們正處於全國緊急狀態中。
2	Pregnancy is a difficult and tiring process.	懷孕是辛苦而疲憊的過程。
3	The frequency of her absences have increased.	她缺席的頻率增加了。
4	He answered all of the questions with incredible accuracy.	他以一種不可思議的準確度，回答了所有的問題。

● 11. 名詞字尾（11）學科

中級
Level

➡ 表示「學科、學門」的字尾有很多種，包括-ology、-ics、-ry、-my等，看過一次就把它們記起來吧！

Macro-economics is a complex subject.
總體經濟學是一門複雜的科目。

➡ 例句

1	Have you ever heard of color psychology?	你聽過色彩心理學嗎？
2	I don't know the first thing about electronics.	我對電子學一竅不通。
3	She wasn't able to pass chemistry this semester.	她這個學期的化學無法及格了。
4	I don't like discussing politics because everyone gets too worked up.	我不喜歡討論政治，因為大家會變得太過於激動。

中級 Level

英語文法・句型詳解

● 12. 形容詞字尾（1）-ary

➡️ 搭配名詞，-ary字尾可以組合成形容詞或是名詞，其中以形容詞最常見，表示「有關...的」的意思，像是literary就表示「與文學（literature）有關的」的意思。

Contrary to popular belief, he is a nice man.
與現在眾所周知的相反，他是個非常好的人。

➡️ 例句

1	The *Iliad* is my favorite piece of literary work.	伊里亞德是我最喜愛的文學作品。
2	Our primary concern is the safety of the children.	我們主要關心的問題是兒童安全。
3	The business dinner is voluntary; you don't have to go if you don't want to.	這商務晚餐會是自願參加，你如果不想去，可以不要去。
4	The invention of the Internet was a revolutionary change in human history.	網路的發明是人類史上一個革命性的改變。

● 13. 形容詞字尾（2）-ous　　　CD2- 64

➡️ 形容詞字尾-ous表示「有...的性質」的意思，像是vigour（精力）→vigorous（精力旺盛的）、ambition（野心）→ambitious（有野心的）、anxiety（焦慮）→anxious（焦慮的）等都是實例。

I feel very anxious about the job interview.
我對這個工作的面試感到極為焦慮不安。

➡️ 例句

1	Paul is a very vigorous and focused worker.	包爾是一位精力充沛而且專注的工作者。

2 The man fell down unconscious after I punched him.

我揍了他之後，他就昏倒了。

3 Ben does well in school because he's very ambitious.

班因為抱有雄心壯志，而在學校表現得很好。

4 There are numerous reasons why I don't think this is wise.

有很多原因讓我覺得這不是個明智之舉。

● 14. 形容詞字尾（3）-cal

➡ 形容詞字尾-cal其實就是-al的延伸，配合前面的名詞，表示「...相關的」的意思，像是medicine（醫學）→medical（醫學的）。

The way he is acting is very typical for him.
這是他特有的舉止。

➡ 例句

1 I just don't like solving mathematical equations.

我就是不喜歡解數學方程式。

2 The house burned down due to an electrical fire.

由於電器走火，導致房子被燒毀了。

3 *Harry Potter* is a magical story about a young wizard.

哈利波特一書是關於一位年輕巫師的神奇故事。

4 The professor encourages us to develop our critical thinking skills.

教授鼓勵我們提升批判性思維的技巧。

● 15. 形容詞字尾（4）-ic

➡ 最常見的形容詞字尾之一就是-ic了。前面通常是名詞，加上-ic變成「...的」的意思。有時候因為單字字尾的關係，在和-ic組合的時候會增減一些字母以利發音，不過通常還是可以看出來原本的字根是什麼喔！

That is a tragic story.
那是個悲慘的故事。

⮕ 例句

1 He can't keep a job because he's an alcoholic. | 因為他是個酒鬼，所以一直無法保住工作。

2 Dong Hai University is an academic institution. | 東華大學是一個學術機構。

3 They have a very systematic way of dealing with this kind of problem. | 他們以極有系統的方式處理這類問題。

4 The judge wasn't sympathetic when the criminal tried to explain his actions. | 當罪犯試圖解釋他的行為時，法官並不表示同情。

● 16. 形容詞字尾（5）-less　　CD2- 65

⮕ 放在尾巴的否定詞-less，表示「沒有...」的意思，前面總是名詞，結合後變成「沒有...的」這樣的形容詞。有時候還會在以結合後的形容詞加上-ly變成副詞喔！

This thing is useless to me if it's broken.
若是壞了，這東西對我來說就毫無價值了。

⮕ 例句

1 It is meaningless to be stubborn over this matter. | 對這件事這麼堅持，實在很沒意義。

2 She cried because she was powerless to change the situation. | 她哭了，因為她無力改變情況。

3 I felt worthless after my boss yelled at me in front of everyone. | 老闆當著眾人面前對我咆哮，讓我覺得自己很沒用。

4 He was restless while waiting for the results of the examination. | 他焦躁不安地等待考試成績的公佈。

● 17. 形容詞字尾（6）-able

➡ 還記得《be able＋to＋V》這個句型嗎？Able本身就表示「有能力做...」的意思，因此變成字尾的時候，可以用來對前半段的字彙表示肯定、允許、有能力如此等意義，變成「可以...的」的意思喔！

They had the best vacation imaginable.
他們度過了一個所能想像到的最愉快的假期。

➡ 例句

1 I hate to admit it, but defeat is inevitable. | 我真不願承認，但失敗確實是無可避免的。

2 I like working with him because he's very dependable. | 我喜歡跟他工作，因為他非常可靠。

3 This brand is more expensive, but it's also more durable. | 這牌子比較貴，但也比較耐用。

4 The honorable student didn't cheat when he had the opportunity. | 那位可敬的學生有機會作弊卻沒這麼做。

中級 Level

● 18. 動詞字尾（1）-ize

➡ 動詞字尾-ize象徵「把事物...化」、「把事物變成...」、的意思，例如表示記憶的memorize，不就是要把事物變成記憶（memory）嗎？

I can sympathize with you in your situation.
我能理解你的情況。

➡ 例句

1 This hospital offers specialized care for cancer patients. | 這家醫院提供癌症病患特別的照顧。

2 Can you please summarize the main points of the meeting?

你能否總結會議的主要重點？

3 Foreign explorers helped to civilize that area of the world.

外來的探險者幫助開化啓迪了那個地區。

4 I have to memorize forty vocabulary words before tomorrow.

我明天以前得背完四十個單字。

19. 動詞字尾（2）-fy（-ify） CD2- 66

➡ 動詞字尾-fy表示「使事物變成...」的意思，配合前面的名詞，成為「讓...變成...」的動詞，例如clarify（澄清）就是要把事情變得「清晰」（clarity）的意思。

Could you please clarify what you just said?
可以請你把你剛剛說的話講清楚一點嗎？

➡ 例句

1 Can you identify the man who stole your purse?

你可以認出偷你錢包的男人嗎？

2 The tension between the two countries has intensified.

兩國之間的緊張關係加劇了。

3 Do I qualify for any type of scholarship or financial aid?

我有資格申請任何獎學金或費用補助嗎？

4 She looked horrified when you jumped out and startled her.

當你跳出來嚇她的時候，她看起來很害怕。

20. 動詞字尾（3）-en

➡ 動詞字尾-en與前面名詞搭配，表示「使事物有...的性質」的意思，像是weaken（削弱），不就是「使事物變得虛弱（weak）」的意思嗎？

Swimming strengthens your entire body.
游泳會增強你全身的體能。

➡ 例句

1 I need a wrench so I can tighten this bolt.
我需要扳手好拴緊這個螺絲。

As the temperature dropped, the liquid

2 hardened.
溫度下降時,液體變硬了。

We decided to shorten our stay at the resort

3 due to the typhoon.
由於颱風,我們決定縮短在渡假村的行程。

The woman went to the tailor to see about

4 getting her skirt lengthened.
那女士到了裁縫那裡,看看要不要把裙子加

長。

21. 形容詞、名詞

中級
Level

● 字尾 -ive

➡ 同時為名詞和形容詞字尾的-ive表示「有...特質的」、「有...傾向的」之意。像是動詞alter(交替)就變成了alternative(交替的、替代選擇)。

Is there an alternative plan?
有其他的計畫嗎?

➡ 例句

1 This is a small country with a progressive economy.
這是一個經濟發展中的小國。

2 Those were objective opinions from other group members.
那些是其他組員的客觀意見。

3 Be careful about what you say to her because she's overly sensitive.
你跟她說話時要小心,因為她太敏感了。

4 The archeologists uncovered ancient artifacts from a primitive civilization.
考古學家從某個上古文明中,發現古老的工藝品。

英語文法・句型詳解

● 22.否定字首（1）Un-　　　　CD2- 67

➡ 常用在形容詞或副詞中，並且表示否定的就是un-囉！例如expected（預期的）→unexpected（預期之外的）、known（已知的）→unknown（未知的）等。

Your surprise visit was unexpected.
你的突然造訪，令人感到意外。

➡ 例句

1	The way he treated me was unbelievable!	他對待我的方式，令人無法置信！
2	The author of this ancient text is unknown.	這篇古文的作者不詳。
3	It's unfortunate that you couldn't stay longer.	你無法待久一點，真令人遺憾。
4	It is quite unusual for it to be this cool in June.	六月天，天氣這麼冷，真是異常。

● 23. 否定字首（2）Dis-

➡ 帶有否定意味的字首中，其中一個就是dis-，常常表示對於後半段字彙意義的否定，名詞、形容詞、動詞等都常看到它的蹤跡。

I think our phone has been disconnected.
我想我們的電話被斷線了。

➡ 例句

1	Today, public places must have facilities for the disabled.	現在，公共場所必須設置殘障人士專用設施。

2 The finance department disapproved of our financial plan for the year. | 財務部沒有核准我們的年度財務計畫。

3 Playing away from home usually puts a team at a disadvantage. | 在外地比賽通常會讓一個隊伍陷入劣勢之中。

4 I quit my job because of the dissatisfaction of doing the same thing every day. | 我辭職是因為不滿每天做同樣的事。

24. 否定字首（3）Mis-

另一個否定字根mis-，則帶有「錯誤」的意思，和單純的「不...」有些不同喔！像是lead（引導）→mislead（誤導），understand（了解）→misunderstand（誤解）等。

中級
Level

The media often misleads the general public.
媒體經常誤導大眾。

例句

1 I think you've misunderstood what I've been saying. | 我認為你誤會了我說的話。

2 The boys got themselves into mischief last night. | 男孩們昨晚又在搗蛋了。

3 You must suffer the consequences of your actions. | 你必須要承擔你的行為所造成的後果。

4 We have experienced the misfortune of a tropical storm. | 我們經歷過熱帶風暴的災難。

25. 否定字首（4）　　　　CD2- 68

➔ 除了前面提到的幾個un-，以下再列出幾個常用來表示否定意義的字根。但要記得喔！並不是所有以這些字首開頭的單字，都可以這樣來解釋的，例如important表示「重要」，可是personal（個人的）→impersonal卻表示「非個人的」呢！

Not coming to the meeting is abnormal for him.
他沒有出席會議，是很反常的一件事。

➔ 例句

1 The weather is quite irregular for a midsummer day. | 仲夏的天氣，變化極不穩定。

2 The service at this hospital seems very impersonal. | 這家醫院的服務看起來很不近人情。

3 Getting a flat tire on the way here was very inconvenient. | 在往這裡的路上，車子爆胎，實在很不方便。

4 You can wear whatever you'd like because tonight's event is informal. | 你可以隨意打扮，因為今晚的活動是非正式的。

26. 常用字首（1）re-和pre-

➔ 常見並且只相差一字的re-和pre-兩個字首，分別表示「重複」和「預先」的意思，常常是動作的修飾詞。

Would you please remove that sofa?
能不能請你把那張沙發移走？

➔ 例句

1 The man apologized in order to restore their friendship. | 這男人道歉，為的是要修復他們的友誼。

2 The fortuneteller predicted that I would get married this year. | 算命師算我今年會結婚。

3 It will be better if you both preview and review your textbook. | 如果你預習並且複習你的課本，會比較好。

4 The man was reunited with his son after thirty years of being apart. | 這男人與他兒子分離了三十年後重聚了。

27. 常用字首（2）Over-

➜ Over在當作介系詞使用時，原本就可以用來說明「越過...上方」、「超越（數量、程度）」的意思，因此變成字首的時候，也帶有同樣的意味喔！

中級
Level

The lake overflowed due to the torrential rains.
由於豪雨，湖水氾濫。

➜ 例句

1 The revolutionaries overthrew the tyrant king. | 革命者推翻了暴君。

2 I sent the important package via overnight delivery. | 我用隔夜抵達的送貨方式，寄出重要包裹。

3 We had to pay extra because our baggage was overweight. | 我們得額外付費，因為我們的行李超重了。

4 I left my bag inside the overhead compartment on the airplane. | 我把我的袋子留在飛機座位上方的置物櫃裡了。

28. 常用字首（3）Trans-

➜ Trans-這個字根常代表「橫越」、「轉換」的意思，舉例來說，transplant（移植）這個字就是將另一件事物「轉換」（trans-）並且「植入」（plant）另一個地方的意思啊！

We have to transfer at the next station.
我們得在下一站轉車。

➡ 例句

1	He has to get a liver transplant in order to survive.	他必須接受肝移植才能存活。
2	That vacation transformed him into a happier person.	他渡完假變得更快樂了。
3	We need somebody to translate this into Mandarin.	我們需要一個人來把這個翻譯成中文。
4	Public transportation in this city is really convenient.	這個城市的大眾運輸系統非常方便。

29. 其他常用字首

➡ 再補充以下幾個常用字首：sub-（…底下的）、non-（沒有…的）、mini-（微小的）、inter-（交互的）以及co-（共同的、合作的）。

Have you ever been in a submarine before?
你坐過潛水艇嗎？

➡ 例句

1	She works for a major cosmetics corporation.	她在一家大型的化妝品公司上班。
2	They will pay me a minimum of $10,000 for the job.	這份工作他們最少會付我一萬元。
3	She didn't make herself clear, so let me interpret for you.	她自己無法說清楚，因此我來代替她解釋給你聽。
4	Our vacation was two weeks of non-stop fun and excitement.	我們連續過了兩週快樂又興奮的假期。

MEMO

MEMO

MEMO

MEMO

MEMO

英檢攻略　17

完全攻略英檢初級、中級必考文法320
（25K+2MP3）

2016年5月　初版

著者 ● 里昂

出版發行 ● 山田社文化事業有限公司
臺北市大安區安和路一段112巷17號7樓
電話　02-2755-7622
傳真　02-2700-1887

郵政劃撥 ● 19867160號　　大原文化事業有限公司
網路購書 ● 日語英語學習網　http://www. daybooks. com. tw

總經銷 ● 聯合發行股份有限公司
新北市新店區寶橋路235巷6弄6號2樓
電話　02-2917-8022
傳真　02-2915-6275

印刷 ● 上鎰數位科技印刷有限公司
法律顧問 ● 林長振法律事務所　林長振律師

定價 ● **新台幣399元**
ISBN ● 978-986-246-095-5

STS

山田社

STS

山田社

STS

山田社